A Christmas
Candy Killing

A Christmas Candy Killing

A KILLER CHOCOLATE MYSTERY

Christina Romeril

CROOKED
LANE

NEW YORK

Published in the United States by Crooked Lane Books, an imprint of The Quick Brown Fox & Company LLC.

Crooked Lane Books and its logo are trademarks of The Quick Brown Fox & Company LLC.

Library of Congress Catalog-in-Publication data available upon request.

ISBN (hardcover): 978-1-63910-166-5
ISBN (ebook): 978-1-63910-167-2

Cover design by Mary Ann Lasher

Printed in the United States.

www.crookedlanebooks.com

Crooked Lane Books
34 West 27th St., 10th Floor
New York, NY 10001

First Edition: October 2022

10 9 8 7 6 5 4 3 2 1

This book is dedicated with much love to Jordan, Josh, Spencer, and Justin. You are my cheer squad. You believed in me long before I ever finished this book. You love me despite all the mistakes I've made. I love you all to the moon and back!

Chapter One

What was an alliterative word that worked with *cyanide*? They'd used Strychnine Strawberry. Was there anything that went with *hemlock*? The only thing better than naming Murder and Mayhem's Killer Chocolates was eating them. When Alex had come up with the idea of naming chocolates after poisons used in murder mysteries, she'd had no idea how popular those chocolates would become. Each month, the bookshop featured one of their Killer Chocolates in conjunction with a mystery novel. In December they featured all their Christmas seasonal chocolates.

Alex Wright dragged her attention back to the woman speaking to the group and made a valiant attempt to restrain her wandering thoughts. The speaker was known for her sharp gaze and tongue, and heaven forbid someone was caught daydreaming.

"It's been said that anyone is capable of murder in the right circumstances, but I disagree. To commit murder, conceal it, and then go merrily along, as if all is well, requires a certain type of character. When an individual's character tends toward weakness or evil, there can be a definite disregard for the rules of society."

The statement hung in the air for a moment. It was as if the occupants of the cozy room needed time to digest it. Alex's gaze traveled around the small space, and she noticed that at least one person seemed to squirm uncomfortably in their chair. Alex had to admit she occasionally pushed the boundaries when she didn't think rules made sense.

A few minutes later, Alex's concentration faded almost completely. Jane Burrows's presentation on this month's book club choice was interesting, but it was eleven days before Christmas and her mind was on chocolate, not murder. The waft of vanilla-and-cinnamon-scented air from a candle, mingled with the tantalizing aroma of chocolate infused with nuts, fruits, and spices, brought to mind nostalgic Christmas daydreams, however far from reality they might be.

Most of Alex's daydreams seemed to revolve around her two favorite topics: poison and murder. Well, three, if you included chocolate. And you had to include chocolate. Two years ago, Jane had asked if the Sleuth Book Club could hold their monthly meetings at Murder and Mayhem: Killer Chocolates and Bookshop. Sleuth was devoted to dissecting the motives, clues, and methods of murder in mystery novels. This month M. C. Beaton's *The Wizard of Evesham* was under discussion. Alex sat up a little straighter and tried to focus on Jane's explanation.

"This novel was certainly entertaining, and I love Agatha Raisin. She's so feisty, if she'd only quit smoking. Most mysteries seem to focus on motive, means, and opportunity, and they have their place, but character shouldn't be discounted. In *The Wizard of Evesham*, the murderer's motivation was jealousy, but greed, lust, revenge, or even the protection of a secret are all possible motives for a killer. As yet, I haven't murdered anyone, but I've been known to give killer looks to my students who I catch daydreaming." Jane looked pointedly at Alex, whose eyes had glazed over.

After everyone had a chuckle, Jane continued, "Honestly, I can't imagine a circumstance that would induce me to kill anyone, but I'd hazard a guess we all know someone who that might not be true for."

"I think most married men would agree they know someone who regularly looks at them with murder in their eyes." Drew Fletcher, a retired pharmacist, flinched under his wife's glare after making the comment.

Alex's gaze lingered on the couple, and Maggie was indeed giving Drew a death stare. But Alex had to agree: men did seem to bring out the worst in some women. Her own brief marriage, right out of college, had ended, in part, because her ex-husband had been more interested in partying than creating a lasting relationship with his spouse. She in turn had become the worst version of herself, complaining all the time. Less than a year after their vows, they'd parted ways.

Sensing a pause in the discussion and wanting to end the meeting on time, Alex stood. "Thank you, Jane, for your presentation. I'm sure we'll all be looking at each other much more suspiciously from now on. Thanks to the rest of you for braving the cold this frosty Monday evening. Once again, I apologize for rescheduling book club and the conflict it created with the horticultural society's meeting for some of you.

"If I'm not mistaken, there were a few noses sniffing the air, no doubt detecting the aroma of chocolate. Hanna made more of December's featured chocolates, including Candy Cane Coniine, a subtly flavored white-chocolate peppermint ganache with crushed candy canes in a white-chocolate shell. Samples of those and a few others are on the counter."

The book and chocolate shop was located in the quaint village of Harriston, nestled along the southwest shore of Echo

Lake in the Rocky Mountains of Montana. Alex had purchased the building for a song three years earlier, as the previous owners had long before moved to Florida and were desperate to sell. With a great deal of hard work, she and her identical-twin sister, Hanna, had turned the antiquated home, built in 1926, from an outdated quilt and fabric store into an homage to the Victorian era of the early twentieth century. The store allowed their customers to escape the modern world for a short time.

The two front rooms, with the entry hall between, constituted the sales floor. The smaller, east room had a bay window with a built-in bench, covered in a heavy, striped fabric of ruby red, ochre, and green that matched all the curtains. At the end of the hall was a large kitchen, where their handcrafted cocoa confections were created. Sleuth met in a room off the hall adjacent to the east room that had likely been the library or den when the house was built.

Alex gestured to the counter in the main room, where the chocolates and other goodies had been laid out. "Please help yourselves before you go, and merry Christmas, everyone."

She stepped aside, into the hall, as the group stampeded toward the treats. It was like watching the running of the bulls in Pamplona. It always amazed Alex how the offer of free food turned the most civilized individuals into a horde of wildlife.

Only Jane stayed behind, and Alex wondered if she was about to be chastised for not paying attention; that had happened often enough in school when she was growing up in Michigan. Barely of average height, Jane had an imposing presence that could just as easily corral a roomful of grown men as a class of elementary school children and commandeer them into singing Christmas carols or completing a despised service project. Her short, gray hair was sensibly styled, and closing in on eighty, she still had a penetrating gaze that could see a lie a mile away. It was these qualities that had made her such an excellent fourth-grade teacher for more than thirty-five years.

"What a wonderful way to end the year. It seems fortuitous that we finished with *The Wizard of Evesham*. Though I must admit, I am a tiny bit disappointed I missed the horticultural meeting tonight. Of course, book club certainly has its compensations." Jane's gaze traveled to the other room, where two hunky members of the club, Zach and Everett, were chatting as they munched on chocolates.

Alex looked at the fine male specimens and had to agree.

Jane was a driving force in the community, spearheading many of the events in the village. She was also president of both the horticultural and historical societies in Harriston. Jane gazed fondly at her surroundings. "You know, dear, I hate to sound sentimental, but I'm very grateful you moved to our little village and opened Murder and Mayhem."

The specialty bookshop was devoted almost entirely to mystery novels as well as the handmade, poison-themed chocolates. Hanna, also the store's co-owner, was primarily in charge of the time-consuming process of making the hand-dipped and molded chocolates.

Jane laid her hand on Alex's arm. "It has also been such a blessing having you visit me every month. Your friendship has meant a great deal to me. I don't know what I would have done without you. Before you came along, the most exciting part of my day was counting the liver spots on my hands. You've helped bring meaning back into a washed-up old teacher's life that had become quite dull."

"I don't buy that for a second, but thank you for the sentiment. I'm the one who should be grateful. If you hadn't taken me under your wing and been such an avid supporter when we first opened, Murder and Mayhem might not still be around. I love our visits as well."

Jane pulled her closer. "Speaking of which, would you be able to come over tomorrow morning for some tea and a little visit?"

"Of course. I'll get Hanna to open the store. What time would you like me there?"

"Eight. I can have everything ready by then. I watched one of my true-crime shows recently." With a furtive glance toward the others, she led Alex back into the conference room and lowered her voice. "It was a reenactment of a cold case. I'm certain the killer is living in our village." She raised her palm to Alex. "Now I realize I've said this before, but I am really quite certain this time. I'm not unaware of the reputation I've developed due to a few errors in judgment. Upon mentioning my theory to Netta Griffin, she had the impertinence to laugh for several minutes. I want you to know, the photograph alone didn't form the base of my conclusion this time. In fact, the picture they showed on television was quite useless. It was more than a little out of focus and at least seventeen years old, but something in the details of the story and the character of the killer reminded me of someone here in the village." Her body tensed, and she grasped Alex's arm with small but strong fingers. "The individual is suspected of four murders, the last over ten years ago. I want you to watch the episode and tell me what you think."

"I'm not sure I'll be of much help. I don't know everyone in the village the way you do. When you've taught almost one-third of the village's residents, you tend to have a different perspective."

"Don't worry, my dear. You know this particular person, and if you don't agree with me, I won't say another word about it. In fact, I'm intentionally saying very little so I don't sway you in any way. Without sounding like I'm trying to flatter you, I think you're one of the most observant people I know—besides myself, of course." Jane's shoulders sagged a bit, and she seemed to relax. With a smile, she patted Alex on the arm. "Well, I must run. There's something I want to check on before it gets too late."

Alex walked Jane into the hall. "I put out a few Veronal Vanilla Creams. Make sure you have one. I know they're your favorite."

"A sweet Christmas elf left a box of four Vanilla Creams on my doorstep earlier today." Jane gave an exaggerated wink. "It's a bad habit, but I always eat a chocolate or two before bed. I'm planning to have a couple tonight. They remind me of my grandmother."

Jane often recounted memories of her English grandmother, who had come to live with the family when Jane was a toddler. The woman had arrived with a small suitcase packed full of veronal for her occasional bouts of insomnia, something Jane had inherited. The barbiturate's heyday was over by the 1950s, but Jane often laughed that her grandmother's supply would last well into the millennium. Though veronal was no longer available, the hand-dipped milk chocolate vanilla fondants were a staple throughout the year.

As everyone said their good-byes to Jane, Harriston's charismatic mayor and local lawyer, Everett Pearson, strode over to Alex as she contemplated what her septuagenarian friend had just shared.

"Hanna mentioned you're looking for someone to replace a window in the shop?"

Alex tilted her head in assent. Everett had the pulse of the village. He took every facet of economic development seriously, and businesses had flourished as a result, rendering him one of the most well-regarded mayors in decades.

"Zach Roberts could use the work. Things are a bit slow for him right now with Christmas just around the corner." Everett put on his gloves. "He's done some excellent work for me. I highly recommend him." He retrieved his car keys from the pocket of his jacket. "I just wanted to put in a plug for a local business. The chocolates were delicious, by the way. I'll have my secretary order some of the Killer Chocolate boxes for the law firm's clients as Christmas gifts." With a salute, he headed to the door.

Alex's business partner and twin wandered over. "Jane looked a little intense. What did she want?"

"She wants me to go over to her place at eight tomorrow morning so we can have one of our teatime chats. Do you mind opening?"

Hanna rearranged Alex's bangs and fluffed her sister's hair. "Not at all. I wanted to tweak the window display a bit anyway. I think it can use more twinkle lights. I don't think there can ever be too many twinkle lights at this time of year."

"That's why we get along so well. We see eye to eye on Christmas." Alex laughed as she bent down to pet the brown-and-white dog lying just inside the conference room door. "Well, Miss Watson, you've been your usual quiet self. I don't think I've ever met a dog with a sweeter disposition." Alex grabbed half a shortbread cookie from Hanna's plate and fed it to the dog. Miss Watson was their Staffordshire terrier, adopted two years earlier from a rescue shelter. Watson was the only name she would respond to after they'd brought her home, so they had officially called her Miss Watson, but they usually dropped the Miss.

Hanna bent down and gave Watson the other half of the cookie. "You'd never know how abused and neglected she was when we got her. She's gone from skin and bones to almost pudgy. We may need to put her on a diet if we don't stop giving her these treats."

The canine in question quickly looked up at Hanna's words and gave a pitiful whine. Alex completely understood. Initially, Watson had been extremely timid and terrified of almost everything. By bringing her to the store occasionally and taking her to doggy parks, they had gradually helped her enjoy the company of people and other animals alike. These days she rarely cowered behind the counter when customers came into the store.

"I think I'll be going on that diet as well if I gain any more weight." Alex looked down and patted her still-slim hips as she pictured the inches accumulating there.

Hanna peered at her sister before looking back at the treat-covered counter. "I don't know what you're talking about. You look fine." Hanna often lamented her own slightly rounder curves and wished she didn't have such a fondness for sweets. "Let's hope we didn't inherit Mom's genes. She started gaining weight around our age. We'd better refill the Christmas Caramel Cupcakes. It looks like Trixie is about to arm wrestle Clive for the last one."

Alex looked wistfully at the trim, athletic couple. "They seem to be able to eat whatever they want and never gain a pound. Maybe I need to become an avid hiker and hit the trails in Glacier with them."

Filled with ancient forests, deep valleys, and alpine scenery, Glacier National Park, a forty-five-minute drive away, was in the heart of the Rocky Mountains and offered a plethora of trails that Clive and Trixie Hanson regularly hiked. Alex had gone with them once last summer and had struggled to keep up with the hiking enthusiasts as they climbed what they had euphemistically referred to as an "easy trail." She had vowed to get in better shape for next summer before joining them again.

"Forget hiking. There are bears out there that eat the slowest hiker. Come to yoga with me instead."

"I'll think about it when I make my New Year's resolutions." Fat chance, Alex thought. She figured if she was going to huff and puff, she'd do it in the comfort of her own home. "I'll help you in a minute. I'm just going to talk to Zach about replacing that window in the bathroom." Alex walked over to a dark-haired, burly man standing by himself.

The sleeves of his red flannel shirt were rolled up, revealing muscular forearms as he popped a Belladonna Black Currant chocolate into his mouth. Belladonna, also known as deadly nightshade, and its main poisonous compound, atropine, had been used in several murder mysteries. It had inspired an—obviously!—nonfatal, delicious creation of white chocolate and black-currant ganache enrobed in a dark-chocolate shell.

Alex led Zach to the window they wanted to replace as she explained the need to slowly upgrade and modernize some of the elements of the house to make it more economical to heat. "I've got a tape measure if you want to take measurements now."

He examined the window for a moment. "This looks fairly straightforward. No rot that I can see. Sorry, I've got to be somewhere shortly. Let me check my schedule." Zach pulled his phone from his pocket and touched the screen several times. "Today is the fourteenth." He seemed to be talking to himself. "I'll be here first thing tomorrow morning, if that's okay?"

She nodded. "Hanna should be here by eight thirty, so any time after that."

The handsome handyman was a bit of an unknown entity. He had joined Sleuth Book Club the year before, at Everett's urging, but rarely contributed to the group discussions. He seemed shy and didn't usually stay long after the meetings to engage in

10

the village's favorite pastime: gossip. Hanna had found out his age—thirty-five—and had pointed out, regretfully, that he was too young to be in either of their dating pools.

He glanced at his watch. "I should be off. Those Christmas chocolates are good, but my favorite is still the Belladonna Black Currant. Thanks for the treats. I'll see you tomorrow morning."

Rejoining Hanna, Alex whispered, "Okay, Zach's on board. Now let's get everyone out of here so we can clean up and go home."

Chapter Two

After the meeting, Alex, no fan of winter, went out to start and warm up her car for the short drive to their two-story home, even though the process took longer than walking the few blocks. She went back inside and asked her sister, "Are you sure you don't want a ride? This has been the coldest December since we moved here."

Hanna wrapped a scarf around her neck. "Watson needs a walk before bed. I'll see you at home in a few minutes. By the time you drop off those chocolates to Tom, I'll be there." Hanna paused as she looked at her sister and let out an exaggerated sigh. Putting down the dog's leash, she fussed with Alex's long, blond strands for a moment and adjusted the scarf that had been haphazardly thrown on. She stepped back and looked at her handiwork with a critical eye. "I wish you would make more of an effort when you're going to see a man. In the Victorian era, you would have been known as the spinster Wright. You're pretty, but even a Rembrandt looks better when it's hung in the right light. One failed marriage two decades ago is hardly grounds to act like you've joined a convent."

Alex was used to these assessments. She and Hanna had almost identical features, but Hanna always looked more put together. Alex wasn't averse to dating, in theory. Unfortunately, the reality had been a rather lengthy string of unacceptable suitors. After her brief marriage, she had put her time and energy into her career, and by the time she was in her thirties and ready to find an eligible mate, the dating pool had dried up considerably. As the years passed, finding potential mates that met her minimum criteria of being employed, having a sense of humor, and not looking for a surrogate mother or therapist became a significant challenge.

She meekly hung her head for a moment. "Yes, Mom." Alex glanced at her reflection in the mirror nearby. She narrowed her cool gray eyes—which sometimes turned more green or blue, like nearby sky-reflecting Echo Lake—as she looked back at her sister. "You know, you're only fifteen minutes younger than me, spinster Eastham. Shouldn't you be worried about catching your own Mr. Right? It's been five years since your divorce."

Hanna fluffed her thick, blond hair, which fell in loose waves past her shoulders. She wore her hair slightly shorter and usually curled it, which helped people tell them apart. "Don't you worry about me. I have a grand master plan that's coming along just fine."

Alex stood inside the heavy front door, watching her sister cross the porch and head to the sidewalk, and reflected on their contrasting natures. Hanna's playful, fun-loving personality was the perfect balance to her own more serious, reserved-and-analytical disposition. Despite their differences, they rarely disagreed over anything major. Even as children, they'd always stuck together.

After turning off all the lights except those in the front windows, Alex returned to her car. A towering bur oak stood like a sentinel in the front yard. The sixty-foot tree provided cooling shade in the summer, though it was currently leafless and harboring snow on its branches.

Alex drove along the festively decorated Main Street and turned the corner at Harriston's K–12 school, which served the community of twelve hundred. The conservative, sleepy village also had a community center, a handful of businesses, its fair share of secrets, and gossip, as well as strong family loyalties. Alex had quickly learned to watch her tongue, as almost half the village was related to the other half, and news spread faster than chicken pox in a kindergarten class once did.

After twenty years as a banker in Missoula, she had quit her job and opened the bookshop. The money she made selling her house in the city had allowed her to buy a modest home as well as the shop and begin a new life doing what she loved. At the same time Hanna had decided it was time to cut the apron strings and move away from her childhood hometown. Alex had welcomed Hanna's idea that the two of them go into business together.

Once she'd parked in her driveway, she tromped through the snow and up the steps of her next-door neighbor's house, clutching a plate of leftover treats. Moments after she rang the doorbell, Tom, a tall man with graying hair and blue eyes the color of forget-me-nots, answered the door.

"Hello, neighbor." Tom's gaze traveled to the plate Alex was holding. "I see you have some mighty fine-looking cookies and chocolates. I don't suppose those could be for me?"

"As a matter of fact, they are." Alex smiled at the man.

His lean frame was dressed casually in jeans and a flannel shirt, and he shivered as the cold night air rushed through the doorway.

Tom ushered her inside. "I think I offended Maggie and Drew at dinner today. I told them you're my favorite neighbor.

Apparently, since she's my sister, she's supposed to be my favorite." He took the proffered plate and lowered his voice confidentially, even though they were alone. "Mrs. Matthews brought over a few cookies earlier today. They're delicious, but she's over eighty, and the cost of getting the cookies was a conversation about her gout. I don't suppose you'd like to come in and visit for a bit, assuming you'll keep your health problems to yourself?"

Alex laughed. "As it happens, I don't have any current health concerns. Unfortunately, I still have quite a bit to do tonight. Can I take a rain check?"

He studied her face for a moment. "I'm going to hold you to that."

At fifty-eight, Tom Kennedy was pastor of the largest congregation in town. He had worked at the jail in Kalispell for over thirty years, the last ten as warden, until his retirement three years ago. Since his wife passed away six months earlier, Alex had been bringing meals or desserts over regularly. Tom wasn't a particularly pious man, but he was a kind one. His sermons tended toward the mild, Good Samaritan versions rather than the pulpit-thumping, repent-or-be-damned type.

Just as Alex was getting ready to announce her departure, the doorbell rang. Tom's brow furrowed, and he gave a small lift of his shoulders as she moved aside so he could open the door.

She recognized the cloying, sickeningly sweet perfume assaulting her nose before the simpering drawl of their neighbor from across the street oozed into the air.

"Oh, Tom, I'm sorry. I had no idea you had a visitor." The new arrival glared at Alex and walked in uninvited. She snuggled a little closer to Tom than convention allowed between acquaintances. "I know how hard it is being alone, so I wanted to bring you a little something I whipped up yesterday."

Penelope Shaw was a divorcée in her late fifties who favored tight clothing, high heels, and available men, not necessarily in that order. She was hunting for a new husband with the skill of a mountain lion. Ever since Tom's wife passed away, Penelope had been stalking him with a vengeance.

She was notorious for her terrible cooking and had managed to give almost the entire ladies auxiliary food poisoning several years ago when she served a chicken pasta salad that had been left out on her counter in the heat of a summer afternoon. By the looks of the freezer-burnt dish she was trying to offer Tom, it had seen a lot of yesterdays. He stood awkwardly between the two women, still holding the plate from Alex.

"I can see your hands are full. I'd be happy to bring this to the kitchen for you and explain how to reheat it." Penelope practically purred as she batted her heavily mascaraed lashes.

Alex studied the newcomer. "You're back early from the horticultural meeting, Penelope. I thought they usually lasted well into the night."

The divorcée was silent for a moment. "Well, they always go off on tangents after the main presentation, and I wanted to get this meal to Tom tonight." She smiled at him and put her hand on his arm possessively. A second later she was glaring at Alex again. "We mustn't hold you up. I'm sure you're busy."

Alex tried to suppress a smile as Tom gave her a look that said he was prey about to be devoured. "You're absolutely right. I'll leave you two to your culinary endeavors." With a wave, she was out the door as Penelope shepherded Tom down the hall.

* * *

Later, as Alex and Hanna did some Christmas baking for the village's elderly widows and widowers, Alex pondered Tom's invitation to come in for a visit. Was he interested in more than her baked goods? Did she want him to be interested?

"How many of the *Vanillekipferl* and *Zimtsterne* do you want to make?" Hanna's voice brought her back to the present.

Vanillekipferl, crescent-shaped shortbread cookies covered in powdered sugar, and *Zimtsterne*, delicious cutout cinnamon stars, had been a Christmas tradition growing up. Their mother had raised them on authentic German cuisine and insisted they speak German at home. Thanks to daily conversations and Saturday mornings spent in the basement of a church conjugating German verbs instead of watching cartoons, they were both fluent in their parents' native tongue.

"I think we should make seven dozen of each."

Alex had fond memories of her mother's cooking, though not so much for some other aspects of her childhood. Her mother, while devoted to her children, had also been overbearing and hard to please. Alex's parents and *Oma* had immigrated to the United States in the early seventies and opened an authentic German restaurant and gift shop in Frankenmuth. Alex and Hanna, followed by Stephan, had been born in quick succession in Michigan's Little Bavaria and were expected to help with the family business from a young age. Alex had preferred reading her Nancy Drew and Agatha Christie novels and took every opportunity to hide from her mother's tutelage. Despite that, she had become a proficient baker, chocolatier, and cook, but had never gotten the hang of making the Bavarian soft pretzels the restaurant was famous for. Her mother claimed the results of Alex's attempts to bake bread could have been used to stone sinners in biblical times.

Alex carefully measured out her ingredients into a large bowl and cast a sideways glance at Hanna. "Tom invited me to stay for a while when I dropped off the leftovers from our meeting. I told him I was too busy tonight, and he seemed intent that I commit to going over another time."

Hanna stopped measuring her ingredients and looked at Alex. "What did you say to that?"

"Nothing—we got interrupted. Penelope showed up." She recounted their neighbor's untimely visit. "*Geschmack wie ein Eimer,* that one." Taste like a bucket. The nuances in language didn't translate well but certainly expressed Penelope's poor taste in clothes.

Shaking her head and grabbing the cinnamon, Hanna went back to work. "She brings a whole new meaning to neighborhood watch. I saw her at her window this morning, with binoculars, focused on Tom's house. But unless I'm mistaken, which I doubt, Tom seems to have eyes for a certain other woman."

"You're crazy. He only lost his wife six months ago. Besides, isn't he too old for me?"

"Duncan was a widower less than that when he asked me out. As for age, it's just a number. It's not like he's got a reservation at the old folks' home."

"Yes, and after dating for only two months, Duncan said he wasn't ready and broke it off. Sorry. I didn't mean to be insensitive. You know what I mean."

Duncan Fletcher was Tom's nephew and lived across the street with his parents, Drew and Maggie. He and Hanna had hit it off when she moved to the village, but as they were getting serious, Duncan had told Hanna they should just be friends. Hanna had been devastated.

"It's okay. I'm over it. But I'm telling you, Tom is interested. I've seen the way he's been looking at you the past couple months. Mark my words, he's going to ask you on a date one of these days."

"Not if Penelope has anything to say about it." Alex smiled broadly, remembering Tom being led down the hall. "I should make a pros-and-cons list of whether to date an older man or not. In case he ever asks."

"Or you could just go and see if you enjoy being with him." Hanna checked the oven temperature and turned to face Alex. "I forgot to mention I saw Penelope earlier tonight as well. While Everett was talking to you, I was putting a couple of Christmas mysteries in the window display and saw Jane leave. Penelope's car was parked out front, and when Jane reached the sidewalk, Penelope sprang out in front of her. I don't know what was said, but Penelope was facing the shop, and whatever she was saying wasn't a festive greeting."

"She must have left the horticultural meeting quite early to have managed that. I've heard Jane say Penelope's usually one of the last to leave, since she's always fawning all over Gary Jenkins."

"She certainly casts a wide net. I don't think any man in Montana over the age of fifty is safe."

* * *

Later, when everything was cleaned up, Alex made her way upstairs to her bedroom. As she contemplated tomorrow morning's visit, she wondered if Jane was right this time. Could there be a murderer living in the village? It didn't seem likely. Jane wanted to solve murders so badly that she accused someone almost every six months.

Alex had spent many hours at Jane's house discussing novels written by contemporary and golden-age writers and trying to solve intricately plotted murders. It was one of Alex's favorite ways for killers to dispatch their victims—poison—that had inspired the idea of Killer Chocolates.

Handmade chocolates had always been part of the business plan for Murder and Mayhem. From her time banking, she knew how important it was to have a diverse product line. She and Hanna had been able to capitalize on tourists from Whitefish and Swanson with their unique offering, and their efforts were coming to fruition from the marketing of their chocolates. The resulting sales were keeping Alex and Hanna very busy as chocolatiers.

Alex enjoyed running the bookshop and was much happier now that she'd left her banking career. Her mother still mourned her daughter's giving up a steady and secure job in favor of being a shop owner, which mystified Alex, since their family came from a long line of retail merchants.

As a teenager, Alex had briefly considered law enforcement, but her mother had so strongly discouraged it as an inappropriate career that she had gone into finance instead. She hadn't particularly enjoyed it, but it had provided her with a healthy nest egg. Part of that nest egg had been used to start her and Hanna's business. Over the years, she had gone on a few ride-alongs with sheriff's department deputies and had thoroughly enjoyed those experiences. She still wondered, occasionally, how her life would have been if she'd followed her own dreams instead of her parents'.

Chapter Three

The next morning, Alex knocked on Jane's door at eight sharp; the former schoolteacher was a stickler for punctuality. Bundled in her parka and winter boots, eyes watering, cheeks stinging from the short walk between driveway and porch, she waited for Jane to answer the door. There was no response. She rang the doorbell, buried her face in her coat, and continued to wait.

After another minute, Alex knocked on the door with some force. *Come on, Jane, it's freezing out here.* Tentatively, she reached out and turned the handle. The door opened, and without waiting for an invitation, she stepped into the hall and called out for her friend. She reasoned that Jane must be busy and had probably left the door unlocked in expectation of Alex's arrival. Alex was just happy to be back in a heated environment. The house was very quiet, and there was no aroma of fresh-baked goodies, which usually accompanied their morning chats.

After calling out again, she removed her boots and put them on the boot tray next to the umbrella stand. As she walked down the hall into the kitchen, a flash of movement on the back deck caught her eye. Looking through the French doors in the semi-darkness of early morning, she glimpsed someone's back as they rushed off the deck and out of sight.

Curious, she looked around the kitchen, but everything seemed to be in order. The counters and sink were clean, without so much as a dirty cup in sight.

Jane's purse sat on the table with a bulging envelope beside it. By the back door was a puddle of water. Carefully avoiding the puddle, Alex tried to open the French doors, but they were locked with the dead bolt.

Moving into the dining room, she stopped abruptly at the sight of drawers pulled open in the breakfront that held Jane's Royal Doulton dishes and her silver cutlery. On one of the shelves of the breakfront sat the antique silver tea service. It should have been on the coffee table, filled with peppermint tea, alongside a plate of freshly baked scones or muffins, awaiting Alex's visit.

Walking through an archway into the living room, she spied more open drawers in the end tables and an antique escritoire. There were a few books, pulled out of a bookcase, lying on the floor, and some papers scattered about. Alex wondered what was going on. Jane's house was always in perfect order.

In the middle of the coffee table was a poinsettia, its large red leaves providing beautiful festive color, and beside it a crystal bowl filled with delicate vintage Christmas ornaments. An exquisite miniature Christmas tree sat on a table in front of the window, decorated with small, glittering, mercury glass baubles. Except for the minor disarray, everything looked normal. Could Jane have been searching for something and even now be upstairs, not having heard Alex call?

Complete stillness pervaded the house; the only sound—*ticktock*—came from the clock hanging on the wall. Leaving the living room, Alex reentered the hall where she had started, completing a full circle without any sign of Jane. As she stood there uncertainly, a sense of disquiet filled her. Perhaps Jane wasn't feeling well?

She slowly ascended the stairs, the silence pressing in on her with each step. One of the stairs creaked, and it sounded like the crack of a bullwhip in the silence. She was pretty sure her heart skipped a beat.

She had been upstairs many times in the murder room, as Jane called it. It was simply a bedroom converted into an office, where Jane kept her extensive collection of mystery and true-crime books as well as her computer and files. There was a comfortable leather recliner in a corner, where she liked to puzzle out the identity of the murderer in her mystery books. Peering into the murder room, Alex noted M. C. Beaton's *The Wizard of Evesham* on the small side table beside the reading chair. The room seemed to be in order.

A few steps farther down the hall and a quick glance into the spare bedroom didn't yield any more information. She called out Jane's name again. Her voice seemed to echo in the hallway. Why was she holding her breath? With a sense of foreboding, she headed to Jane's bedroom.

Peeking into the room, she noticed the bed was unmade and Jane's cell phone was on the nightstand, along with a mini box of Killer Chocolates. There was a faint metallic smell in the air. She took a step into the room, and her hand flew to her mouth to stifle a cry. Her eyes widened, and her heart pounded so hard it was in danger of escaping her chest. On the floor lay the owner of the home. She looked as if she had simply crumpled beside her bed. It could have been a heart attack except for the large quantity of blood staining the front of the once-pristine white nightgown and the beige carpet around the body.

After staring at Jane's pallid, still form for what felt like an eternity, Alex bent down to check for a pulse. The body was cold, and there was no heartbeat, not that she had expected one. The blood on the nightgown appeared to be almost dry.

She couldn't seem to tear her gaze away from the frayed holes of the fabric covering Jane's chest in the midst of the dark-crimson stain. It was surreal; the room began to spin, and she stood to lean against the wall. Her legs were still a bit wobbly, but after several shaky breaths, she looked around the room to distract herself from the cold shell that had so recently been a warm, kind human being.

There didn't appear to be any drawers open or items out of place, other than an unmade bed. The room seemed in perfect order. Alex dropped to her knees and looked under the bed, thinking perhaps the weapon that had killed her friend might have rolled or slid underneath it, but all she found were a few dust bunnies. Very few. Jane had obviously been a diligent housekeeper.

She squeezed her eyes shut and forced herself to take deep breaths until her heart rate slowed to near normal. What should she do? As one part of her mind grappled with the horror of what she had discovered, another part seemed to take over and began recalling all the things she had learned on the ride-alongs with the deputies as well as in the many mystery books she had read. *Dummy. Call Duncan.* He'd know what to do. He was a deputy sheriff with the Lakehead County Sheriff's Department in Swanson, the county seat. After several failed attempts—it was like one of those dreams where you couldn't seem to press any of the right buttons—she finally managed to get the call through and apprise him of what she'd found.

"Could anyone still be in the house?" he asked.

Alex looked around and shook her head, even though Duncan couldn't see her. "I don't think so. It looks like Jane's been dead for some time, but I haven't checked the basement." She glanced at Jane's body again, wishing her friend would open her eyes and say it was all a macabre joke.

"I want you to go outside right now. Wait in your car with the doors locked. I'm still at home, so I'll be there shortly."

Taking some liberty with Duncan's instructions regarding the words *right now*, she walked to the nightstand and pressed the home button on Jane's cell phone. The phone was locked, but a reminder appeared: *Tues 8:00 a.m. Alex to watch true-crime show.*

She decided to take some pictures of the scene in Jane's bedroom as well as the office. She wasn't sure it could be called the murder room anymore, since that was what the bedroom had become. She took one more look around, with a quick peek into the bathroom off the hall, but everything looked exactly as it should on any normal day.

Except this was no normal day.

Once she was inside her car, her mind reeled. She was slightly numb as she thought about Jane, but tears wouldn't come. Jane was one of her best friends, and Alex was going to miss her so much.

Who would do such a thing to such a lovely lady? She pictured the person she'd seen leaving the deck when she arrived. She couldn't say absolutely, but she was fairly certain it had been a man, based on the person's size and gait. He'd been wearing dark pants, an old, possibly brown coat, and one of those hats with flaps to cover the ears, but it had been too dark to distinguish colors with certainty.

Rats! Why hadn't she run after him? Practically speaking, it was because her boots had been at the front door and there was about a foot of snow outside, and besides, at that point, there hadn't been anything particularly sinister about his presence. But the impractical part of her mind kept saying, *If only.*

Before she could muse any further, Duncan arrived with the lights on his cruiser flashing but no siren on. He approached her car. He had the same blue eyes, height, and build of his uncle Tom. She lowered the window of her car as Duncan walked up beside it.

"Are you okay?"

She nodded. Okay, at this point, was a relative term.

"I'm going inside. I've already called the sheriff. She'll be here at some point, but it may take a while. Just stay in your car and wait for me."

Fifteen minutes later, Duncan asked her to recount her movements in the house. She told him about checking Jane's phone. Duncan frowned, but she quickly mentioned the person she'd seen leaving the back deck. "He was hurrying, and it was too dark to be certain of what he was wearing. Sorry."

"He? You think it was a man?"

"Just an impression. I can't say for sure."

Taking a notebook out of his pocket, he gave Alex an understanding nod. "What time did you get here this morning?"

It felt like a lifetime had passed since she'd gone into Jane's house, but the car's clock said it had been less than forty minutes. "It was about one minute to eight when I pulled up. I checked the time just before I went to the front door."

Duncan made a note. "You said Jane was expecting you?"

"Yes. She was at the Sleuth meeting last night and asked me to drop by today at eight. She wanted to show me something. When she didn't answer, I tried the door. It was unlocked, and I assumed it was okay for me to go in. Normally she keeps things locked up tight, but she was expecting me, so . . ."

Duncan looked up from his notebook and gave a curt nod to Stella DeJong, who was watching them from the front of her house across the street, no doubt wondering why a sheriff's department cruiser was parked in front of Jane's house with its lights flashing. Stella was a stout woman, highly efficient, in her midsixties, though she'd never admit it, and had been at the Sleuth meeting the night before.

"Did you see anything that seemed out of place?"

Alex considered a moment. "Well, there was a puddle just inside the back door, as if someone had come in from outside and stood there or left their boots there. I checked, and the door was locked. There were things scattered around downstairs, but nothing was out of place upstairs, which seemed odd. Sorry, nothing else comes to mind."

"All right. You can head to the store now, and I'll come by later for your official statement. Could you please try not to talk about what's happened to anyone? I know you're going to tell Hanna, but otherwise, keep it under wraps for now. We don't want her family getting wind of this before we can do an official notification."

Somberly, she gave a nod. "Jane didn't really have any family to speak of. Her parents are dead, and her brother died a year ago. She has an ex-husband, but she's been divorced over fifty years, so I'm not sure if he's even alive anymore. I think she has a cousin in the old folks' home in Swanson. I'll keep it quiet, though."

Chapter Four

As the initial shock of finding Jane began to wear off, tears threatened. Alex's chin trembled as she drove through the village and saw the cheery Christmas decorations everywhere. Why did bad things have to happen at Christmas? It would have been horrible at any time; nonetheless, she wished there could be a moratorium on death during December.

By the time she had left Jane's, there had been numerous neighbors braving the cold for a juicy bit of gossip. They were huddled together like crows on a telephone pole, no doubt guessing at what tragedy had occurred. It wouldn't be long before everyone in the village knew; after all, Jane had lived alone. When the ambulance arrived and took Jane away, the simplest of persons could deduce whose body it was.

This was the kind of day that needed sugar-laden comfort food. Of course, in her opinion, most days needed sugar-laden comfort food; that was probably why some of her pants were getting tight. At forty-five, she was starting to notice the scale's indicator move in an undesirable direction. She pulled into a parking spot in front of Cookies 'n Crumbs.

Opening the door of the shop, she was assailed by the heavenly aroma of freshly baked goods. The display cases were filled with cookies, cakes, muffins, cupcakes, tarts, and more. The walls of the cozy little bakery and coffee shop were a combination of white shiplap and reclaimed wood. Six days out of seven, there were several tables filled with regulars who liked to start their day with some delicious baking and local gossip. By tomorrow, the gossip would be fast and furious about one topic.

It took her a moment to assimilate the contrast between the cold reality of death at Jane's and the convivial atmosphere at the coffee shop. When she saw who was behind the counter, she almost turned around and left. She didn't want to endure the surly and abrupt manner of the bakery's only employee, Louise Sweet. While her name might seem perfect for someone working in a bakery, there simply couldn't have been more of a dissonance between the name and the person.

Gathering her resolve, Alex approached Louise optimistically, doing her best to summon a weak smile with her greeting.

Louise wore an expression suggesting she had just bitten into a lemon, her lips pursed together disapprovingly and her skin, the texture of old paper, stretched taut over her face as if there wasn't quite enough of it to cover her skull. "What do ya want?" She managed to make it sound like she was about to be asked to do a huge favor instead of provide the service she'd been hired to do.

Alex bit her tongue and tried to maintain a friendly smile, but it may have verged on a snarl. "I'd like two each of the Gingersnap Sandwich Cookies and the Chocolate Mint Sandwich Cookies. Please."

Louise didn't bother responding; she merely pressed her lips together grimly and went straight to the display case to fill the order. In exchange for a white bakery bag, Alex gave her a large bill. "Keep the change, and merry Christmas!" *You old bat.*

Louise muttered under her breath, "What's so blasted merry about it?" And went to help the next customer.

* * *

At Murder and Mayhem, Alex made a cup of mint tea and filled Hanna in on the morning's events, showing her the pictures of the murder scene and warning her not to mention them to Duncan. She suspected that if he knew about those, she would have to delete them or, worse, turn over her phone.

Alex spread the holiday baking she'd bought on the table in the conference room. "Have something. It will make you feel better." She felt a little like a drug dealer, only she was pedaling sugar for the dopamine rush.

Hanna nodded, taking a Gingersnap Sandwich Cookie, her expressive gray eyes still teary. "You're the one that found the body. I should be comforting you."

As the older twin, if only by fifteen minutes, Alex had always been the one to take charge and offer reassurance. Even when she'd needed five stitches in her shin after an accident caused by her sister, she'd been the one to console Hanna on the way home from the playground. Being identical twins didn't make them telepathic, but they did tend to be on the same wavelength. So when one of them was in distress, the other seemed to feel it more acutely.

Hanna paused in her chewing. "I can't believe it. I don't think there's ever been a murder in Harriston. Just last night Jane said there hasn't been a serious crime in the village for over a hundred years. Could the guy you saw have done it?"

Staring into her oversized Christmas mug for a moment, Alex considered before responding. "I don't think so. When I checked for Jane's pulse, she was cold. She'd been dead a while.

The blood on her nightgown looked dry around the edges too." She shuddered, recalling the cold and waxy feel of Jane's skin.

Hanna wrapped her arms tightly around herself. "Why would anyone kill her? She was such a nice lady. I mean, she certainly knew everyone's business, but she wasn't a gossip per se. She was always helping people. I just don't understand." Hanna's eyes were bright with unshed tears.

Alex, who now had her emotions firmly under control, gave Hanna a hug and recalled her last conversation with Jane. "I wonder if it has something to do with what she wanted to talk to me about. Maybe she was right and there is someone living in Harriston wanted for murder. Do you think that person found out what Jane suspected? She said she only told Netta."

"Let's consider for a moment how likely it is that she was right this time." Hanna frowned. "Remember last summer? She thought the serial killer from the *Most Wanted* show was Dr. Hanson. That was about the fourth person in the village she thought she recognized from one of her true-crime shows."

Clive, an attendee at book club the previous evening, was a semiretired doctor who maintained a small practice in the village and worked a few mornings each week. He and his wife, Trixie, also ran a small bed-and-breakfast out of a converted barn: Hanson's Heavenly Haven.

Hanna continued, "He used to be an army doc, and it's a good thing he was stationed out of the country when those killings happened, or she would have been calling the FBI."

"In all fairness, he did bear a remarkable resemblance to the pictures of the killer they showed on television. You know the story of *Peter and the Wolf*? Eventually a wolf really did show up. I think we'll just have to wait to hear what Duncan has to say. For now, let's add some more lights to the window display to take our minds off Jane's death." Over the years Alex had had her share of ups and downs, and she'd learned that keeping busy and helping others was the best way to deal with life's challenges. "Did Zach come take measurements for the new window?"

"I arrived a little after eight, but he hasn't been here."

"Maybe something came up. I'm sure we'll hear from him later."

As they worked on the window display, a blast of cold air heralded the entrance of Duncan and a tall, angular woman he introduced as Sheriff Summers. Alex took them into the conference room for privacy, as there were a few customers openly curious as to what the sheriff and deputy were doing in the shop. Within the next twenty minutes, Alex was willing to bet half the village would know the two were here.

The sheriff, with her cropped salt-and-pepper hair, oozed restraint and efficiency. She barked out her commands like a drill sergeant at basic training. "This morning. You were at the victim's house? Start from the beginning. Don't embellish. Just the facts."

Feeling as nervous as a first-day recruit who might be ordered to get down and do fifty push-ups for an inadvertent comment, Alex did her best to recite just the facts. Starting from the night before, with Jane's cryptic comment about a murderer in the village, Alex told Duncan and the sheriff everything pertinent that had led to the discovery of the body that morning.

Sheriff Summers had a tough, steely-eyed look that didn't encourage familiarity and made Alex feel like she was being carefully weighed and measured. Alex sat up straight and didn't fidget while she answered the sheriff's questions. A thesis defense to obtain a PhD couldn't have been any more nerve-racking. It looked like the sheriff was about to put her notebook away when she paused. "One more thing. Where were you last night after you left the meeting here?"

Alex swallowed hard. "I went to my neighbor's briefly and then back to my house for the rest of the night. I was baking cookies with my sister until eleven."

After Sheriff Summers left, Alex blinked. "Wow. Where did she learn her interrogation techniques? The Kremlin?"

Duncan shrugged. "I think she was in the Marines before she joined the sheriff's office."

No surprise there. "What do you think happened?"

"Sorry, Alex, I can't tell you anything about an ongoing investigation."

Alex leaned forward in her chair and put her clasped hands on the table. She looked Hanna's ex-boyfriend in the eye. "Duncan, when you were planning your first date with Hanna, who gave you the inside scoop on all her favorite things? Who told her what a great guy you were? Who comforted her when you broke her heart? Who insisted the two of you remain friends?" She looked at him with her best impression of her mother's guilt-inducing stare. She raised her left eyebrow for good measure.

Duncan hung his head in defeat. "You know anything I tell you is for your ears only?"

She gave him a long-suffering look. "Of course."

"Right now, forensics is still at the house. We're not ruling anything out, but it looks like it could have been a robbery gone wrong. Someone may have broken in, Jane woke up, and they killed her. There was blood on her sheets, so we think she was probably stabbed in bed and tried to get up for help before she collapsed and died. We'll also be looking for anyone who may have had a motive to kill her. Once the medical examiner and the forensics team are done, we'll have a better idea what happened."

"So she was stabbed?"

"Until the autopsy is done, nothing is certain, but that's what it looks like."

"What about the person I saw out back when I got there? Jane was obviously killed much earlier. You don't think the killer came back?" Her eyes widened and her eyebrows shot up. "If robbery was the motive, it didn't look like much could have been taken. There was an envelope full of cash from the historical society's Christmas bake sale on the table beside Jane's purse, her cell phone was sitting on her nightstand, her computer was still in her office, and none of her silver or antiques seemed to be missing. Surely, if it was a robbery, at least some of those things would have been taken."

Duncan slid the written statement and a pen in front of Alex. "Since we don't have an inventory of Jane's belongings, it's hard to figure out what might be missing. There are too many unknowns right now. It's early in the investigation. We're still questioning neighbors, and we'll have to wait for the ME to establish a time of death. It'll be a little while before we have anything concrete."

With the signed statement in hand, Duncan stood. "I'm just glad you're okay. No telling what might have happened if the intruder was still inside when you got there."

Alex had another thought. "How did the intruder get in? I didn't see any sign of forced entry. If Jane was in bed, then the door should have been locked. She was fanatical about keeping her doors locked. I can't imagine her forgetting to do that."

Duncan hesitated. "The intruder probably left the door unlocked when he exited the house."

"That makes sense, but it still doesn't explain how he got in. Were there any basement windows broken?"

Duncan shook his head. "No broken windows, but it's possible the lock was picked." Before he opened the door, he turned around. "Forensics should be done tomorrow sometime. Can you come to Jane's when they're finished and go through the house and retrace your steps from this morning?"

She nodded.

"I'll call you tomorrow." He opened the door and left.

Chapter Five

A lex had barely stepped out of the conference room and back onto the sales floor when Gary Jenkins, owner of Harriston Blooms greenhouse and longtime member of the horticultural society, approached her. An unimposing man with a well-established paunch and a receding hairline, Gary leaned on the side of laconic, bordering on rudeness at times. A county road map couldn't have had more lines than his weary face today.

"I heard Jane passed away and you found her? I just spoke to her yesterday morning." Gary sighed heavily. "What happened? Was it an accident?"

Alex couldn't believe how fast news had spread. That was village life for you. People knew everyone's comings and goings almost instantly. "I found her this morning. I can't say much about it because the sheriff's department wants to notify her family, but it was no accident."

Gary's eyes widened. "Well. This . . . this is a shock. It looked like they had half the sheriff's department out there this morning. I talked to a few of the neighbors. No one knew what was going on. We were all standing around outside, watching." He ran a hand through his thinning gray hair. "I'd like to know what happened. Yes indeed, I'd really like to know."

Gary would have had a front-row seat to all the action; his house was next door to Jane's. Alex knew he led a solitary life. Other than the people he dealt with at the greenhouse, he didn't seem to have any friends or family.

Alex had barely said good-bye to Gary when Yvonne, a well-dressed woman in her midseventies with beautifully coiffed short, silver hair reminiscent of Helen Mirren, demanded Alex's attention. She grasped Alex's hand and gave it a squeeze. "Such distressing rumors. Tell me it isn't so. Not our dear Jane, gone so soon! Why, just yesterday she brought me a beautiful poinsettia—but of course, at our age, you know your days are numbered."

Alex looked at the influx of customers milling around the store. Realizing this would be the day's theme, she resigned herself to commiserating with her customers. "Yvonne, I don't know quite what to say. She was just speaking to us last night at the Sleuth meeting. We're going to miss her."

Yvonne's mouth stretched into a thin line, and an edge crept into her voice. "Yes, she missed the last horticultural meeting of the year in favor of your little club. It seemed an odd choice as the society's president. I've never missed a meeting. Did you know it was originally my idea to start the horticultural society?"

"I wasn't aware of that fact. It was well before my time here in the village."

"Well, with my expertise with plants and my love of gardening, it just seemed the perfect avenue to allow those of us with so much knowledge to share it with amateurs. Of course, I had assumed I'd be elected president, but there it is." She held her palms up, as if there was no accounting for the vagaries of a small village. "I heard from a reliable source that you found Jane. What a shock! What's the sheriff's department saying? There seem to be quite a few of them milling about at Jane's house right now."

Leaning a little closer, Alex spoke in a whisper. "They've asked me not to talk about it until family has been notified. You understand?"

"Of course, of course. We'll have to talk another time, once the sheriff's department has released the details." Yvonne looked at her watch. "Oh, look at that. I've got to run or I'll be late for my appointment with Tanya at Lavish Locks." Giving Alex's arm a squeeze, she limped out the door, leaning heavily on her black walking stick.

If Harriston had boasted a class system, Yvonne Crawford would have been its aristocracy, or at least she would have thought of herself as such. Her parents had been intellectuals, professors at a prestigious university, and as the only offspring of an older couple, she had been thoroughly spoiled. It was reputed she had married well and was quite wealthy. Jane had done much eye rolling at the airs Yvonne liked to give herself.

After helping several customers, who all had questions about the goings-on in the village, there was finally a lull in traffic. Alex was able to fix up a display decimated by people who only wanted information on Jane's death but had happily purchased something to justify their presence in the store. Alex suspected there wasn't a sole person within the village who didn't know Jane had died by this time.

That afternoon, she discussed the murder with Hanna as they piped filling into their molded chocolates. "I don't see how it could have been a robbery that ended in murder. This isn't Detroit or New York. Why would anyone even rob Jane's house? Actual break-ins here are rare. Rowdy teens, feuding neighbors, and stolen bicycles abound, but a robbery and murder? If someone was looking to rob the place, then why didn't they touch Jane's purse or the money right beside it?"

"Maybe they were looking for jewelry? That's something usually kept in a bedroom." Hanna started moving the filled chocolates back into their special fridge.

"Okay, but why pick Jane's house? It's hardly one of the fancier houses in town. Certainly not the kind where you would find expensive jewels. And how did he get in? Jane was obviously in bed, and there were no signs of forced entry. Do people really know how to pick a dead bolt? And why dump books and papers on the floor in the dining and living room but leave the silver and her purse sitting right there, in plain view, on the kitchen table?"

Hanna shrugged. "I can see your point, but the sheriff's department will figure it out."

"I'm not so sure. You didn't see the look Sheriff Summers gave Duncan when I pointed out that Jane's death followed hard on the heels of her telling me her suspicion of a killer in the village from that true-crime show. The sheriff rolled her eyes so far back in her head I thought they might get stuck."

Hanna grinned as she pulled chocolates that were ready to be sealed out of the fridge. "Even if that theory was true, how would that person know Jane was onto them? You said other than you, she only told Netta about her suspicions, and she didn't even mention who she thought it was."

"True, but Netta is the biggest local gossip, and that's saying something in a town that seems to have the highest number of gossips per capita in the state. I'm sure Netta told everyone far and wide what Jane said, so it's quite possible it could have gotten back to the wrong person. I'm not saying that's what happened, but I don't think any theory can be dismissed out of hand."

Staring intently at the chocolates on the counter for a moment, Hanna turned and looked at her sister. "I've got an idea! You have a point that all theories should be considered.

Let's look at the possibilities and see if we can figure this out, just like we do in Sleuth."

Alex paused in her work. "No. You just finished saying the sheriff's department is handling this. They'll find Jane's killer. This isn't a mystery in a book, you know."

Hanna's eyes gleamed. "I know, but all we'd be doing is considering what could have happened. It's just theoretical." She gave a huge shrug. "What harm can it do?"

Alex stopped filling the chocolates and gave her sister an appraising look. "I'm certainly no detective, but I guess it wouldn't hurt to talk through what might have happened. It's not like we'll be the only ones in town discussing the murder."

Hanna cocked her head to one side. "I haven't had a date in months, and I could use some excitement."

"All right, but then let's do this right. We should create a murder board to organize all the information."

In the kitchen was a large, old-fashioned blackboard attached to one wall, usually used for recipes they were creating or lists of what needed to be made. After they finished the chocolates, Hanna erased the board. Alex got sticky notes from a drawer, then wrote Jane's name at the top of the board and labeled her as the victim. She continued with headings along the top of the board: *Day and Time of Death, Motives, Suspects,* and *Alibis.* Underneath *Motives,* Alex wrote, *Burglary and to protect murderer's identity.*

"I have no idea who the suspects might be," she said. "Jane said the picture she saw on television was at least seventeen years old and not very helpful in identifying the killer. Presumably, that was the best picture the police had of the murderer. According to Jane, the last murder happened about a decade ago, so I think we can safely assume the murderer moved here after that. We've only lived here three years, and the only person I know for certain who moved here in the past ten years is Oliver Robins."

Hanna looked at Alex blankly.

"The writer. His yard backs onto Jane's."

"Oh, right. I don't think I've ever met him."

"He's a little reclusive. He writes some kind of self-help books, and I see him at the library occasionally." Alex paused for a second. "I've always thought he's rather good-looking."

"Why have I not run into him?"

"Because you don't ever go to the library. I need to talk to Tom and Maggie. They keep pretty close tabs on the comings and goings in town. Can you try to stay close to Duncan to see what he finds out? I guilted him into telling me what he knew today, but just in case there's any information that might not technically be for our ears, you can snoop around."

When Duncan's wife died of cancer, he had moved back in with his parents to help pay off some of the accumulated medical bills. Somehow he had never left their house, and Hanna often went across the street to visit, even after she and Duncan stopped dating. Alex had been encouraging Hanna to go out more, but after a string of bad dates, Hanna had decided to become more selective, which had resulted in the dry spell.

Later that afternoon, Murder and Mayhem had another surge of customers hoping to hear the details of how Alex had found the body. When Netta Griffin came in, she immediately approached Alex.

"Netta, I love the new hairdo." Alex admired the elderly woman's freshly styled hair.

"Thank you. I had it done this morning at Lavish Locks." Netta tilted her head to one side and patted her short gray curls.

Netta's eyes sparkled, and she practically bounced while she spoke to Alex. "When Stella called first thing this morning, I said she must be mistaken. I couldn't believe it. I just saw Jane yesterday, and she looked fine. Of course, I hurried over to Stella's and watched the deputies and all those crime-scene people come and go. As soon as Stella said you were there when Duncan's cruiser arrived, I knew I had to come see you to get the details. Stabbed to death, poor soul. Don't be afraid to tell me everything. I'm used to blood and carnage. I've read Stephen King. It can't be worse than that." The petite woman looked at Alex expectantly.

"I'm afraid I can't say much. Duncan has asked me to keep things to myself until the family has been notified. Last night, Jane mentioned she told you she had a new true-crime candidate from the village. Did you happen to mention that to anyone else?"

Netta looked like a ball with a slow leak and lost some of her bounce. "You know she's accused several people of being killers from the true-crime shows she watches? I'm afraid I laughed when she mentioned it, and I do feel rather badly about that. It's just so absurd to think a serial killer, or some such person, is going to move here." Netta paused and took a breath. "I may have told one or two people what Jane said to me. Why?"

"Do you remember specifically who you told?"

Netta averted her gaze. "Of course I remember. I'm old, not feebleminded. I mentioned it to Stella earlier today." She paused in her narrative, tilted her head like a bird, and pursed her lips. "I was telling Gary last night at the horticultural society meeting, so I suppose anyone there might have overheard." Netta had the decency to blush. "I seem to remember mentioning it to Eudora when I mailed a parcel on Friday morning. There were some other people in the post office at the time. I can't think who they all were. I do recall the person behind me seemed quite interested in what I was saying, but then they left before I did."

Netta seemed to realize she wasn't likely to get any more information from Alex and made a hasty exit.

After she left, Alex turned to Hanna, who had been trying to listen in. "I can't believe that woman. I'm sure almost every person in Harriston knows about Jane's suspicions. Jane knew what Netta was like. Why would she have said anything to her?"

Hanna shook her head. "I can't even begin to imagine, but you have to admit, there aren't many in the village who would have kept it to themselves."

Alex had to agree.

Promptly at five, Alex turned the sign on the door to CLOSED. As she counted cash and reconciled credit card receipts, Hanna's cell phone rang in the kitchen. Sounds were too muffled to hear what was being said, but it seemed as if Hanna was pleased to hear from whoever was calling. By five thirty, both sisters were done with their tasks and ready to leave.

Hanna was dressed in workout gear and heading to the community center for her yoga class. She would find out what she could from Duncan later, and Alex would gather the names of possible suspects from their neighbors.

"Who called earlier?" Alex locked the front door as Hanna waited for her.

"Just Mom." Hanna tucked a strand of hair behind her ear.

"Oh, did she want anything in particular? She doesn't usually call us at work."

Hanna dug into her pocket for her keys. "Um, nothing in particular. Don't forget to let Watson out. I'm not sure when I'll be home."

Curious. Hanna seemed almost evasive, which was unusual. As twins, their lives were like open books to each other. Alex would have to remember to ask her about it later.

Chapter Six

Walking into her kitchen, Alex saw the light flashing on the answering machine. She hit the play button and listened. "This is Tom. I know about Jane. Don't make dinner. I've got it covered. You and Hanna come to my place when you get home. Maggie and Drew will be here too."

She relaxed and thought how nice it was to have such friendly neighbors—the perks of living in a small village and everyone knowing your business. She really didn't want to cook tonight, and this would make it easy to question the three of them. She had fed Tom numerous times in the past several months, but this would be a first, being invited to his house for a meal.

While Watson was in the backyard, Alex poured dog food into a bowl and changed the dog's water.

Quickly running a brush through her hair in deference to Hanna's admonishment last night, she left a note in case her sister returned early. After letting the dog in and giving her a few cuddles, she put on her boots, grabbed a box of chocolates, and ran over to Tom's.

* * *

Half an hour later, Alex dabbed at her mouth and put her napkin down. "What a delicious dinner. I thought I'd be preparing a peanut-butter-and-jam sandwich when I got home from work, so this was a wonderful surprise."

Drew gave a discreet cough. "I was rather frightened at the prospect of eating anything Tom cooked, but it was surprisingly good. With all my digestive issues, I'm wondering if I might have developed celiac disease or irritable bowel syndrome."

Alex glanced at Tom, who had snorted and tried to cover it with a cough.

"Maybe I shouldn't have dessert?" Drew had developed some hypochondriacal tendencies since retiring last year. So far he'd come up with a new self-diagnosis each month. In September, he'd been sure he had dengue fever. It ended up being a mild bout of flu.

Tom scowled at Drew and then looked at Alex with a kind smile. "I thought you might not want to be alone tonight, under the circumstances. Just wait until you see dessert." Tom started clearing the dishes. Maggie and Alex started to get up and help, but Tom shooed them back into their seats. "This is my night to treat you."

Maggie put her hand on Alex's arm. "We better take advantage of this. Knowing my brother, this won't happen again until the next ice age."

Tom sent his sister an icy glare.

After tidying up, Tom brought a perfect lemon merengue pie out of the fridge and put it on the table.

"Don't tell me you made that." Maggie's eyes widened.

"What? You don't believe I'm capable of baking a pie?"

"No!" Maggie and Drew said in unison.

Looking sheepish, Tom sat down and started serving everyone a piece. "It may have come from the bakery. Drew, if you're concerned about celiac disease, you probably shouldn't have any."

Drew frowned and crossed his arms.

After everybody finished the delicious pie, including Drew, who decided his system might be able to tolerate it, Tom looked at Alex. "Let's head into the family room. I won't pretend we don't want to hear what happened."

During dinner, Alex had indicated she was looking for some information tied to Jane's death but had suggested they wait until after eating to delve into it, so everyone was anxious to hear firsthand details of what had happened. Once they were settled in the cozy space, with a welcoming fire burning, Alex asked how they had found out about Jane's death.

Maggie, two years older than Tom, had the same blue eyes and lean frame but was at least eight inches shorter than her over-six-foot brother. She was perpetually optimistic and celebrated each holiday with a variety of clothes that had themed motifs. Today she wore a black sweater with a cute penguin sporting a glittering red Santa cap. Maggie rubbed her arms as if she was cold. "Well, I had several calls from people telling me they thought Jane had died, so I went to get the mail and talk to Eudora at the post office. If anyone knows what's going on, she does, and she confirmed it. She said Jane's death had to be suspicious or they wouldn't have had all those crime-scene people there."

Alex nodded and sighed. "The village grapevine strikes again. Duncan asked me not to say anything until the family has been notified. By now, I'm assuming that's been done, but we should still keep it between us"—she waved her hands to include them all—"until it's public knowledge."

Everyone agreed.

"Last night, Jane invited me to visit her this morning. She wanted me to watch one of her true-crime shows to see if it reminded me of someone from the village."

Drew, with his gray hair, wire-rimmed glasses, and serious expression, leaned forward. "You know she's accused several people of being murderers from the true-crime shows she watched?"

"I do. Jane insisted this time was different." Alex recited what Jane had said to her the night before, emphasizing Jane's opinion that this time she wasn't mistaken. "She thought there was a murderer living here, and less than a day later, she's dead. A bit of a coincidence, don't you think? I didn't see a weapon anywhere, but the blood pattern I saw and the wounds would have been consistent with a stabbing."

Maggie snapped her fingers. "I remember, that forensics woman . . . Duncan arranged for her to come talk to us a few months ago. She showed us how blood at the scene can tell investigators a lot about how the crime was committed."

"Exactly, and from what I saw, I think Jane was stabbed several times."

Maggie's brows drew together. "Doesn't that sound like a crime of passion?"

Drew frowned. "Or someone just wanted to make sure she was good and dead."

Alex had already thought stabbing someone several times suggested a more personal connection than a random stranger committing a robbery.

Tom was shaking his head. "But who would have an ax to grind with Jane? She was one of the nicest people I know. We could always count on her to help out with any church or community activity. I can't imagine she had a single enemy in the village."

"She almost single-handedly organized the bake sale to raise money for the historical society last Saturday," Drew added.

Alex chewed on her bottom lip. "If it was a robbery like the sheriff's department thinks, then why was the envelope with the money from the bake sale not touched? It was sitting right in the open on the kitchen table beside her purse. And if she was asleep in bed, why kill her? Also, who was leaving the deck as I entered the kitchen?"

"Do you think that was the murderer?" Maggie asked.

Alex shook her head. "I don't think so. Jane had been dead for quite some time, and it was getting light outside. Why would the killer still be there, or alternatively, why would he have come back? As Poirot said, 'We must use the little gray cells.'" Alex tapped her temple. "So what I'm hoping to discover is, who are the possible suspects? The individual from the true-crime show had to have moved to the village in the last ten years or so. I'm also wondering if anyone might have had a grudge against her."

"Alex, this is just an exercise in curiosity, right? You're not actually going to try and find the murderer?"

She looked at Tom and gave a little shrug. Technically, she and Hanna had agreed their search for the truth was just theoretical. But when did theory turn into practice?

Tom seemed to be getting a bit worked up. "I dealt with real killers at the jail, and I wouldn't like to think of you coming face-to-face with one. You know this is a matter for the sheriff's department, right?"

Everyone was silent a moment, waiting for Alex to reply. She knew this could be a sensitive topic, since Maggie and Drew's son was helping investigate the murder. "You may be right, but it didn't seem to me like the sheriff was looking at Jane's murder with an open mind. I'm just indulging in a little cerebral exercise for now. This is what we do every month at Sleuth. Are you willing to help me or not?"

No one said anything for a minute until Maggie spoke up. "I'm in. I'll help you even if these fuddy-duddies won't."

Drew looked a little uncomfortable. "I don't see what it can hurt to discuss it. It's not like she's pistol-whipping suspects, Tom."

Alex and Maggie chuckled while Tom hung his head and slumped his shoulders. "Fine. I'm obviously outnumbered. I guess it can't hurt to do a little guesswork."

Everyone relaxed and was quiet for a moment. Alex retrieved a pen and her notebook from her backpack.

"If I'm not mistaken, Tanya and her husband moved here a few years ago." Maggie tapped her chin with one finger.

"I think we can safely leave out anyone younger than thirty. Jane said the last murder happened ten years ago." Alex didn't think this was about a teenage killing spree. Later, if their theory of a true-crime killer didn't pan out, they could broaden their search criteria.

Tom looked at Drew. "I seem to recall that property developer, Joe something or other, has been here about ten years."

Drew tilted his head and was quiet a moment. "Joe Cameron. I think I recall hearing he moved here after a nasty divorce."

Alex wrinkled her nose and frowned. "I know who he is. He seems like a bit of a jerk. He doesn't come across as nice, if you know what I mean. The way he talks about women makes it sound like we're inferior."

Maggie frowned in agreement. "Gary Jenkins has been here for about ten years. You know who he is?"

Alex nodded. "He was in the shop today. He's the star of the horticultural society, but he can be a little abrupt, and outside of anything plant related, he keeps pretty much to himself." She rose and moved away from the fire. "I know he doesn't like getting his picture taken. Jane wanted him featured in the *Swanson Sun* last year for the gorgeous poinsettias he grows at Christmas.

He refused to be photographed. He said the poinsettias were the stars, not him."

Maggie snapped her fingers. "Penelope Shaw only moved here about seven or eight years ago. I've never seen a woman so desperate to snag a husband. She's gone after almost every handsome, well-off, and cultured man in these parts."

"I take umbrage to that. She hasn't gone after me," Drew sulked.

"Sorry. I meant handsome, cultured, well-off, and single." Maggie emphasized *single*.

"Well, I guess I'm not single," Drew fired back, and Maggie grimaced.

"I'm single," Tom added.

"Yes, but not cultured or handsome." Maggie's eyes twinkled. "And neither one of you two men is that well-off."

Alex, her tone implying mischief, said, "I have to disagree. I'd say Penelope has Tom set firmly in her sights, even if he isn't cultured. She's not bringing him freezer-burnt leftovers because she feels sorry for him. I'd be careful about eating any of those meals she brings, Tom. She's got a reputation as a poisoner here in the village."

Alex thought Maggie was wrong on one other count as well. Tom was definitely handsome in a rugged sort of way. He had a nose that looked like it had weathered a few breaks, and his skin had a ruddiness to it that made him look like he always had a bit of a tan. Maybe he didn't have conventional good looks, but she could definitely see why Penelope was in hot pursuit.

Drew cautiously bit into one of the chocolates Alex had brought and chewed for a moment. "Louise Sweet has lived here about ten years. But she's an elderly woman, so I'm not sure we need to add her to the list."

"What do you mean we shouldn't add her to the list? Just because she's a woman?" Maggie asked indignantly. "Women are murderers too. You've almost driven me to it any number of times." She made a face at Drew and helped herself to a chocolate as well. While she had happily been a stay-at-home wife and mother all her life, she had taught her daughters they could be whatever they wanted. One of her daughters was a doctor in Boston, and another was a diver with the Coast Guard. Maggie was one proud mama.

Drew looked sheepish. "You know what I mean, and I did say *elderly*. Statistically, women are less likely to commit murder. You all are much more sensible than us men. Besides, Louise looks like she's at least eighty, and her disposition is anything but sweet. She's about the crankiest person I've ever met and has about a dozen cats around her place. Maybe that makes her the perfect candidate to be a serial killer."

"Actually, Louise is only about sixty-eight. I issued her a library card when I first moved here and was working at the library part-time. I remember being shocked, because she does look quite a bit older. I'm keeping her and Penelope on the list." Alex glanced at the others, looking for general agreement. "You never know what's hiding in someone's past. I'm adding Oliver Robins to the list, even though it doesn't seem very likely he could be the murderer. Being a published author, it's unlikely he's being featured on a cold-case show. I can't imagine having such a public profile if you were wanted somewhere for murder."

"I just thought of someone else," Tom said. "Zach Roberts moved here about ten years ago. I've gotten to know him a bit, since he's done a few projects around the house for me, and he's far too nice to be a murderer."

"Now he's a good-looking man." Alex winked at Maggie.

"You are so right." Maggie got up and high-fived Alex. "If I was ten years younger . . ."

Alex laughed, "You go, girl."

"Easy there, cougar. Don't forget you've got a husband," Drew said dryly.

Before Drew said any more, Alex mused, "He's certainly good-looking, but I don't think he's all that well-off. As far as I know, he rents a basement apartment over by the softball fields. After the meeting last night, I asked him about installing a new window at the shop. He said he didn't have time to take measurements last night because he had to meet someone, and he never showed up this morning."

"Just remember, Ted Bundy was a good-looking and charming man too." Drew smirked.

Alex looked at her friends. "Can you think of anyone who might have had a grudge against Jane for any reason? Maybe something that happened a long time ago?"

"Honestly, I can't think of anyone that didn't like her," Maggie said thoughtfully. "I've known her most of my life. She taught me in school, I've worked with her in auxiliaries, and I can't think of anyone who disliked her enough to kill her."

"Maggie's right," Drew agreed. "Everyone in the historical society thought highly of her. Even Fenton Carver, who has to be the most cantankerous man I know."

Tom helped himself to a chocolate on the coffee table. "Recap your list, Alex."

"Okay, here goes. I've got Joe Cameron, the slightly misogynistic property developer. Oliver Robins, reclusive self-help writer. Gary Jenkins, gruff, picture-shy greenhouse owner. Zach Roberts, young, attractive, nice but not well-off handyman. Penelope Shaw, husband hunter and poisoner. Lastly, Louise

Sweet, cranky, older but not quite elderly cat lady. Does that cover it?"

Maggie was laughing. "I think that sums it up."

"Well then, it's time to break out the cookies Mrs. Matthews made. She's a great baker, but I'm not partial to her topics of conversation." Tom had a pained expression as he got up and headed for the kitchen.

* * *

Two hours later, Alex was in bed reading when Hanna came in and raced up the stairs. Breathless, Hanna sat on the edge of the bed. Watson, who had been sleeping beside Alex, shook herself awake and snuggled up to the new arrival.

Alex put her book down. "What's up?"

"You're not going to believe this. I was having tea with Duncan—in Swanson, because he was working late. While I was there, he got a call, and I shamelessly listened in, of course. They've taken in a suspect for questioning in Jane's murder!"

Chapter Seven

Only nine days before Christmas, and it was another bitterly cold day, though thankfully there was no snow in the forecast. Wearing tight black jeans and a chunky red turtleneck, Alex ran out and started her car so it could warm up for five minutes before she left for work. The air was clean and crisp, and she could still see stars glittering in the sky. Alex had considered walking to work for a millisecond, before sanity returned.

At eight, it was only starting to get light out. There was a tiny band of pale orange on the eastern horizon, graduating to a pale blue gray and deepening into an intense indigo to the west. Another five days and it would be the shortest day of the year. Alex could tolerate the snow and cold until Christmas, but after that she'd be longing for hot, sunny days.

After a restless night, Alex was weighed down with thoughts of Jane. Could anyone from their village really be a killer?

Still in her coat, Hanna had blurted out the news. "They just took Zach in for questioning in Jane's murder. His fingerprints were found on both sides of the doorknob of the French doors in Jane's kitchen. But that's not the big news. You'll never guess why they were able to identify Zach's prints so quickly." Before

Alex could even try, Hanna said, "He has a criminal record for robbery and assault!"

Character. That was what Jane had said was as important as means, motive, and opportunity. Alex couldn't believe Zach was a stone-cold killer. Who had the sort of character that would allow them to kill and then carry on as if everything were normal? And who had a reason compelling enough to kill Jane? What would Agatha Raisin do?

Agatha would march straight to a suspect's house and grill them. Alex had a better idea.

Stopping at Cookies 'n Crumbs on her way to work, she decided to pick up a couple of Christmas Spirit Scones for herself and Hanna. The scones had cranberries and white-chocolate bits in them, with the lightest of sugar glaze coatings, and were delicious.

The tables were all occupied, and all eyes turned toward her when she walked through the doorway. For a moment, everyone was quiet and stared. She felt like a specimen in a jar, but thankfully the moment passed, and everyone went back to their coffee and gossip.

Sam O'Connor, the owner, was wearing a red apron over a red-and-white-striped top and jeans, making her look a little like an elf, as she was barely five feet tall and had a cap of dark-brown curls held back by a ponytail. Her usually bright blue eyes were downcast as she exclaimed over the fact that even in this little village, people weren't safe in their own beds.

"People have been coming in since yesterday morning talking about it. Of course, no one knew it was murder right off, but when all those crime-scene people started showing up, it got around pretty quick that there was something more to it than a heart attack or a fall down the stairs. I don't think I've had a chair empty for more than five minutes while I've been open for business." All this was said in one breath. Sam talked as fast as she moved, and that was fast, since her only employee didn't always show up for work.

She handed Alex her bag of treats. "Sorry, gotta run. Louise called in sick again, and with being so busy—" She shrugged and went to refill coffee and take orders at a table that had barely been vacant for a minute before new customers sat down.

Driving the short distance to the bookshop, Alex couldn't imagine why Sam didn't fire Louise. She called in sick more often than she was at work, and when she was at work, she was as surly and miserable as anyone could be.

Fortunately, things were more consistent at Murder and Mayhem, mostly because Alex and Hanna didn't have a regular employee. Balancing her backpack and scones, Alex let herself in the front door and smiled. The air was filled with the crisp scent of paper and ink, mingled with hints of cedar and vanilla. Rich, dark mahogany bookshelves lined most of the walls, and a matching counter ran half the length of one wall in the main room. Alex had salvaged them from an ancient bookstore long gone out of business that was being torn down. She could never have afforded such well-made fixtures otherwise.

There were little festive touches of pine, cedar, and colorful ornaments everywhere. A tall but slender Christmas tree, covered in white lights and delicate crystal, white, and silver snowflakes of all sizes, stood on the floor at the end of the counter, where there was just enough room for it. Alex put her coat and boots away and lit one of their homemade candles. The shop would be scented with cinnamon and vanilla for the rest of the day.

Alex had never dreamed she would own her own store. She had worked with many business owners for years in her banking career and had seen the ups and downs that came with business ownership. It had been a big step to quit her steady job and venture into the risky world of entrepreneurship, but she and Hanna had been able to stay in the black since they opened.

Hanna came into the kitchen twenty minutes later, wearing a red buffalo-check flannel shirt under an oversized gray sweater with snug-fitting faded jeans. She'd pulled her hair into a ponytail and looked great, even though she wore only mascara and lip gloss.

"Can you believe it? I still can't get over Zach being brought in for questioning last night. Mmm, those scones look delish." Hanna hung up her coat and sat on a stool.

Alex had thought of little else since last night. "Why was Zach at Jane's house yesterday morning? There has to be more to it. He's lived here for years. There are a lot of homes in the village that would be much better candidates for robbery, and some of them will be empty in another week as people go away for the holidays to visit family. I've been thinking about it, and I think the pulled-out drawers and scattered papers were a distraction to make it look like an attempted robbery."

Hanna took a sip of the tea Alex had put in front of her. "Isn't it possible he needed money right away? Maybe he has a drug addiction? Or gambling debts?"

Transferring the scones from the clear plastic bag to a plate, Alex set them near Hanna. "I don't think so. His behavior certainly doesn't suggest that. He's never shown any signs he's doing drugs or gambling. And why leave Jane's purse and the envelope full of money if you're looking for cash to buy drugs? Also, he couldn't have killed her just before I arrived. It was obvious she'd been dead for hours."

Hanna looked crestfallen. "Well, darn. That means there's still a murderer out there." She took a bite of her scone and sighed.

"I feel certain this wasn't random. I think Jane was killed for a reason, so we need to find out why someone wanted her dead, but my money is still on our unknown true-crime killer at this point. According to Tom, Maggie, and Drew, Jane was well liked and didn't have any enemies. They came up with names for possible suspects based on individuals who have moved to the village in the past ten years."

They stared at the murder board Alex had updated. Taking a bite of her scone, Alex closed her eyes and savored the combination of sweet and tart flavors. If only they could enjoy this little taste of Christmas heaven and forget about murder for a moment.

Alex opened her eyes. "I just figured out the show Jane wanted me to watch yesterday should be taped on her DVR. If I can check it when Duncan has me walk through the house, we might be able to solve the murder by the end of today!"

As they looked at their list on the murder board and debated the best way to tackle their shortage of information, especially alibis, Duncan called and asked Alex to meet him at Jane's house. The forensics team was done.

Chapter Eight

J oe Cameron, a tall, fiftyish man with sandy-colored hair in a ponytail and the athletic build of a runner, was hurrying out of the Black Currant, a health food store next to the bookshop, as Alex walked out the front door of Murder and Mayhem.

"Hi, Joe. You're shopping early." Alex waved her arm. She'd almost said *yoo-hoo*.

For a moment, she didn't think he was going to respond, but stopping abruptly, he turned to face her on the sidewalk. "Yeah, no choice. I was going to make my protein shake this morning after my run and forgot I hadn't picked up my protein mix because I got hung up in a meeting last night, so here I am."

It was obvious Joe wasn't interested in chatting, but Alex wasn't going to waste an opportunity. "Did you hear about Jane Burrows?"

His jaw tightened, and he looked annoyed. Joe shrugged under his black puffer jacket. "The old lady that died? The ladies in my office didn't talk about much else yesterday. Hardly got any work done. Even dead, the old broad is causing me grief. Listen, I'm late for a meeting. See ya."

Without waiting for a reply, he practically ran the rest of the way to his car and took off.

Rats! She'd hoped to get him talking. What did he mean by Jane causing him grief? Alex didn't have time to ponder it further; she was now running behind as well.

Duncan and Sheriff Summers were waiting for her outside Jane's house. In the same gruff manner as yesterday, Sheriff Summers instructed Alex to go through the steps she had taken when she arrived the morning of the murder. They followed her as she took them through the house, describing exactly what she had done the day before.

Alex paused in Jane's bedroom. The body was gone, but there was also a section of carpet removed where Jane's blood had stained it the day before. A mixture of anger and revulsion filled her as she looked at the missing area of flooring, and then a deep wave of sadness rippled through her.

This was where her friend had spent her last moments on earth. As much as Alex believed in an afterlife, she also wanted to see justice meted out in this world.

They ended back in the living room after completing the tour; Alex had answered questions as they went. On the coffee table, Jane's beautiful poinsettia was drooping pitifully and had lost some of its leaves since yesterday morning. Alex checked the soil, but it was still damp.

"Do you mind if I try to find the television show Jane was going to show me? It might explain who did this to her."

Sheriff Summers smirked. "Oh, absolutely. Please do. I wish all our victims would be kind enough to leave taped evidence of their killers."

Ignoring the sarcasm from the sheriff, Alex turned on the television and checked the listing of taped shows. She was confused. There weren't any shows taped. "That doesn't make sense. Jane wanted me to watch the show that had made her suspicious of someone in town. Why would she have erased it?"

Sheriff Summers assured Alex in her smug tone that she was sure Jane had probably realized her error. "No doubt she was going to let you know she was mistaken when you got here yesterday. Hadn't she accused several people in the past of being killers she'd seen on a true-crime show?"

Alex had to concede that was true.

The sheriff's gaze bored into Alex. "I just want to verify your whereabouts for the night of the murder. You said you went to your neighbor's house briefly? We checked with him, and he said it was about five minutes. Is that correct?"

"Yes."

"And after that, you spent the evening with your sister? Until eleven?"

"Yes." Alex began to wonder what the sheriff was getting at, but the woman thanked Alex for her cooperation and told Duncan to lock up the house.

Alex waited until the sheriff was out the door. "Do you still think Zach had any part in Jane's death?"

Duncan sighed. "Do you know how much trouble I can get in for telling you about the investigation?"

"I promise I'll keep it to myself. Besides, I could ask Zach, and I bet he'll tell me what happened last night."

Duncan ran his hand through his hair. "He doesn't have an alibi and says he was home alone."

"So does that mean you have a time of death?"

Duncan cringed. "Yes. Jane died between eight thirty and ten on Monday night. Zach also said he's been working for Jane, which we corroborated with a neighbor who has seen him putting up Christmas lights. There's also a record in Jane's checkbook indicating she's paid him several times."

"So he had a reason to be in the house?"

"Yes. But unfortunately, he does have a criminal record involving robbery and assault, and he lied to us. He initially told us he wasn't anywhere near the house yesterday, but when we said we had an eyewitness . . ."

Alex raised her eyebrows.

Duncan shrugged. "We don't always tell a suspect everything. You're an eyewitness. You just didn't see his face. The clothes you described on the person you saw matched clothes hanging by his door when we went to question him. Based on that, we brought him to the detachment for further questioning. He admitted he'd been in the house to get some of his tools for a job that morning, and when Jane didn't answer his knock, using a spare key for the back door, he went into the kitchen, as was his custom.

"Zach said he was a little worried because she was usually up and about well before he arrived. He thought maybe she'd fallen or something. When he didn't see her anywhere on the main floor, he went upstairs and found Jane in the bedroom, where you saw her. He said he freaked out and knew he'd be a suspect because of his record. He left and had planned to call in an anonymous tip. He didn't realize you'd seen him. We matched his fingerprints on the doorknob."

"That explains the puddle at the back door. Jane would kill anyone who wore shoes into her house. His explanation seems reasonable. Is he still in custody?"

"Technically, he never was in custody. We just brought him in for questioning. We don't have enough evidence to hold him at this point."

"Zach was at the Sleuth meeting until about eight thirty and said he was meeting someone after that."

"We know, but he was alone after nine, which gave him plenty of time to kill Jane."

"So how many times was Jane stabbed?"

Duncan rubbed his face with his hand. "After this, we're square, okay?"

"There were a lot of nights I had to comfort my sister after you broke her heart." Alex was surprised at how quickly inducements of guilt slipped off her tongue to help Duncan overcome his reluctance to share details of the investigation. Maybe she was more like her mother than she'd thought.

Duncan gave another deep sigh. "The ME and the forensic team's initial findings suggest Jane was lying in her bed when she was stabbed three times, which would be consistent with her being asleep. It doesn't appear she fought her attacker. She may have been getting up to try and get help, but she died very quickly from her wounds."

"I appreciate you answering my questions. I still can't believe she's gone. Would you mind if I took this poinsettia home? It's looking kind of distressed today. Not that I'm much of a plant expert."

"Sure." A shadow flickered across his face.

"I'll just grab a plastic bag out of the kitchen to cover it on the way back to the store. Poinsettias don't like the cold."

Holding up his hand to prevent her from going anywhere, Duncan looked at her. "There's one more thing you should know. The sheriff is looking to put someone behind bars, fast. It's an election year. Just remember that."

Alex wasn't sure what Duncan meant by that comment, but it sounded like the sheriff might be more concerned with her image than putting the right person in jail.

* * *

Alex dropped off the poinsettia at the store before she walked across the street to the post office. Eudora Harris had been the postmistress as long as anyone could remember. Alex knew she had to be near eighty, but she still had ramrod-straight posture and dark, shrewd eyes, in sharp contrast to the wispy white hair she kept in a bun and the delicate scent of talcum powder that permeated the air around her. She was also a prolific reader and frequent customer of the bookshop, as well as a whiz with technology.

The spinster was a descendant of Steven Harris, the founder of Harriston. She seemed to have a network of spies and knew just about everything that went on in the village. She and Jane had been friends since childhood.

Alex greeted the postmistress in the empty room. "I brought a few chocolates over." Alex handed her a box. "I put two Ricin Raspberry Creams in. I know they're your favorite. Do you have a second to answer a couple of questions?"

"You didn't have to butter me up with chocolates, but I'm going to enjoy them nonetheless. I'm guessing you're here to ask me about Jane." Eudora responded in a hushed tone, pointing to the area out of sight where the mail was sorted.

Alex understood someone else must be working and lowered her voice. "How on earth did you know that?"

"I happen to know you found Jane's body and were inside her house with Duncan and the sheriff this morning. I'm also aware of Zach's trip to the sheriff's department late last night. It stands to reason your sudden need to ask me some questions might have something to do with Jane."

"Jane thought she and I were observant, but we've got nothing on you. How on earth did you know I was at Jane's today?"

"I have my sources." Eudora winked. "Now, what would you like to know?"

If the CIA ever lost its spy network, they could recruit the seniors of Harriston. "The night she died, Jane asked me to visit her the next morning. She wanted me to watch a true-crime show. She thought she recognized someone from our town on the episode."

"You know she's made a few wild guesses in the past after seeing those shows and they've all turned out to be nothing?"

"I know." Alex leaned closer to the counter. "But it seems a bit too coincidental that she was murdered right after talking to me about it. I find it difficult to believe that Zach could have done it. He's too nice to go around murdering old ladies."

"As Jane and I were of a similar age, I take offense to your referring to her as old. I prefer to think of us as mature. They say seventy is the new sixty, and I wholeheartedly agree."

Alex looked closely at Eudora. Seventy! She had to be a breath away from eighty if she was a day. Jane would have been eighty in January, and Eudora couldn't possibly be far behind.

Eudora lowered her voice again. "I also agree with your assessment of Mr. Roberts. He's done quite a bit of work at my home, both inside and out, and there are quite a few valuable antiques in my home as well as a considerable array of electronics, and I have never had any issue with his honesty or his work."

"Can you think of any other reason someone would want to kill Jane? I took a good look around before I found the body, and I don't think this started as a robbery."

"It would be unpleasant to think we must start locking our doors, but I can't imagine anyone wanting to kill Jane. She was a kind soul and helped so many people in the village. Certainly, there may have been some minor jealousies. I know Yvonne and Netta both wished to be president of the horticultural society, and, while both are certainly knowledgeable, I don't think anyone quite surpassed Jane's mastery of the subject, other than Gary, perhaps. But of course, he has no desire to replace Jane as the society's president. To answer your question, I'm not aware of anyone who had a reason to kill Jane."

"Netta mentioned she was here on Friday and told you Jane had another killer from a true-crime show in her sights. She said there was someone behind her in line when she told you. Do you remember who it was?"

Eudora closed her eyes for a moment. "I'm sorry. I know there was someone else present, but I can't picture who it was. They left while Netta was still talking to me, so I never actually spoke to them. Give me some time, and it might come to me."

"One other thing. Did Jane give you a poinsettia?"

"Yes. She gives one to all of the ladies in the horticultural society each year at the last meeting before Christmas. This year she missed the meeting, so she delivered them earlier that day. I believe she brings each of the men a container of her homemade fudge. Why do you ask?"

"I brought Jane's to the shop because it had so many leaves drop overnight. It looks like it's dying."

"Hmm, I can't imagine why. Perhaps there was a draft from all the comings and goings of the deputies?"

"Possibly. She kept it where she always does in the living room, and the door to the hall was closed when I was there. I'll have to ask Duncan whether it was left open earlier."

"My guess would be a draft. It's unlikely it was anything Jane had control over." Eudora leaned across the counter and continued quietly. "Sheriff Summers talked to Everett Pearson early this morning. Your name came up in the conversation. It sounds like the sheriff has another suspect in addition to Mr. Roberts. You."

Chapter Nine

Returning to the shop from the post office, Alex was grateful none of the customers seemed to need help; one young woman was sitting on the bench by the window reading, and the others were browsing the shelves in both rooms. She related the events at Jane's house and Eudora's revelation to Hanna.

Hanna burst out in anger. "I can't believe the sheriff would suspect you in Jane's death. It's an utterly ridiculous idea! You don't have a motive. Jane was your friend."

"True. And I was with you and Tom all night. Trust me, if I killed someone, I'd try and make it look like an accident. But why would they suspect me? I don't have a motive. Eudora's source must be mistaken."

The door jingled, and a customer exited.

"Did that look like Penelope?" Alex asked. "I thought I recognized her perfume."

Hanna shrugged. "I was in the kitchen when some of the customers came in. We should really have a camera in there. When someone is behind the shelves, you can't see them."

"I agree, but it might put people off, having a camera in the shop. Maybe one of those hidden nanny cams?" Alex turned to the desk behind the counter. "This poinsettia of Jane's really isn't looking great. I need to ask Duncan if the door was open the whole time the forensics and crime-scene people were going in and out."

"I can answer that for you," Hanna said. "They had to close the door to the living room because they were worried about drafts disturbing potential evidence in the living and dining rooms. Someone closed and locked it with the skeleton key sticking out of the keyhole and then put it in the escritory, or whatever it's called—you know, the secretary desk thing."

Alex smiled. "Escritoire?"

"Yes, that one. Why would they call it an escritoire instead of a desk? Anyway, later no one could find the key to unlock the door. They found it eventually, but Duncan was annoyed because it wasted time. He was complaining about it last night. That's why I knew."

"Then I'm stumped. I'm not sure what to do for it." Alex pointed to where she had put it on the desk by the window. The plant's remaining leaves were hanging down as if they were in deep mourning for their owner.

Hanna shrugged. "Don't worry about it. My plants always die on me. Everett called while you were at the post office and wanted to know when you'd be back. I told him to come by in twenty minutes. He should be here soon."

Tall, with dark eyes that could melt your soul, his Afro cut short, Everett was dressed in a dark-gray suit and arrived promptly. Alex led him to the conference room. Everett's wife, Isabelle, and Hanna were close friends, and Alex knew them well, but Everett was all business on this occasion.

"I won't waste any time—I'm sure you're busy—so I'll start by saying I was Jane's attorney. About a year ago, after her brother passed away, she made a new will, and at that time, she also made me the executor of her estate."

Everett pulled a file folder out of his briefcase and put it on the table in front of him. "In the will she named you as one of the beneficiaries. As such, you are to receive half the proceeds of the house when it's sold. The other half is to be split between a few charities and her cousin. She has also named you as the beneficiary of any remaining moneys in her bank accounts, after all estate costs have been processed. Additionally, she indicated you're to have any of the items in the house you would like. Anything you don't want is to be auctioned off, and the proceeds are to go to the horticultural and historical societies she was a member of." Everett looked at Alex. "She's asked if you would handle that part of the arrangements. I can provide you the name of an auction company in Kalispell that handles estate sales."

Alex was dumbfounded. Why would Jane do this? They were friends but not family. Of course, Jane didn't have any close family anymore. She'd often said she couldn't stand her nieces and nephews, who were all in their fifties and "couldn't come up with an IQ between them." But still.

Alex finally said, "I'm shocked. I don't know what to say."

"I know Jane thought very highly of you, if that helps explain her decision. I'll talk to you again once the sheriff's department is finished with the house, but for now, know that Jane considered you a very close friend. I should also mention the sheriff came to see me earlier today and is also now aware of the contents of Jane's will. I'm afraid Jane inadvertently made you a suspect in her murder."

With a sympathetic smile, Everett left.

A few minutes later, Alex had shared everything with Hanna, who looked at her incredulously. "Why would Jane have done such a thing?"

"I don't know. That's what I keep asking myself."

"That explains why you're a suspect. You benefit financially from Jane's death. Now you have to investigate her death to clear your name."

Alex could only nod. Hanna was right. Alex needed to make sure the right person was held accountable for Jane's death. "That must be why Duncan made that comment about the sheriff looking to put someone in jail quickly. He knew I was a suspect."

Yesterday morning she'd awoken as an ordinary shopkeeper. The most pressing thing in her life was ensuring they had enough Killer Chocolates on the shelves. Now she needed to add amateur detective to her to-do list. "I guess I'm going to have to channel my inner Miss Marple until this is solved."

"Interesting that you want to channel a white-haired old lady. Me, I'd be Nancy Drew."

"Miss Marple was an astute observer of human nature. She was usually underestimated. Whoever the killer is, they've been leading a duplicitous life that has now been threatened with exposure. They're going to fight to keep their true identity a secret. They've already killed once to that end. I don't want to close myself off to any possible motives, but one option isn't viable."

"What option?"

"Follow the money. That's what I usually say. I'm an ex-banker, after all. But in this case, that would lead to me, so I know that isn't it. Unfortunately, Sheriff Summers hasn't come to the same conclusion." Alex's stomach growled. "All this talk of murder is making me hungry. I'm going to go grab a burger from the General Store. I didn't bring a lunch today. Before I go over there, I think I'll stop at Harriston Blooms and get a poinsettia for the shop. That gives me a good reason to ask Gary a few questions. With this turn of events, we're going to have to amp up our theoretical investigating. Do you want me to bring you something for lunch?"

After taking Hanna's order, Alex got into her car and drove to Harriston Blooms. Despite living in a tiny community, Alex rarely walked anywhere farther than a block away during the winter. She was going to have to reconsider her drive-everywhere policy when the weather warmed up. The greenhouse was situated virtually alone, on a block with a few old crumbling buildings and ancient lawns that had been reclaimed by weeds and brush and a couple of old houses on the north end of the street. Gary ran the greenhouse and plant store year-round and held the horticultural society meetings there. This year he had provided all the greenery the village's businesses used in their planters on Main Street, at a discount, so they would have a cohesive look.

She didn't know much about his personal life. He wasn't married, but she didn't know if he ever had been or if he had any children. Drew said he was seventy, but Alex would have tacked on an extra ten years if she hadn't known.

Pulling into a parking spot, she observed Gary kneeling on a small piece of rubber in front of the door. Dressed in his usual garb, a sweatshirt and baggy jeans, with an old parka for warmth, he was breaking up a large slab of ice with a pick and sprinkling salt on the area as he removed the chunks of ice. Alex stepped out of her car and called out a greeting.

Gary's face creased in a larger frown than usual. "What brings you here on such a cold day?"

"Actually, I was wondering if you had another one of those poinsettias Jane gave to the ladies in the horticultural society? They're so beautiful, I want one for the shop."

"Sure, let me get this stuff out of the way, and then you can come in." He spread another handful of salt on the cement and gathered his tools. "I had a customer almost fall this morning. If she'd been wearing sensible footwear, she would have been fine."

Gary shook his head in disapproval as he looked at Alex's designer boots. He got up and held the door open for her to precede him inside. "Jane was a sensible woman. She did more in a day than women half her age. This village won't be the same without her. I can't quite get over it. She picked up those plants early Monday morning to deliver them in person, since she wouldn't be coming to the horticultural society meeting."

"Can you imagine why anyone would have wanted to kill her?"

He scratched his chin. "You know, I helped her load her car with those poinsettias, and as I went back inside, Joe Cameron pulled up right beside Jane and got out of his truck and started yelling at her. He was pointing and waving his arms. I thought he might hit her. I was about to go out and see what it was all about when he got back in his truck and pulled out of the parking lot so fast his tires spit ice and gravel. I was afraid he'd run into someone. I went to the door and asked Jane if she was okay, but she said she was fine and got in her car. That was the last time I saw her."

"You didn't hear what they were talking about, by any chance?"

Gary shook his head. "Not really. It sounded like Joe was angry about something Jane had done, but I don't have any idea what it was. They're saying Jane was killed during a robbery."

"That's one possible theory, but I don't think it seems all that likely. Do you?"

He was silent a moment. "More likely than any other reason. Jane was a good person. I can't imagine anyone from around here hurting her. I'm sure whatever Joe was yelling at her about wasn't anything serious."

"Since Joe doesn't seem to be a huge fan of Jane's, maybe there were others who felt like him?"

Gary scratched his head. "I can't think of anyone that could have hated her that much. But I guess it's possible."

"How long did the horticultural meeting go the other night?"

"We started at seven, and I had a few people linger until eleven. Once we start talking about plants, we lose track of time."

"Penelope must have left the meeting early that night?"

"Yeah. It was odd. I think she left shortly before eight. She's usually hanging around until I close. I practically have to kick her out."

"You don't have a wife or kids to keep you busy?"

"Nope. Never got around to getting married. I was always too busy with work, and then one day I was fifty-nine and all I'd done was work in a job I didn't even like anymore. Within a year, I'd left it all behind and moved here."

"What career did you leave behind? Was it in Montana?"

"Nothing interesting, just a boring job in a big city. Let's get you that poinsettia. I'll wrap it for you. You'll want to go start your car right now so it'll be warm by the time you put the plant in."

Gary had worn a veneer of cheerfulness—rather determined cheerfulness, it seemed. There was a decided coolness that had come over his manner when she asked about his past.

Upon her return to the shop, she parked in the narrow driveway beside Murder and Mayhem and dashed in the back door to drop off the poinsettia before heading right back out.

The General Store had been around in one form or another for almost as long as the village had existed. By the look of the interior, not much had changed in the last eighty years. The main counter was fronted by a row of vintage glass containers filled with candy, and there were faded old signs on the walls advertising soda and ice cream that had been there since those items cost pennies, not dollars. One side of the store had a counter with a long chalkboard attached to the wall behind it with a handwritten menu that featured mainly fast food. There were several round stools at the counter and a few tables and chairs at the back of the store.

After giving her order, Alex joined Trixie and Clive, who were lunching at one of the small tables. Trixie had a maternal nature that belied her tough, fit exterior, and as head of the ladies church auxiliary, knew just about everybody in the village. She and Clive were both at the end of middle age but looked younger than most of their contemporaries.

The standard greetings and sad expressions over Jane's passing were conveyed before Alex could probe what she really wanted to know. "I wonder if either of you heard about Jane's recent claim of a killer in Harriston?"

Trixie erupted in laughter. "Yes. A couple of people mentioned it in the past few days. Clive still hasn't quite gotten over his close call with the FBI last time."

"You go ahead and laugh, but Jane was serious about calling them," Clive interjected. "If I hadn't had those pictures to prove I was out of the country when those murders happened, I'd probably be in Guantanamo Bay right now." His face flushed.

Alex tried to look appropriately sympathetic, but she wondered if he was being a bit melodramatic. She tried to steer the conversation away from Jane's accusations. "It seems there were a few people that had recent run-ins with Jane." She mentioned Jane's encounters with Joe and Penelope. "I was always under the impression Jane was universally liked."

"She was, generally," Trixie agreed. "You know how it is in the village. There are always some petty grievances and disputes happening. Last week I walked into the post office and Louise

Sweet was practically shouting at Jane. Something about letting sleeping dogs lie. At any rate, when I came in, Louise left and Jane said she might have opened a can of worms."

"It does seem a few people had words with Jane in the past week."

Trixie shrugged. "Small towns."

It had been an adjustment for Alex when she moved to Harriston. She wasn't used to the level of scrutiny residents of a small village were exposed to. Every little thing a person did became fodder for the gossip mill. While she and Hanna were renovating Murder and Mayhem, almost every resident of the village had happened to wander by. On the bright side, they'd had several people insist on helping without remuneration. Hanna had made lots of Bavarian pretzels for the helpers, but no one had taken a dime for their help.

Chapter Ten

After finishing her lunch, Hanna gathered up the wrappers. "I'm going to be making chocolates for the rest of the day. You'll be on your own in the store."

Hanna and Alex had learned the art of chocolate making from their mother, who had learned it from their *Oma*. They kept their selection small, changing it up according to the season. During the end of November, they sold an Advent Calendar with a box for each day, containing a special seasonal chocolate or one of their signature Killer Chocolates. They had a dozen varieties now in their regular Killer Chocolate line and would be adding Hemlock Hazelnut in January. Of course, none of the chocolates actually had poison in them, but customers loved the theme. A poster on the wall listed all the poisons the chocolates were named after, including the symptoms produced if ingested.

"I think we should see if Maggie can help out in the store until Christmas," Alex said. "With you making chocolates and me needing to get out and investigate, we need someone helping run the shop."

"I agree. She was great last summer. Why don't you call her and see if she can start right away?"

Alex made the call and was thrilled to hear Maggie would be there within an hour.

After ensuring no one in the store needed her help, Alex turned to her computer. She decided research into her suspects' pasts was needed; she would start with Joe, the property developer.

Unfortunately, the website for his company, Heritage Homes, didn't offer much information, other than indicating that his career had spanned two decades in Montana and on the West Coast. There were pictures of some attractive homes, a couple of which Alex recognized from Harriston. But aside from a few mentions related to his business, she couldn't find anything about Joe as an individual. While she knew not everyone had an online social media presence, it was odd not to find anything for someone his age.

She had expected to find at least a reference in an obituary for a parent or grandparent, though it was certainly possible Joe still had all his family living. Her *Oma* was ninety-two and very much alive and working part-time at her parents' restaurant.

She moved on in her research. Oliver Robins's car had been parked at the library when she returned from the General Store. He drove an immaculately maintained silver Mercedes, the only one in Harriston, making it easy to spot.

She looked up Oliver's biography on his website and read it through. He'd been raised in Australia until he was sixteen and then was sent to a boarding school in England. After university he struggled with a drug and alcohol addiction for several years, before turning to meditation, Buddhism, and veganism to overcome his addictions. His self-help books were a guide to living a healthier physical, mental, and spiritual life. There was no mention of a wife or children. It said he continued his healthy practices in a small village in Montana and was still writing.

Alex found a social media account that seemed to revolve around his books but didn't really provide any personal information; it just showed a handsome, smiling man in his early forties performing yoga and meditation in a lot of tropical settings. She decided she would head to the library and have a chat with him when Maggie arrived.

True to her word, Maggie showed up within the hour. Alex gave her a quick rundown of the pertinent things that had changed since the summer. "If you have any questions while I'm out, check with Hanna."

"I'm so glad you called. Drew has been researching every one of his imagined symptoms on the internet and weighing himself every hour. We have delivery trucks coming every day to drop off supposed cures for all that ails you. And now he's brewing some kind of concoction he found online that has the house smelling like a cabbage-filled sewer."

Alex laughed. "We're just grateful you're here. It looks like I may be a suspect in Jane's murder, so I've got a vested interest in finding out who killed her. I'm going to the library to talk to Oliver."

Maggie spoke hesitantly. "I've been thinking about people who have moved into town in the past ten years. Technically, Netta fits that list. She grew up in Swanson, but her husband was from Harriston, and they lived here the first few years after they married. She moved back from Texas ten years ago, after her husband passed away. I suppose since we knew her before she went away, she can't really be a suspect?"

Alex expressed her appreciation to Maggie. At this point, she didn't think anyone could be completely ruled out. Even if Jane had been wrong, again, in her obsession to recognize a village resident from a true-crime show, there was no disputing someone had wanted her dead.

The library was on the second floor of an old brick building beside Murder and Mayhem; the spacious first floor housed the village offices. After climbing a creaky flight of stairs to the library, Alex was a little breathless. She definitely needed to get into better shape.

Things were quiet in the library now, but come summer, it as well as the rest of the village would be hopping with tourists and cottagers. Sure enough, the tall, lanky writer was in the nonfiction room. His sun-lightened, milk-chocolate-colored hair touched his shoulders, and he had the look of someone with a perpetual tan. There were books piled on a table in the corner of the reference section, where he seemed intent on his work. Alex quietly greeted the librarian, then went straight to Oliver's table and drew a chair across from him.

Alex introduced herself to the slightly startled author. It seemed she remembered him better than he remembered her. She got the impression he initially thought she was some middle-aged groupie stalking him. Fortunately, he was familiar with Murder and Mayhem, and she was able to establish herself as a legitimate library patron.

After his first few words, Alex drew a breath in pleasure. She loved an English accent. It was so sexy to listen to, but there was a purpose to the interview. She snapped her mouth shut, it having momentarily hung open. "Are you working on another book?"

The table was strewn with books, and he was taking notes; thus, the answer seemed obvious, but better to lead with something less accusatory than *Did you kill your neighbor?*

"I've got an advance to do a book on better sleep to fight addiction. It's been a bit of a struggle to work on it at home, so I came to the library."

"That sounds interesting." *Probably still too soon to ask for an alibi.* "Where did you go to school?" Alex was terrible at small talk and never knew what to say.

Oliver became more animated. "I studied neurobiology at Oxford, and I'm fascinated by the two-way relationship between addiction and sleep. People often treat sleep problems with drugs and alcohol, which can lead to addiction. If they're already addicted to drugs and alcohol, that can impact their sleep patterns and make them more reliant on their addiction in order to sleep. It's a vicious cycle. Of course, you're not here to listen to me talk about my book . . ."

Oliver looked at her expectantly.

Finally, the moment she had been waiting for. "I won't keep you long. I'm assuming you've heard about Jane Burrows's murder? Her backyard adjoins yours."

"Some deputies actually came by my house and asked if I'd seen anything suspicious the last couple of days. It's terrible. She was such a nice lady. It's one of the reasons I'm working here today. Every time I look at her house, I think about what happened, and I can't focus. I tried meditating but finally gave up."

"So, did you see anything suspicious?"

Oliver's demeanor changed slightly, and he became more sullen. "As I told the deputies, the only thing I noticed was Jane's handyman doing some work around the house. He hung her Christmas lights a couple of weeks ago and has been doing some repairs and other work on her deck. He must have been working on things inside as well, because he was carrying tools and supplies in and out for the last few days." Oliver scrutinized his hands, which were clasped on the table. He glanced at Alex with an edge of apprehension before lowering his gaze. "I didn't hear or see anything the night of the murder."

That's a lie if I ever heard one. "That's too bad. I happened to be the one to find Jane's body, and I saw someone leaving the back deck as I got there. You never noticed anyone going in or out Monday night?"

Oliver straightened the books on the desk and shook his head. "As I said, I didn't see anything. I didn't get home until after ten that night. I wish I could be more help." His tone belied his words, and it was obvious he really wished the conversation would come to an end.

"You look like you've been away somewhere warm recently?" Alex admired Oliver's tan.

His cheeks flushed. "I go to Bermuda a few times a year, so I never seem to lose the tan. I do videos and take pictures I can use for social media."

There was nothing to be gained in keeping Oliver from his research any longer.

Alex chatted a few minutes with the librarian before heading back to the store. She hadn't bothered with a coat because of the short distance, and the frigid air assaulted her and was sharp in her lungs the moment she stepped outside. An area of Arctic air was hanging over Montana and causing particularly low temperatures, and there was no relief in sight for at least a few more days. Hopefully, temperatures would go back to something more seasonal by Christmas.

Despite the cold, Alex lingered beside the building, admiring the picturesque scene before her. A wave of nostalgia washed over her. She loved Christmas and missed her Bavarian-themed hometown at this time of year. With Everett's help as mayor, she had been pushing the village to make more of an effort to draw tourists. This year Main Street looked like something from a Currier and Ives postcard. All the businesses had large black planters in front of their doors, filled with festive greenery and red velvet bows. On each lamppost hung a large green wreath lined with white twinkle lights and adorned with a red bow, and there was a huge Christmas tree in the middle of the village's main intersection, decorated with white lights and giant round ornaments.

Murder and Mayhem and several other businesses had lined their large picture windows overlooking Main Street with cedar garlands and white twinkle lights. A photographer from Kalispell had come the week before, during Harriston's Christmas festival, to take pictures of the village for the lifestyle section of a Kalispell magazine that had published yesterday. During the festival, carolers dressed in Victorian-style clothes had sung along Main Street. The retail shops had sponsored a hot-chocolate-and-cookie booth and, when there was enough snow, a snowman contest. There had also been a bazaar in the community center for individual crafters and small businesses and a family dinner and dance on Saturday night.

It was only three, but the light was waning, and in another hour the Christmas lights would be turning on outside. *It always gets dark so early in December.*

On impulse, Alex ran past Murder and Mayhem and stopped at Penelope's antique store. She pushed the door open and inhaled the musty odor of old furniture. Each square inch of the dingy room was crammed full with every imaginable kind of antique.

Penelope was sitting behind the counter of the empty store, cleaning an old clock. On the floor at the end of the counter, on a plush dog bed, a miniature schnauzer growled low in its throat and then proceeded with a riot of yapping. Penelope breathed in sharply when Alex entered. She told the dog to be quiet, and he shut up immediately. "Why are you here?"

Alex hadn't expected a friendly greeting and wasn't going to mince words. "I won't stay long. I'm curious what you said to Jane on Monday night when she left the Sleuth meeting. Someone saw you waylay her, and you seemed to be quite angry with her. I'm sure the sheriff would be interested in hearing about that."

Penelope's face turned white, and the lines around her mouth deepened. "I'm sure it's none of your business. She and I had a difference of opinion regarding a small matter, and that's all I'm prepared to say."

The door opened and several ladies came in, chattering happily. The dog started its raucous barking again, and Penelope quieted him.

She looked at Alex. "Is there anything else?"

"Not at the moment." This wasn't over. Without another word, Alex turned on her heel and left the overly warm shop.

Shivering, she ran the last few steps back to Murder and Mayhem. Inside, business was brisk. Apparently, people from Kalispell had seen the pictures in the magazine and were driving out to see the bakery and other shops decorated so traditionally for Christmas. It was a good thing Hanna was making more chocolates; this was promising to be their best Christmas for sales since the store had opened.

At five, Alex shut the door behind their last customer, locked it, and turned the sign to CLOSED.

"We had a pretty good day, I think. Those ladies from Kalispell bought several boxes of chocolates as well as a bunch of our gift items and a stack of books." Alex walked behind the counter to start tidying up.

Maggie straightened the boxes in the chocolate display. "One of the ladies asked about the Advent Calendar and was very disappointed when I told her they were only available the last two weeks of November. I gave her a sample of the Candy Cane Coniine. She loved it and ended up buying four boxes of the Christmas Killer Chocolates."

Alex had decided that since the Advent Calendar had been so popular last year, they would sell a special Christmas Killer Chocolate collection that featured Candy Cane Coniine, Gingerbread Gelsemine, and Fruitcake Fluorine chocolates.

"I'd better get home. Drew said he needs to eat before six to keep his digestive system on track. Just thinking about all the stuff he's been concocting gives me the trots." Maggie put on her coat. "I'll see y'all later."

Alex was starting to count the day's cash. "We'd better hurry too," she called out to Hanna in the kitchen. "Watson will need to be let out and fed before the ladies arrive for our class on how to make chocolates."

Alex was a competent chocolatier, but she didn't have the flair Hanna had developed as she continued to study chocolate making long after Alex had moved away. Alex was excited to help teach the mysterious and precise art of creating tiny, delectable masterpieces. Hanna's chocolates had won awards for Most Delectable Ingredient Combinations and Best Artistic Design at a bridal awards competition a few years before she moved to Montana. Their mother was still nursing a little bitterness over losing Hanna's chocolate-making skills to Alex's business venture.

When Alex had described her plans to quit banking and open a bookshop, Hanna had suggested she move to Montana and make chocolates at the bookshop. Hanna had total creative control over that part of the business, and their chocolates were already becoming famous in the area. The past several weeks had seen tourists skiing in Whitefish come to Harriston to purchase them.

Alex had great hopes for the evening. Not only was she planning to finally crack the secret of Hanna's award-winning chocolates, she was also expecting to glean some helpful information to help solve Jane's murder from a few of Harriston's leading gossips.

Chapter Eleven

Arriving home, Alex set the house aglow with hundreds of twinkle lights. Coming from Frankenmuth, where Christmas was celebrated year-round to some extent, Alex and Hanna usually had every inch of the house decorated within the first week of November. It was almost heartbreaking to put all the decorations away in January.

Rummaging through the freezer, Alex found some soup and put it in the microwave before letting Watson into the backyard. Hanna prepared all the things they would need for the evening's lesson. The previous year, they had done a special evening of German cookie baking with friends. This year Alex had suggested they teach their friends how to make hand-molded chocolates.

Trixie, Maggie, Netta, and Stella would be coming, as well as Sam from Cookies 'n Crumbs. Hanna and Alex had already prepared certain things ahead of time to make the process quicker tonight.

The kitchen was large, with ample counter space and a large quartz island that allowed plenty of room for each person. Like the rest of the house, the kitchen was done in whites and light grays. Alex had added touches of natural wood and other textures that made the house warm and inviting.

Centered in front of the living room window was a large, flocked Christmas tree decorated in silver, gold, and white, with hundreds of small, white twinkle lights. Incorporated in the tree were natural elements like pinecones that gave it a winter wonderland effect.

*   *   *

Christmas music was playing in the background when the women arrived at six thirty. Alex and Hanna both had their hair up in a ponytail.

When Stella walked in, she put her hands on her hips and looked at them both. "You know I can hardly tell you apart when you put your hair up like that."

"Hanna's the prettier one." Alex nudged her sister in the ribs. They used to hate it when people compared them, especially when it was suggested that one was prettier, or smarter, or heavier than the other. More secure in themselves now, they occasionally teased each other that way.

Hanna crossed her eyes at Alex, then gathered everyone around the kitchen island and exhibited two different chocolates. "Chocolate needs to be tempered, or it won't have that beautiful shiny finish." She pointed to the first chocolate. "We want to be especially careful not to have sugar bloom. See the whitish spots on this other chocolate? Sugar bloom is caused by moisture in the chocolate-making or storing process. Water isn't our friend today, ladies."

"Can that chocolate still be eaten?" Trixie pointed to the second chocolate.

"Absolutely. It will still taste fine. It just doesn't look as appealing. There will be no casualties tonight. Even if things don't'turn out perfectly, it's still chocolate."

The ladies went through the process of melting the chocolate over double boilers to the right temperature. Alex checked the candy thermometer while Sam stirred. "Sam, you know Zach, right?"

Sam had lived in Harriston all her life. Her family had helped establish the village and continued to be some of its most prominent residents. "Pretty well. He did most of the work on the bakery when I bought it, and he does any maintenance that comes up."

Alex hated to spread gossip, but the needs of the investigation took precedence, so she dove in. "Did you know he had a criminal record? He just doesn't seem the type to have committed robbery and assault."

Sam shook her head. "I had no idea. He's always been really great, though. He's a hard worker and very fair on his quotes. I accidentally left the safe open once after getting out the float, and he pointed it out to me and told me to be careful about keeping cash out. He said, 'Crime happens everywhere, even in small towns.'"

Stella spoke up. "Did you know Zach's dating that pretty teacher from the school, Jennifer something or other? Someone said they were talking marriage. I don't think he had anything to do with Jane's death. Even if he is a suspect."

"Jennifer called in sick Tuesday morning and said she'd be out for the rest of the week. They were a little put out at the school, but she's so good with those kids, she can get away with a little extension on her holidays," Netta added.

"Speaking of dating." Sam was looking meaningfully at Hanna. "Have you been out on a date lately? I'm only asking because I was asked to organize the school reunion dance, and I need volunteers to help. The renovations to the school gym and theater are almost finished. Many of the alumni donated to it, and the school is celebrating with a reunion to recognize their generosity. I want to organize a special speed-dating activity prior to the dance. It will be a fun way to help singles get to know each other. Please say yes. I really need the help, and there aren't many singles in Harriston. Many of the alumni won't get into town until just before the dance."

Reluctantly, Hanna agreed to help out. "Why don't you ask Alex? She's single."

"I know, but Alex doesn't give off a very receptive vibe for dating. No offense." Sam looked at Alex apologetically.

"None taken. And you're right. After the last date I had, I've sworn off romance."

Hanna held up a clear mold. "Okay, ladies. Now we let the chocolate cool until it reaches about eighty-eight degrees Fahrenheit. In the meantime, we'll prepare our polycarbonate chocolate molds. We want to ensure they're sparkly clean. Make sure you don't leave any fingerprints inside the mold, where the chocolate goes. And remember, water isn't our friend. Make sure the molds are completely dry."

Alex headed to the stove. "Once that's done, we'll start our ganache. Essentially, it's just a chocolate-and-cream filling. Of course, there are other ingredients as well, and we made the pear puree ahead to save time tonight. The recipes we give you will have all the ingredients and instructions."

Hanna held up a perfect chocolate. "Tonight we're making a special chocolate I've created just for us, Poison Pear Ganache. It's a subtly flavored white-chocolate pear ganache enrobed in a dark-chocolate shell. The key to having a spectacular chocolate is ensuring it has a smooth mouthfeel and has the prefect infusion of flavors."

As they cleaned their molds, Alex managed to position herself beside Stella, who was renowned for knowing something about everyone in the village. "Do you know where Penelope's from? I heard she's been divorced a couple of times."

"Far be it from me to gossip." Stella looked at Alex over her half glasses as she spoke. Alex had to look down at her mold so Stella didn't see her eyes bulge. "But I think she's been divorced more than a couple of times. Netta told me Penelope let it slip the last one was number four. She must have moved here from North Carolina, but the plates on her car were changed lickety-split. Most people wait awhile, but she had new ones a couple days later."

"Ladies, it's time to coat your molds." Hanna showed them how to heat and then fill the molds, scrape them, get the air bubbles out, and pour out the excess chocolate and scrape them again.

Making chocolate was an exacting skill. Hanna shared an experience from the year they were fourteen and their mother had asked Alex to watch the thermometer as the chocolate was heating. Alex had been reading one of her mysteries and became so engrossed she'd missed the temperature starting to escalate. By the time she realized what had happened, the chocolate had burned and turned into a dry, discolored paste. After that, her mother had patted her down each time they were baking or making chocolate to make sure she didn't have one of her novels with her in the kitchen.

Near the end of the night, Alex managed to corner Netta. "Stella mentioned you told her Penelope had actually been married four times. I thought she'd only been divorced twice."

Netta's eyes brightened. "Well, just after she moved here, I brought her some buns. You know, a little welcome-to-the-village visit."

Anyone moving into the village could count on at least one or two visits from the old biddies in town, baked goods in hand. Gossip was a commodity in the village, bought and sold like coffee bean futures on the New York Mercantile Exchange. There couldn't have been more intensity and furor in the trading pit of the NYME for a futures contract than in the living rooms and kitchens of Harriston for a juicy bit of information.

When a moving truck pulled in, husbands were sent out to help unload with strict instructions to find out anything and everything. In the meantime, more than a few ovens in the village were set to 350 degrees. The power company must occasionally wonder at the sudden surge in usage. It was a race to be the first to get your banana loaf in.

"While we were chatting, I asked her what brought her to the area. She said she'd just had a nasty split with her ex. Naturally, I asked if it was her first divorce, and she said she'd been married four times, 'not that the last one counted'—her words. She seemed to realize what she'd said and corrected herself. She said, 'Silly me, I mean I'm twice divorced,' and then told me about her first two husbands. She's told everyone else she's only been divorced twice, but I think she's lying. Of course, I can't prove it, but I'm sure I heard her correctly." Netta sniffed, her chin seeming to recede even farther, giving her a petulant look.

Hanna had several molds of chocolates already prepared, and she and Alex showed the ladies how to fill the chocolates from a pastry bag with the ganache.

"Make sure you avoid getting the filling on the rims of your chocolate molds. It can cause leaks in your chocolate shells. Also, make sure you don't fill them to the top. Leave about a sixteenth of an inch so you can seal them properly." Hanna held up a mold that already had the ganache piped into the shells.

By the end of the night, they had gone through the entire process, and everyone was delighted with the new concoction Hanna had created.

After the newly minted chocolatiers left, the sisters sat down on the living room sofa, exhausted. Alex recounted for Hanna the things she'd discovered.

"Why would Penelope lie about the number of times she's been married?" Hanna stretched out her legs on the coffee table, and Watson jumped onto the sofa beside her.

"Maybe she's embarrassed or thinks it will impair her chances of getting number five? Or maybe she killed numbers one through four and is on the run?"

Hanna laughed. "Well, you should warn Tom. Just in case." She continued laughing.

Alex threw a pillow at her. "Be serious. I'm going to talk to Zach tomorrow. After Duncan's warning, I'm wondering how hard the sheriff is looking at other suspects." She yawned and grabbed another Poison Pear chocolate. "We need to figure out who has an alibi. It would seem Oliver and Gary each have one. Do you think you can find out if there's anything new in the investigation from Duncan?"

"I'll do my best." Hanna walked over to the window and peered out across the street. "I don't see his car yet."

"Be careful. You're starting to remind me of Penelope."

Hanna made a face.

"I'm sorry you got stuck helping out with the reunion dance."

Moving away from the window, Hanna shrugged, "Don't worry about it. It's funny. When you reach a certain age and you're unmarried, people either want to set you up with someone they think will be perfect for you or you're that person they can ask to help with every committee because you're single and therefore must have lots of time on your hands."

"I know. It's not as bad for me because, apparently, I give more of a back-off vibe than you do." Alex laughed.

Hanna started chuckling. "Remember that guy Stella set you up with?"

"How could I forget? We were halfway to Kalispell when he pulled over in a truck turnout, put his cell phone on the dash, and said there was a basketball game on that he had to listen to. We sat there for almost two hours, and when it was over, I told him to just take me home. I couldn't believe he actually called and asked me on a second date." Alex shook her head. "Then there was the guy you went out with who showed up in slippers and decided it would be fun to go back to his mother's, where he was living, and watch home movies." She smiled broadly.

"Don't remind me. Maggie set me up with him through a friend of hers after Duncan and I split up. It was her friend's grandson, and he'd just finalized his divorce. Maggie had no idea what he was like. She felt awful for making me go through that," Hanna said good-naturedly.

"I'm not going to promise I'll never try and set you up, but I promise not to set you up with anyone I wouldn't go out with myself. Who knows? If I get desperate enough, maybe I'll give slipper-guy a call."

Hanna guffawed. "I'll save you from yourself if you start making those kinds of choices! Besides, you're going to find the perfect guy and get married and live happily ever after."

"Maybe I should ask Penelope for pointers," Alex said, her expression deadpan.

Hanna burst out laughing. "Don't worry. Things always have a way of working out the way they're meant to. That's why I'm not too worried about my dating status. I'll meet the right guy at the right time."

"I'm not even sure I want to get married again. Once bitten, twice shy. I'm set in my ways, and I don't know if I could handle a second divorce. Failing at marriage isn't something I want to experience again, and with one divorce under my belt, I'm not sure I want to take a chance."

"You're too young to give up on marriage. Even though you're older than me."

Alex threw a cushion at Hanna.

"It looks like Duncan's home." Hanna was peeking out the window again. "I'll go up to my room and call him. It's always best to question men at the end of the day when they're not thinking as clearly."

Alex finished tidying up. She looked out her window at Tom's house. Lights were on, and she decided to call and see if he wanted to go with her to question Zach tomorrow.

"I'm glad you asked me," he told her. "I think it would be an excellent idea to check on a member of my flock. I can give him a call and arrange a time for tomorrow when you're done working."

"I keep forgetting to ask if you have any true-crime episodes taped. When I checked Jane's DVR, there wasn't a single episode taped, which seemed strange. The killer must have erased them all. Nothing else makes sense."

"That is strange. Jane enjoyed watching those types of shows even more than I do, if that's possible. I have at least half a dozen on my DVR."

"Can you please not erase them until I've seen them? I'm hoping you might have the same episode Jane wanted to show me."

"How are you going to know if it's the same episode?"

"I guess if it's about a four-time murderer with a blurry picture, I'll know it's the right one."

Tom cleared his throat a couple of times. "Maybe you'd like to come over tomorrow after we see Zach and watch one of those episodes?"

"That would be great. If it's not imposing too much on you?"

After Tom gave Alex several assurances that he would be delighted to have her watch any number of episodes at his house without being inconvenienced in the least, she rang off.

As she walked past Hanna's bedroom on her way to bed, she stuck her head in to say good-night and let Watson in. The dog usually slept with Hanna if they were both home. Hanna was on the phone with someone and looked like she had been caught with her hand in the proverbial cookie jar. She told whoever it was to "hang on" and said good-night to Alex, then waited until the door was shut to start talking again.

What on earth was that about? Since when did they have secrets?

Staring at her reflection while she brushed her teeth, Alex wondered about all that had happened in the past few days. Who was, even now, sitting in their warm and cozy home, secure in the knowledge that, with Jane's demise, their secret was safe?

Alex hadn't learned much today. Neither Gary nor Oliver had been very forthcoming. Both had something to hide, but was it anything pertinent to Jane's death? Gary had mentioned the incident between Joe and Jane on Monday. What had Jane done to arouse that kind of anger? The same could be asked about Penelope. Hanna's description of Penelope shouting at

Jane suggested something more than a minor difference of opinion. Didn't it?

In her mind's eye, she recalled Gary's hands when she asked about his past. Despite the casual tone, his knuckles had gone white as he'd gripped the counter. Unsure what it meant, she made a note to find out more about him.

Chapter Twelve

Before going to sleep last night, Alex had resolved to head in to work early to get some paperwork done that she'd been putting off. Walking past her sister's room, she heard Watson moving around. Quietly, Alex opened the door and let the dog follow her downstairs.

When Alex let Watson into the yard, Tom already had his lights on. She wondered what she'd say if he asked her on a date. She was really too old to have children anymore. That door had pretty much closed, but if she started dating someone older, it would be like putting a lock on it. Someone his age wouldn't want to have little children running around. Of course, that was probably true for most men her age; realistically, her childbearing days were past. She'd known her biological clock was ticking, but at this point, it was dying a not-so-slow death. She needed to make peace with that fact. With Tom, at least, there would be a ready-made family with grandchildren. She shook her head. She'd better stop this line of musing. If she wasn't careful, she'd have herself married to him by the time she gave the dog breakfast, without ever having gone on a date. Watson heard Alex laughing and came running back to the house for some quick cuddles and kibble.

Opening the garbage can lid, Alex was about to throw out an empty cereal box when she saw a partially crumpled note in her sister's handwriting. The words *when Alex isn't around* caught her eye. She pulled the note out and smoothed it on the counter. It was a short to-do list, the last item being *Call Mom when Alex isn't around*. There was a big star beside it. Her brow furrowed. She threw the note and the cereal box into the garbage. Alex looked at Watson. "Do you know what that means?"

Why would Hanna wait until she wasn't around to call Mom? Unable to come up with anything that made sense, she left Watson curled up in her doggy bed and headed to work.

In their rush to get home for the chocolate-making class the night before, they hadn't done their usual thorough cleanup. At the shop, Alex quickly tidied things up and was restocking their chocolate display case and bookshelves when there was a knock at the door. Duncan was on the doorstep. She ushered him in and offered him a peppermint tea.

"No, thanks. I was heading out of town and saw your lights on and wanted to pop in for a second."

"Sure. What's up?"

"You said you spent the evening with Hanna the night of Jane's murder?"

"That's right. I left Tom's, then Hanna and I spent the evening baking, and then I went to bed."

"We spoke to Penelope yesterday. She said she saw Hanna take Watson for a walk from about nine thirty until ten."

"I don't remember the time exactly, but Hanna did take the dog out. At that point, we were taking cookie sheets out of the oven and putting new ones in. She took Watson for a walk. I really don't know how long she was gone. Why does that matter?"

"With the time of death between eight thirty and ten, that means you could have left the house while Hanna was out and killed Jane and returned home again before she returned."

"That's crazy. Why would I want to kill Jane? She was a friend. Besides, I don't walk anywhere in the winter. I would have taken my car, and I can't imagine Penelope would have missed that. Even if I was inclined, which I wasn't, Jane's house is a bit far to have gone on foot in that short span of time. You know me, Duncan. I'm not even capable of running that distance. Her place is at least half a mile from my house. Plus, how would I have gotten into the house? I certainly don't know how to pick a lock."

"I'll grant you the timeline would have been tight, but anyone can Google how to do just about anything these days, including how to pick a lock. We've confirmed you stand to inherit a substantial portion of Jane's estate. That's a pretty good motive. Do you take any sleeping pills?"

That's a non sequitur. "What has that got to do with anything?"

"Jane had eszopiclone in her system when she died. It's a strong sedative. There was a box of Killer Chocolates on her nightstand, and every single one of them was laced with the stuff. That suggests Jane wasn't killed in a random burglary. Someone set out to sedate her and, quite possibly, kill her.

"She ate one of those chocolates shortly before she died. It would have knocked her out within minutes, and even if the killer was playing the drums all the way to her room, it's unlikely she would have heard it. Did you give her those chocolates?"

"Absolutely not!" Alex's pulse escalated, and her face warmed. "At the Sleuth Book Club, Jane mentioned a Christmas elf left them for her earlier that day. She winked at me when she said it. I guess she thought I gave them to her, but I didn't. She told me

100

she planned to have one before bed. They're her favorite," she said hoarsely.

"Can you think of anyone who has purchased a box of them recently?"

"No. That would have been a custom order."

Duncan stared at her.

Alex gave a shake of her head. "We don't usually sell a box of only one kind of chocolate. Someone would have had to ask for them specifically or bought several boxes and picked out all the Veronal Vanilla Creams. I can ask Hanna if she remembers making up a box like that for anyone."

"Veronal?"

"It was a barbiturate that was sold by the name veronal in Europe and England until the fifties. It was used as a sedative, but because it was so addictive and led to quite a few overdoses, it was taken off the market."

"Look, Alex. I don't think you did it, but the sheriff is determined to find a quick resolution to the murder. You and Zach have solid motives and opportunities, and that's where she's putting her efforts. Unless something more obvious comes across her desk, she's got the two of you as her top suspects."

Alex couldn't believe what she was hearing. Clearly, the sheriff wasn't going to do a proper investigation or search for the real killer. Alex had discovered two people in the past forty-eight hours who had engaged in heated arguments with Jane shortly before her death. But it looked like the sheriff had tunnel vision as far as this murder was concerned.

"Do you have any more details on the murder?"

"Hanna asked me the same thing last night. I shouldn't be telling either of you anything, but I don't necessarily agree with the sheriff's list of suspects. The ME confirmed Jane was stabbed three times with a long, narrow blade, something like an ice pick, though they haven't found anything that could have been the murder weapon so far. Since Zach was at the scene when you arrived and doesn't have an alibi, he's become our number-one suspect."

Duncan headed for the door. "I need to get going. Say hi to Hanna for me when she comes in."

Hanna arrived thirty minutes later with Watson, and the sisters sat down with tea while Alex replayed her conversation with Duncan. "Do you remember anyone buying a box of four Vanilla Creams?"

"No, but anyone who bought two of our full-size boxes would have had four of them."

Alex guzzled the last of her tea. "Easy enough for anyone determined to kill Jane and put suspicion on us. If Zach hadn't come by that morning, I'd be the number-one suspect right now."

Hanna didn't seem surprised. "Duncan told me they aren't even considering the theory that someone from a true-crime show killed Jane. He didn't come right out and say so, but I got the impression Sheriff Summers thought your idea was ridiculous." Hanna put her mug in the dishwasher and started wiping down the counter.

"I guess our investigation is the only way we'll find the real killer."

"The sheriff is trying to build a case against you or Zach. She's trying to close the case by Christmas," Hanna said.

Alex looked at the calendar. It was Thursday, December seventeenth. That gave her a week to solve this. She got up and updated the murder board, and they reviewed their list of suspects. "If we can confirm Gary and Oliver's alibis, then they're off our list. Penelope appears to have been watching us, but who was watching her? She could have slipped over there easily enough." Alex gave an account of her impromptu visit to the antique shop yesterday. "Penelope could have killed Jane."

"Definitely. In fact, she bought three boxes of chocolates last week. I remember because she rarely buys anything from us."

In an effort at civility, Alex occasionally purchased antiques for the store at Penelope's shop. On rare occasions, Penelope reciprocated, though usually she made an effort to shop when Alex wasn't in the bookshop.

"You know, I'm curious about one thing. Jane had obviously been in bed. I know she wasn't a night owl, but would she have been sleeping by ten?"

"After eating one of those drugged chocolates, it's possible," Hanna offered.

"But why did someone want her asleep? Was it so they could break in unheard and steal something? Or did they come solely to kill her?"

"I don't know, but we'd better open up. Maggie will be here any minute."

Alex couldn't put Jane's death out of her mind. If Jane had intentionally been sedated with the chocolates, which had to have been purchased beforehand, her murder was premeditated. And since she would have been sound asleep, there wouldn't have been any reason for a thief to kill Jane. Whoever had gone into Jane's house had done so with the intent of murdering her.

* * *

It was only one week before Christmas Eve, and it seemed like everyone was out doing last-minute Christmas shopping with a vengeance. Midmorning, Alex was coming out of the kitchen with several boxes of Killer Chocolates when the chimes jingled as the door opened. Tall and elegant, Yvonne looked like she'd just come from Park Avenue in New York. She was dressed in gray wool slacks with a matching turtleneck and an elegantly cut, dark-gray car coat. She wore black leather gloves and carried her walking stick.

She limped straight for Alex. "Darling, how are you holding up? This must all be so awful for you. I don't know what I'd do if I found a dead body. I've come to invite you for a visit this afternoon at my home. We'll have tea. You simply must tell me what's been happening with this dreadful murder."

Though they were well acquainted, Alex had never received so much attention from the elderly woman. She desperately tried to think of an excuse. "I'd love to, Yvonne, but I'm not sure I can get away."

Maggie was standing nearby and took a step closer. "You go right ahead, Alex. I'll be fine."

"Perfect." Yvonne beamed at Maggie. "That's settled! I'll expect you this afternoon."

When Yvonne had left, Alex turned to Maggie. "Thanks." Her voice dripped with sarcasm.

"I looked at the murder board this morning and saw you need to corroborate Gary's alibi. You can do that when you talk to Yvonne. So you're welcome."

Alex let out a deep sigh. "You're right. I just find it very tiring talking to her. I never know what to say." Alex had never found it easy to talk to people she didn't know well. As a banker, and now as an entrepreneur, she had to make a concerted effort to socialize and network. If she'd had her druthers, she'd have stayed at the shop or at home and let Hanna do all their socializing.

Maggie patted Alex on the shoulder and went to ring up a sale for a customer.

Alex put the chocolates she was holding on the counter. As she headed to the far room to see if anyone needed help, Drew walked in. Maggie was still at the register, so Alex stopped to chat with him until his wife finished with her customer.

"How are you? I hope we haven't upset your routine too much having Maggie work the week before Christmas." As she spoke, she led him closer to the conference room and away from customers who might overhear their conversation.

Drew was patting his stomach. "I'm still having some problems, but I've got something brewing on the stove that should help."

"Maggie mentioned you've been doing some . . . cooking."

"It's dismaying. There's gluten in so many things, but that's not why I came to see you."

"You didn't come to see Maggie?"

"Not at all. I came to tell you Duncan stopped by the house a few minutes ago to grab some papers, and I overheard him talking to the sheriff on the phone. He was in the village because they were doing another search of Jane's house to try and find the murder weapon. This time they used a metal detector and went over the area around Jane's garden shed. They found an ice pick in the snow. It's on its way to the lab now to see if they can get prints off it or find traces of blood."

"Do they have any idea who it belongs to?"

"It didn't sound like it, but I thought you'd want to know."

Done with her customer, Maggie approached them, and Alex went to help another customer who had found a couple of Agatha Raisin novels to add to her two boxes of Killer Chocolates.

The woman gushed, "My daughters are going to love these chocolates with their books. They've been M. C. Beaton fans since they were teenagers. I love how the lid on the chocolates looks like an old-fashioned advertisement for poison."

"If they'll be eaten within a few weeks, store them at a temperature around sixty degrees to keep them at their peak. It's best not to let them get too cold, as that can affect their appearance."

Once the customer was out of the store, Alex returned to Maggie and Drew. The latter was fussing about his digestion. "Then what should I eat?"

"I told you, if you're celiac, you can't have any gluten. That means no stops at the bakery," Maggie was remonstrating as Drew did up his coat.

"Well, maybe it's not celiac disease. I'm going home and searching my symptoms again." Drew gave Maggie a peck on the cheek and headed to the door.

She pressed her palm to her forehead and closed her eyes. "Oh, brother. That man needs more to do. I think he retired too early."

Chapter Thirteen

Alex was actually looking forward to seeing inside Yvonne's large, historic home. She had admired it from the outside since moving to Harriston and had read the bronze plaque telling of its history several times. She stopped on the sidewalk to read it once more.

The Queen Anne Revival dated back to 1912 and had been built by a wealthy banker from Kalispell. His descendants had lived in the home until 1999, when the last family member died and the house was sold.

A large fir wreath decorated with pinecones and a red ribbon adorned the black front door. On either side of the walk at the base of the stoop were two large black planters filled with birch logs, greenery, and red bows, similar to the ones on Main Street.

The single-car garage on the north side of the house had obviously been added later but was still in keeping with the overall Victorian influence of the immaculately maintained dwelling. Yvonne answered the doorbell promptly, looking as pristine as her house.

Inside, Alex presented her with a small box of four Killer Chocolates. "I wasn't sure what you liked, so I put in a Morphine

Mint, Arsenic Almond, Candy Cane Coniine, and Strychnine Strawberry."

"Thank you. They sound delightful. I'm sure they'll be delicious."

After removing her boots, Alex was led into a formal living room off the entry hall. The furniture wasn't new but was obviously expensive, with antique pieces scattered throughout. A Lalique vase filled with artificial flowers and crystal figurines had been placed here and there, but it was largely an impersonal room. The only sign of Christmas was a large poinsettia on the coffee table.

"Your home is very beautiful. I've always wondered what it looked like inside."

"I'd be happy to show you the other rooms before you leave. I didn't decorate in here for Christmas, as I don't often use it."

"The poinsettia is festive. It's really all this room needs." Alex pointed at the cane. "What happened? I noticed you using that when you were at the shop."

Yvonne waved her manicured hand in the air. "Oh, it was nothing, just a little spill going down the steps outside. My ankle is a little sore and swollen."

"That poinsettia must be from Jane." Alex indicated the plant on the coffee table.

"Yes. God rest her—she brought me one each Christmas. So sad what happened. I'm going to miss her. It's devastating to think that while I was at the horticultural meeting, she was killed. Perhaps if she had been there, she'd still be alive."

Alex wasn't sure if that was meant to be a barb, suggesting that if Jane had gone to the horticultural meeting, which ran later into the evening, instead of the Sleuth meeting, she wouldn't have been murdered. Knowing of the doctored chocolates, Alex was aware that Jane's killer had been determined, but she wasn't about to argue with Yvonne. "I guess that could be true. Gary mentioned he was there until about eleven."

"Yes. I'm afraid I held him up. I believe we were the last ones to leave. He was showing us how to prepare foxgloves and a few other plants that need to be started early so they'll be ready for bedding out in spring. Of course, there's nothing he showed us I didn't already know." Yvonne seemed wistful. "Growing up, my family had a beautiful garden and a wooded copse behind our home, and I loved to learn about the plants. My mother was a botanist and taught me everything she knew. I also read and studied a great deal. It's still a great hobby of mine. You probably noticed my greenhouse in the backyard. It's heated, and I grow a wide variety of plants year-round. I guess now with Jane gone, I'll become president of the horticultural society."

"I was told Netta was in the running for that position as well?"

"That's ridiculous. She's an amateur. I was always more knowledgeable than Jane, but you know how it is in these small towns. The people who have lived here all their lives are always chosen for the prestigious positions." Yvonne smiled, but the steely look in her eyes belied any pretense of patience with small-town ways. She made an effort to get up from the sofa. "Would you like some tea?"

"I would love to, but I've got to get back to the store. I'm afraid we've been quite busy today, and with Hanna making chocolates, Maggie is alone."

"Ah, Maggie. Her son is a deputy, I believe? Have they any idea who killed Jane? The rumor is they suspect Zach, though I do hope it wasn't him. He's been such a help keeping up this old house. I had to update so many things when I bought it. I'd be lost not having him to work with me, but of course, you never know people as well as you think you do."

Alex said doubtfully, "I have a hard time believing it was Zach. That seems to be the way the sheriff's department is leaning, though I don't think they have any hard evidence. Unfortunately, he doesn't have an alibi." She wasn't about to mention the fact that she was the sheriff's number-two suspect. "I noticed Penelope was home well before nine on Monday night."

"I'm afraid she's just a dabbler. She isn't really serious about gardening, though I was surprised she left so early." Yvonne curled her lip in disgust. "She seems more interested in Gary than the plants. Have you seen her garden?" Yvonne shuddered. "Her lawn is full of quack grass, and she has overgrown lilacs in most of her flower beds."

"Unbelievable." Alex shook her head. She caught herself before she said *tsk-tsk*.

Picking up a framed picture from an end table, Yvonne held it out for Alex to see. It showed a smiling middle-aged couple, Yvonne lifted her chin a fraction. "My parents. They made sure I had a good education, and I like to think they would be proud of how well I've done."

"Are they still alive?"

"Heavens, no. They've both been gone for years. I'm not all that young, you know."

"How long have you lived in Harriston? I understand you moved here when your husband passed away?"

"I've been here simply ages. My dear husband passed away many years ago, and I found it too lonely living in the city. We didn't have any children, and with my parents gone, I wanted to find a place where I could make friends more easily."

"I suppose it can be difficult to make friends as an adult. For those not naturally outgoing, it can be especially difficult. Where was home for you?"

"Florida. We were married over thirty years, but we were in our own little world. We had so few friends, and with no family of my own, it just wasn't the same after my Ernest died.

"It was funny," she continued. "I happened to see an ad in a magazine that featured the historic railway station in Harriston. They made the village sound so perfect. I just picked up and moved. I'm originally from a small town in New Hampshire, so moving here was quite nice. Well, I should show you those other rooms so you can get back to work."

Yvonne maneuvered off the sofa, using her cane. "Darn thing. It's frustrating moving so slowly."

Across the hall was the study. A large walnut desk faced the entrance, and bookshelves lined the wall behind it. Two leather wing chairs faced the desk. Along one wall was a long sideboard, and on it were an antique decanter and several crystal glasses, an amaryllis in full bloom, and a large wooden carving of a hawk.

There were several large pictures of woodland scenes on the walls, and elegant Santas made of crystal and porcelain sat formally on the bookshelves behind the desk. In front of the window, a large Christmas tree, elegantly decorated with vintage glass ornaments and tinsel, gave the room a slightly nostalgic feeling.

Next, they went down the hall to the kitchen, a combination of old-world charm and modern convenience. The creamy-white cupboards contrasted with the stainless-steel appliances and dark hardwood floor. Everything was immaculate and extremely organized.

The family room, adjoining the kitchen, was much smaller than the living room at the front of the house, though still spacious. On the walls were sketches of plants with their Latin botanical names and pictures with woodland themes. On the wood mantel sat three hand-carved Santas and another picture of Yvonne's parents.

Alex left with promises to return soon and drove to Louise Sweet's home. Not really knowing the woman, aside from seeing her at the bakery, she hoped it wouldn't seem too odd to just drop in this way. Knowing Louise's propensity to call in sick, Alex was counting on her being home. She got another box of chocolates from the back seat of the car.

The paint was peeling from the siding of the modest bungalow, and the small, sagging porch was littered with dried leaves and old lawn chairs. The only acknowledgment of Christmas was a plastic Santa hanging in the front window.

Fortunately, luck was with Alex, and her hand had barely finished knocking when the door was opened abruptly. Whereas Yvonne was tall and attractively slender, Louise was of average height but so thin as to be gaunt. Despite being almost a decade younger, she looked much older than Yvonne. She wore an old, stained pair of pants topped by an *I Love Montana* T-shirt and a drooping cardigan.

"What do ya want?" She stood with the door only partially open and seemed ready to slam it shut at the earliest opportunity.

Alex figured Avon ladies and alarm company salesmen received warmer welcomes. She held out a box of chocolates and explained that Sam had mentioned Louise was under the weather. Louise reluctantly invited her in.

The first thing Alex noticed in the dim foyer was the cats everywhere she looked. Cats of every description walked through the rooms, lay on furniture, and sat in windowsills. The second thing she noticed was the harsh odor of litter boxes. She counted at least ten felines. This presented a problem, as she was highly allergic to cats. A quick visit would be in order here.

Louise led Alex into a brightly lit kitchen, where every surface was covered with stands holding what appeared to be sticks of different sizes, colors, and designs. Some were very intricate, with jewels and carvings in their handles; some even had sharpened points. Alex made to move a box of the finished sticks off a chair, but Louise grabbed her arm.

"No, not there. As ya can see, there's not much room. Have a seat over here." Louise swept a cat off one of the kitchen chairs. She brushed aside a box of cat treats to make space for the chocolates on the Formica-topped kitchen table. "Can I get ya something to drink?" Her pained expression suggested a strong hope Alex would say no.

Looking around, Alex could see clumps of cat hair covering almost every surface. "Thanks, no. I won't be staying long. I just popped over to bring you the chocolates and make sure you're doing okay. It looks like you're quite busy." She glanced around the room. Crammed into every nook and cranny that didn't have wands were knickknacks and signs. One read, *I Was Normal Three Cats Ago*.

Louise swept her hands to encompass the kitchen. "Wands. I'm gettin' ready for a convention next month. Adults with too much time on their hands get all dressed up and pretend to be characters in games. Live-action role play, they call it. Crazy if ya ask me. But I can hardly keep up with making enough wands for my booth. Keeps food in the cupboard, since working at the bakery don't pay that well. I gotta go to all kinds of stupid conventions to sell them, though. More and more people order them off the internet, but still most of the money's made in person."

"How interesting." Alex wouldn't have put Louise down as an entrepreneur, though she could imagine her hunched over a table painting signs that read *Cats are like chocolate. It's hard having just one.* Alex tried to shoo away a cat that had jumped onto her lap. "Did you start doing this before you moved to Harriston?"

Louise's eyes narrowed. "Not really any of your business, but as it happens, I started making these after I moved here. Not a lotta jobs here in the village, and I didn't fancy driving into Kalispell or Swanson every day, so I found something I could do from home."

After wiggling and jiggling her legs with no result, Alex finally picked up the overly friendly cat and put it on the floor. "I guess you know about Jane's murder?"

"I sure do. It didn't surprise me at all. She was one nosy lady, always poking into other people's business. Nope, not surprised at all. Of course, I don't condone killing, but when ya snoop into things, sometimes you find out stuff you oughtn't have."

The cat was still circling Alex's legs, looking ready to pounce on her lap again. Keeping one eye on the cat, she looked at Louise. "What is it Jane was snooping into? Do you think that's why she was killed?"

"I don't rightly know, not that it's any of your business either. She was always asking folks questions about their past, getting them all het up. If people want their business known, they'll tell folks. That internet is as much a curse as a blessing. It invites snooping. I reckon that could be what got her killed. You might want to remember that."

Had Louise just threatened her? "So were you home on Monday evening?"

"Been spending every spare minute at home making wands, like I said, getting ready for a convention next month. Shipped out my last order this past Friday. Won't be any more before Christmas. Can't guarantee shipping. People always pitch a hissy fit if orders don't come when they should." Louise put a hand over her heart. "I'd best sit down for a sec. My heart's fluttering something terrible."

Louise knocked a couple of prescription bottles out of the way and moved a box of wands onto the table so she could sit. "It's got so bad I can't even work some days."

Alex glanced at the labels of the prescription bottles that had rolled in her direction. "I'm sorry to hear that. I can't help noticing you have a bit of a southern accent. Possibly Alabama or Mississippi?" Alex was no linguist, but Louise's accent was from somewhere in the South.

"Land's sake, you're as nosy as Jane was! I got to be getting back to work." Louise stood and waited expectantly for Alex to do the same.

Alex's throat was starting to get scratchy. It was time to get out of here. She'd obviously worn out her welcome anyway. She thanked Louise for her hospitality and left.

There was a kind of itch in her throat, and her breathing had become a bit wheezy. Her pants were covered in cat hair. She'd have to try to fix that back at the shop or she'd have itchy eyes all day. As she drove, she reflected on Louise's comments. It was obvious Jane hadn't been universally liked. Clearly Louise had taken issue with Jane for finding out something and hadn't been too pleased with all the questions Alex was asking. Louise appeared to have heart trouble, which might explain her many absences from work. Alex had noticed one bottle of pills on Louise's table was digoxin, a strong heart medication. The other was a sleeping pill containing eszopiclone.

Chapter Fourteen

The shop was almost overrun with customers for the rest of the day. By the time they closed, did the bookwork, tidied, and restocked, Alex had to get home. She didn't even have time for dinner before she and Tom went to Zach's at six.

On their way, Tom asked how her day had been.

"Busy. I took some chocolates to Louise. She's quite a character. It sounds like she didn't care for Jane. She called her nosy and said she wasn't surprised Jane was murdered. She implied Jane might have found out something she shouldn't have and that caused her death."

"I don't know her well, but I gather she's had a hard life. I think she was in a bad marriage at some point. She may not have the best disposition, but I don't think she'd kill anyone."

"If I have to talk to her again, I'll stay out of her house. I'm only just getting over my allergic reaction to her cats. How was your day?"

"The usual, visiting the poor and the sick. Mrs. Matthews brought by some fresh bread for me today."

"Did you learn any more about her gout?"

"No. It appears the gout is better. Unfortunately, she's been having trouble with her bowels."

Alex looked away and smiled as Tom pulled in front of Zach's place. She handed a plate of cookies over to Zach as he welcomed them into his small apartment.

He gestured for them to sit on an old sofa as he sat in a recliner patched with duct tape. "Sorry. I've never paid much attention to the furniture. I got all this stuff secondhand years ago and just can't be bothered to replace it." Zach blushed.

Alex and Tom admired the trim and flooring. She could see the kitchen had beautifully finished cupboards with quartz countertops. "Did you do the work in here? It's wonderful craftsmanship."

Zach started to turn pink again. "Yeah. Everett provided all the materials, and I did the work. I would have done it for nothing so I'd have a nicer place to live, but he insisted on giving me half off my rent for the first year I lived here. It really helped, because I was just getting my business off the ground."

"Are you going to be able to take care of that window for us?"

"I'm really sorry about that. Things happened, and I completely forgot. I'll be there first thing tomorrow morning, if that's okay?"

"Definitely." Alex looked around the living room as Tom made some benign inquiries. There were pictures of who she imagined were Zach's family, as well as several pictures of a pretty brunette Alex suspected was his girlfriend.

In his best pastor's voice, Tom asked, "How are you doing? Is there anything I can do?"

Zach averted his gaze. "I'm okay. She didn't come right out and say so, but the sheriff thinks I killed Jane. I swear I didn't kill anyone."

Alex leaned forward. "What happened the morning after Jane died?"

He looked uncomfortable. "I knocked on the back door like usual, but Miss Burrows told me a while back if she didn't answer, just get the key from under the flowerpot and let myself in."

He shifted in his chair. "I was doing some work in the basement that day, but I needed to ask Miss Burrows a question. I figured she had to be home. She was usually in the kitchen by seven, but sometimes she worked in her office. I called her name, but she didn't answer, and I thought maybe she couldn't hear me. She wouldn't admit it, but her hearing wasn't as sharp as it used to be. So I went upstairs to check." Zach swallowed hard and squeezed his eyes shut for a second. "I saw her lying there, inside her bedroom. All that blood. I was so scared. I didn't know what to do. I figured I'd leave and then call in an anonymous tip." He looked at Tom beseechingly. "I know I shouldn't have lied to the police, but I figured, with my history, I'd be their top suspect." He sounded bitter as he added, "And that's exactly what I am."

"Did Jane know about your past?" Alex asked.

"Yes." A note of petulance crept into his voice. "I've been dating Jennifer Wolf. She's a first-grade teacher. I wanted to ask her to marry me, but Miss Burrows insisted I needed to tell Jen about my past before I proposed. Monday night, after the Sleuth meeting, I went to Jen's house and told her about my criminal record. She asked me to leave, and I haven't talked to her since. She won't answer her phone or return my texts. If I hadn't listened to Miss Burrows, I'd be proposing next week, and I'd have an alibi because I would have been with Jen."

"If you hadn't told Jennifer about your record, she probably would have found out when the police questioned you. I'm not sure that would have worked out any better," Alex said.

"I suppose."

Tom spoke up. "How did Jane find out about your past? Did you tell her?"

"I don't know how she found out. When she asked me about it, there didn't seem any point in trying to hide it, since she already knew."

"Do you mind telling us what happened?" Tom asked.

Zach began after a deep breath. "It was a long time ago. I was eighteen, and I drove a friend of mine to the store for some cigarettes. He went in, and I waited in the car. It was taking so long. I went in to see what was up. He had a gun pointed at the clerk when I walked in. Without even thinking, I caught the bag of money from the cash register when he tossed it to me. The clerk tried to press the alarm under the counter, and my buddy knocked him on the head with the gun."

He looked defeated. "The clerk ended up with a concussion, and I ended up in jail. I told them I had no idea what my friend was doing in there, something my buddy backed me up on, but my lawyer said a jury would probably convict me and I should take the deal the deputy county attorney was offering, one year in prison and parole for two. I had an athletic scholarship to Montana State to play football that fall. Instead, I went to jail."

Alex felt sorry for Zach. *Talk about being at the wrong place at the wrong time.*

"After I got out, I worked a bunch of construction jobs, but I hated it. About ten years ago, I'd had it. I'd done a job here when they were renovating the school, and I really liked the place. I got some jobs lined up, got this apartment, and here I am."

Zach sounded genuine, and while he seemed to be avoiding eye contact, it appeared to be more from embarrassment over talking about his past than from hiding anything.

Alex was inclined to believe him. But she also knew you couldn't always judge a book by its cover. Guilt and shame could easily be confused. He seemed upset with Jane for insisting he tell his girlfriend about his past. As much as she liked Zach, she couldn't altogether rule out the possibility that he'd murdered Jane, but she believed it highly unlikely. And if he had killed Jane, would he have sent her chocolates laced with a sedative first?

"Did anyone else know where that key was?" Alex asked.

"I'm not sure. I know Miss Burrows was careful about locking up. She moved the key around occasionally too. For a while it was on a hook on the back side of one of the deck posts near the ground, but with the snow, she wanted to keep it handier. I think that neighbor that backs onto her yard saw me get it one morning. He was always sitting in his living room looking out over the backyards."

Alex knew Jane could be a bit paranoid and had always attributed it to all the true-crime shows Jane watched. They talked a little while longer, but Alex didn't learn anything more. Tom offered his help if it was needed, officially or unofficially.

Back in the car, Tom extended an invitation Alex couldn't resist. "Come back to my place and I'll make you something for supper. You must be starving."

"That would be awesome. What are you offering?"

"I've got a delicious dinner of turkey, mashed potatoes, vegetables, and cranberry sauce I can whip up."

At Tom's house, Alex sat on the sofa in front of the gas fireplace he had turned on. The room had been painted a warm beige and was filled with large, comfortable furniture. Family pictures hung on the walls and sat on bookshelves. A Christmas tree stood in front of the picture window. The turkey dinner, it turned out, was a TV dinner. While it cooked in the microwave, she told him about her interview with Yvonne.

"I don't know much about her. I tend to know people who have lived here all their lives or go to church. There aren't many people in the village who don't fit into one of those categories."

As they spoke, Alex went through a true-crime episode Tom had taped. It was about two girls who had gone missing while on a hike; their bodies had been found a month later. The murderer had never been located, though the police had a sketch. Neither the sketch nor any of the details matched anything Jane had talked about. Alex fast-forwarded through another episode, but to no avail. It couldn't be connected to anyone in Harriston.

She was just finishing her dinner when the doorbell rang. She looked at Tom, who shrugged and went to answer the door. When she heard who it was, she had an overwhelming urge to laugh. Penelope was insisting Tom let her in. She had important information.

A second later their neighbor marched into the family room. "Oh, you're here." She didn't seem at all surprised to see Alex. "Tom, I think you should know the police have been asking questions about her"—Penelope thrust out her arm and pointed at Alex—"activities the night of the murder. I'm not sure it's safe for you to be here alone with that woman."

Alex was shocked. Could Penelope really be warning Tom to stay away from her? She decided to keep a sense of humor about it and grinned. "She's right, Tom. I've been told I'm the sheriff's number-two suspect." Alex got up from the sofa and walked up to Penelope. "By the way, how do we know you weren't off killing Jane on Monday night? It seems to me you don't have an alibi for the entire evening either, do you?"

Tom and Alex both looked at Penelope expectantly.

Penelope was turning an unattractive shade of red. "I . . . I . . . can't believe . . . the utter rudeness. Never . . ."

"Tom, in good conscience, I don't think you should be alone with either one of us, for your own safety. I'm sure Penelope agrees. Let's go, Precious." Alex stood behind Penelope and ushered her to the door. Alex quickly put on her boots and grabbed her coat. She silently mouthed *You're welcome* to Tom as she closed the door behind herself and Penelope.

Penelope was still uttering only the first word or two of each sentence as she headed back toward her house. Alex followed her.

"Penelope, I recently discovered you've been married and divorced four times, not two. Is that right?"

The older woman swung around. The fact that she had gone as white as a sheet was evident even with only the streetlight providing illumination.

"How dare you! You have no business discussing my personal life."

Alex arched her eyebrow. "Since you brought up mine at Tom's, I claim dibs on the same privilege. So, is it true? I'm pretty good at research. I can probably find out, whether you tell me or not. And I'm still curious why you were yelling at Jane the other night in front of my shop."

"You're no better than that busybody Jane. It's no wonder she got herself killed. You better watch your step, missy. You don't want to come to the same sticky end as your nosy friend." With that, Penelope turned and stalked to her house without another word.

Back in her own kitchen, Alex saw a note from Hanna on the counter. Her twin was back at Murder and Mayhem finishing some chocolates she'd started earlier in the day. Alex looked at her watch and remembered the note she'd found in the trash that morning. Her stomach twisted into a knot. Had Hanna gone to the store to talk to their mother without worrying about Alex walking in? Why would she need that kind of privacy?

Alex considered heading to the shop to help Hanna, but Watson had been alone for too long today. The dog happily stood still as Alex rubbed her behind the ears. "Let's go upstairs, Watson. I need a distraction, and research should do the trick."

Watson followed Alex to the office, and she sat in front of the computer. The dog curled up on her feet. First, she looked up *Penelope Shaw*, adding *North Carolina* to the search criteria. A long list of references to a commercial realtor came up. Alex went down the results but couldn't find anything for Harriston's Penelope Shaw.

This is crazy. How can people have no internet presence?

Next, she searched on Louise. She found Louise's website for her wands and a social media account, also about her wands—and her cats. She had ten thousand followers. How could so many people be interested in wands and cats? Murder and Mayhem struggled to keep two thousand followers. Alex looked down at Watson. "Maybe we should trade you in for a cat."

Watson let out a whine and covered her eyes with her paw.

Alex and Watson went back downstairs and watched a taped television show about a woman who went to garage sales and ran an antique shop and kept running into dead bodies. Alex hoped watching the television sleuth would give her ideas on how to solve the mystery around Jane's death, but before the TV murder was solved, Hanna came home.

Fifteen minutes later they sat on the sofa, each with hot chocolate in a holiday-themed mug. Hanna had a good chuckle as Alex narrated the evening's events.

"*Sie hat nicht alle Tassen im Schrank.* That's what Mom would say about Penelope."

"Agreed." Alex thought some of the expressions her mother used were perfect. Penelope was indeed one cup short of a full cupboard.

"Do you think Zach could have been angry enough with Jane to kill her?" Hanna had finally stopped laughing.

Alex sighed. "I don't know. If I was deeply in love with someone and in a similar situation, I'd be pretty angry. But I certainly wouldn't kill over it. I keep remembering Jane's words at Sleuth. Does Zach's character suggest he might kill over love? I'm not sure I know him well enough to say for sure. Do we know any of the suspects well enough to judge their character? Though I'm inclined to think Joe could be a killer. But whoever did this has got their act down pat."

Hanna nodded. "Exactly. I don't think we can trust anyone. Whoever it is has been fooling people for a long time."

"I'm not sure what to do next." Alex took Hanna's empty mug and put them both in the sink. "Did you talk to Mom tonight, by any chance?"

There was the briefest hesitation before Hanna shook her head. "No. Why do you ask?"

"I thought something was up, since she called you at work on Tuesday."

"Oh, that." Hanna forced a laugh. "She was having a bad day and wondered if I wanted to reconsider moving back to Frankenmuth to work for them again."

"Are you?"

"Am I what?"

"Considering a move back home?"

Hanna grimaced. "Of course not. I'm happy here." She got up from the sofa. "I guess I'll head to bed. I'm beat. Come on, Watson."

"I'll be going to bed shortly too. Good night."

As Alex trudged up to bed a little later, she wondered about Hanna's explanation of their mother's call. Alex's twintuition told her Hanna wasn't being completely honest. Maybe she wasn't as happy here as she claimed and was considering a move back to Michigan. Not only would Alex miss her sister desperately, it would present a serious problem for Murder and Mayhem. Alex wasn't a professional chocolatier; she would have some work ahead of her to improve her skills to Hanna's level. And more importantly, she would lose her best friend. These past few years together with Hanna had reminded her of the close connection they had as twins. Their relationship went beyond friendship and family ties. Alex would lose a piece of herself if Hanna moved away.

Chapter Fifteen

Alex awoke out of a haze of dreams. She remembered most recently being chased by Penelope, who was clutching a frozen casserole. In the dream, Alex was terrified of that casserole. It all made sense. The way things did in dreams. But before Alex opened her eyes, she sensed she wasn't alone.

Hanna was sitting at the foot of the bed, staring at her. "You must have been having a wild dream. Your eyes were moving like crazy. Did you know you sleep with your mouth open?"

Alex closed her eyes again. *Maybe this is still a dream.*

"Wake up, sleepyhead. I've got news." Hanna gave Alex's legs a shake. "This is important."

Watson jumped up on the bed and flopped onto Alex's legs. Alex finally sat up and leaned against her headboard. Hanna appeared to be anxious to share whatever news had her up at this ridiculously early hour.

After Alex had gone to bed the night before, Hanna had seen Duncan's car leave (Hanna's bedroom faced the street), and she had texted him and asked what was going on. He'd finally gotten back to her in the wee hours of the morning.

"Duncan said they got fingerprints off the ice pick found in the snow by Jane's shed. They were Zach's, so the sheriff was able to get a search warrant for his apartment late last night. They found a coin collection he admitted was Jane's. He claimed she gave it to him the week before as a Christmas gift for all the work he's been doing. But, with no proof of its being a gift, Duncan arrested him for robbery."

Alex drew her eyebrows together and pressed her steepled hands against her mouth.

"When they questioned him about the ice pick, he admitted it could be his. He said he'd been using one at Jane's and had left it on her deck on Friday but couldn't find it Monday morning. They also found a prescription bottle of sleeping pills at the back of a drawer. It was the same kind used to drug Jane's chocolates." Hanna tilted her head and stared at Alex.

Alex rubbed her eyes and took a drink of water from the glass on her nightstand. "The evidence seems to be mounting, but it's all circumstantial. The sheriff seems intent to pin the murder on him. If we want that window replaced in the bathroom at the shop, we'd better find the real killer."

After a few more minutes of discussion, Hanna went to feed the dog and Alex headed for her shower. While she was happy not to be in the sheriff's cross hairs momentarily, she couldn't help but feel the sheriff had it all wrong. If Alex's instincts were right, then a murderer was wandering the streets of Harriston while Zach sat in jail.

At Murder and Mayhem, Alex double-checked the calendar. It was December eighteenth, and she'd almost forgotten her eight-thirty hair appointment at Lavish Locks.

The small beauty salon on Main Street boasted two stylists. When Alex got there, Tanya Baker, the owner, was still with another client, so she sat beside the only other person in the waiting area.

Stella was of retirement age but still worked part-time as a secretary for the Williams Insurance Agency and ran the office with a firm hand. Alex figured Stella would never actually retire, because almost everyone in Harriston used Max Williams as their insurance agent and went to the office at least once a year. Stella would lose her edge on gossip if she ever left her job. She had the hardy constitution of her forebears and would likely be running things into her nineties. Alex saw a fortuitous opportunity to find out more about her suspects. She hadn't been able to question Stella as thoroughly as she would have liked while they made chocolates the other night.

Before Alex could ask anything, Stella launched her own question. "I heard Zach was hauled to jail early this morning. Did you hear anything about that?"

Alex played dumb and instead asked what Stella knew about the writer Oliver Robins.

"Honey, I heard tell he's a drinker. He sells those books of his by telling people how to quit drinking and live healthy, but he's been seen in the liquor store in Kalispell more than once recently. I don't suppose he'd want that to get out. Of course, he's not the only drinker in town, but he's the only one writing books claiming to be a health nut."

In a quiet voice, Alex asked, "Do you know anything about Joe Cameron?"

"Well, you know I don't like to gossip, but he's quite a mystery. I know one of his secretaries, and she said his wife divorced him after some kind of scandal. Chester, Max's son, had Joe build him a big, fancy house in the new development on the north side of the village. Apparently there have been a few issues with the house, and Joe won't do anything about it. There was a sneaky clause in the contract that allowed him to walk away from the problems. Chester's a lawyer, so you'd think he would've looked over the contract more carefully." Stella shook her head.

That certainly speaks to character.

Stella looked at Alex with narrowed eyes. "It's been said Penelope has her eye on Tom and isn't too pleased with your visits over there."

Alex tried to keep her face neutral. The last thing she wanted was a rumor that she was jealous of Penelope over Tom's affections.

Stella frowned and lowered her voice. "I don't know how men fall for women like that. Tom needs to find another good woman, like his first wife." She looked at Alex slyly. "Can you think of anyone who might fit the bill?"

Thankfully, Alex was saved from answering, as Tanya waved her over to the chair. Stella gave Alex's hand a squeeze as she got up.

Tanya wore her straight, dark hair in a long bob, and her dark-brown eyes lit up her face when she smiled. She reminded Alex of a young Connie Chung. Since having her last baby, she'd taken to wearing a smock over her clothes. She said it covered all the spit-up stains that inevitably happened as she was trying to get out the door.

Alex placed a wrapped box on Tanya's workstation. "Our Christmas Killer Chocolates. I know you like the Gingerbread Gelsemine ones, so I made sure I put several of them in there." Gingerbread Gelsemine were milk-chocolate shells filled with a milk-chocolate ganache infused with gingerbread flavor.

"Thank you. That's so kind. I'll keep them here. If I take them home, Wiley and the kids will eat them all, and chocolate this good would be wasted on them." Tanya's slender build had bloomed with her last pregnancy. She claimed half her family was tiny and the other half was chunky, and she didn't care which side she resembled. With three kids under six and her own business, she had more important things to worry about than her panty size.

Wiley, Tanya's husband, was a police officer in Kalispell. Tanya had opened Lavish Locks three years earlier, thinking she and Wiley wouldn't be having any more children. Then, less than a year later, she was pregnant.

"Is Wiley working again this Christmas?"

"No. He was finally able to get a week off over the holidays. We're leaving here as soon as I'm done work tomorrow and heading to his parents' cabin in Whitefish. Wiley said he'd have the kids in the car by the time I get home." Tanya was scrutinizing Alex's split ends. "So what are we doing for you today?"

"Just a trim, please. I want to look presentable for Christmas."

"You're getting an aromatherapy scalp massage first. I've decided to give all my clients one before their services from now on. I started doing it December first as a Christmas bonus, but everyone loves them so much, I'm going to make them part of my regular service."

Tanya had Alex close her eyes and held three different oils under her nose, then asked her to choose one. Alex picked one that smelled of lavender and freshly washed sheets hung outside in the sun to dry. As fingers started working their way over her scalp, massaging the aromatherapy oils in, all thoughts slipped from Alex's mind. It was incredible. She was so relaxed after the scalp massage she hardly wanted to go back to talking about murder.

"A little birdie told me you're looking into Jane's murder."

Alex opened one eye. "Where did you hear that?"

"I'm the stylist for half of the ladies in this village. I hear lots of things. Some would curl your toes. But I never reveal my sources." Tanya laughed as she conditioned Alex's hair. "In fact, I heard Dr. Hanson had a wingding of an argument with Jane at the bake sale last Saturday. Not that I think he would kill anyone. But Jane did think he looked like that serial killer on one of those true-crime shows. They say where there's smoke, there's fire."

Alex wondered why Clive had never mentioned his argument with Jane to Alex. *Something else to look into.*

"I heard Chester Williams wasn't very impressed with Joe after he built his house and wouldn't fix a few minor problems." Alex made the comment as Tanya moved Alex to her chair.

"I heard about that, but Joe also built Everett's house, and I didn't hear of him having any trouble. I think there were a few issues, just the usual kind of stuff, and Joe fixed them all. Everett's pretty happy. Wiley said maybe we could get Joe to build us a house. Not in the new section, of course. We couldn't afford one of those, but there's an empty lot we really like across the street from Louise's house, so maybe in a couple years."

Alex found it interesting that Everett hadn't had any issue getting things fixed with his house but Chester couldn't get anything done because of a contract clause. She'd have to ask Everett about that. It was certainly making Alex question what kind of contractor Joe was. Could there be other unhappy customers? What would Joe do if some of those customers made trouble for him because of the sneaky clauses in his contracts?

Chapter Sixteen

When she was done at Lavish Locks, Alex headed to the post office to see if she could get a little bit more information about the village's self-help author. It was too early to check for mail. It wouldn't be finished sorting for another hour.

"Eudora, I know you can't give out confidential information, but I'm wondering, is it possible that Oliver Robins is a pseudonym and he actually has a different legal name?"

"You're right, I can't give out confidential information. But you might want to check the online system, Montana Cadastral, to see who owns the house he's living in, if you're really that interested. That would show the legal name of the owner. It's been mentioned you've been asking a lot of questions relating to Jane's death. I assume you don't believe the sheriff's department has the right person in custody?"

"You're as astute as ever. I'd love to know where you get your information."

The postmistress looked pleased but didn't reply.

"I suppose it's possible Zach killed Jane, but it seems out of character. Inasmuch as I know his character, of course. I get the impression he's as nice as he seems to be, and maybe the sheriff is hurrying this investigation a bit too much. Being number two on the sheriff's list of suspects gives me a vested interest in how all this shakes out. I was under the impression everyone loved Jane, but it seems I was wrong. Joe and Louise weren't exactly fans, and even Zach and Clive were upset with her. Louise and Joe both called Jane nosy. I'm wondering if they had something to hide that Jane may have been trying to find out about."

"Dear Jane. Even as a child, she was always curious and loved doing research. She saw things as puzzles and never thought she might cause harm. She wanted to figure out people's secrets. I don't think she shared them with anyone. In fact, I think she helped wherever she could, assuming you weren't wanted for murder. I guess if you had something to hide, like being a murderer, then Jane's propensity to dig up secrets would be a concern. I don't know if Louise or Joe has a secret. As I said, Jane wouldn't have shared it with me anyway, and I don't know either of them well. I suppose Netta was always a bit jealous of Jane too."

"Because she wanted to be president of the horticultural society?"

"That, but it goes back further. Netta dated Jane's ex-husband before he met Jane. We were all at a Valentine's Day dance, in the sixties, I believe, and when Netta's boyfriend was introduced to Jane, he lost all interest in Netta. He and Jane had a whirlwind courtship and married soon after. As it turns out, he wasn't a very nice young man, but Netta was quite bitter about it. I don't think she ever really forgave Jane for taking her boyfriend away."

"You don't think Netta killed Jane over that?"

"Oh no. It's just that we all have a history. We may not even realize some of the people we know don't especially like us."

Alex didn't think she was making much progress. She thanked Eudora for her help and headed back to the shop.

A little later she sat behind the counter, ostensibly to look at the inventory order, but instead her mind kept wandering to her remaining suspects. Could a stolen boyfriend so many years ago have been enough to prompt Netta to kill Jane? Unlikely. But that was what Alex kept thinking about each of their suspects, and yet, Jane had undeniably been murdered.

She did another search on Penelope. As she scrolled down the results, her eyes skimmed across something about a man charged with bigamy. She quickly scanned the article. It appeared Penelope, who had a different last name back then, had been one of three women married to the same man, at the same time. He'd neglected to mention his simultaneous marriages to any of his wives. That was probably what Penelope had meant when she'd told Netta, "Not that the last one counted." Her last marriage hadn't ended in a divorce because it had never legally existed. The illegal union had happened ten years ago.

Alex did some more searching and discovered the man had spent six months in jail, but judging from the social media profiles Alex uncovered, it hadn't hurt his social life any. What did women see in a man like that? More to the point, his behavior explained Penelope's reaction. She was probably embarrassed by what had happened to her. Alex was actually a little sorry for the woman.

When Hanna came to the counter to ring through a purchase, it roused Alex out of her reverie, and she went to help Maggie straighten books and share her findings.

"I have a feeling Penelope won't thank you for uncovering that bit of information, even if it does take her off your suspect list," Maggie said.

"Penelope has disliked me almost since the day I moved here. I'm sure you remember how she used to leave her dog outside until late in the evening, yapping its head off and keeping half the neighborhood awake. I asked her—very nicely, I might add—if she could bring her dog in earlier if it was barking. She refused and actually started leaving the dog out even later. When the neighbors all banded together and made a formal complaint to the village, she blamed me for that. I've tried being nice to her, but nothing helps."

"Keep trying. You might get through to her someday." Maggie lowered her voice. "Last night I overheard Duncan on the phone. It seems Clive and Trixie saw Zach at Jane's house at about nine fifteen on Monday evening. They were on their nightly walk after getting home from Sleuth and saw Zach talking to Jane at her front door. He seemed upset, but they were too far down the street to make out what he was saying. After a few minutes, he stormed down the steps, got in his truck, and drove away. They didn't worry about it too much at the time but got to thinking they should probably report what they saw after they heard he'd been arrested."

"Tom and I talked to Zach yesterday evening. He told us he was angry with Jane because she insisted he tell his girlfriend about his criminal record before he proposed. Unfortunately, his girlfriend dumped him. I can understand his being upset, but I don't think he would have killed Jane over it. Let's face it. We all get angry with people at times, and we don't go around killing them."

"That's true, but it would definitely seem like additional motive to the sheriff, I'd bet."

Alex wanted to discuss the case with Hanna, but it wasn't to be. As Hanna's customer left, one of their suspects walked in the door.

Alex greeted Joe and asked if she could be of help.

Joe handed her a list of items. "I was told to come here for this stuff." He scowled. "My staff expects me to give them gifts again this year, and my assistant gave me this list and told me to pick something from it for each person. I need four gifts."

"This shouldn't be hard. How much do you want to spend?"

"As little as possible." Joe had a sour expression.

"In that case, I suggest the cinnamon-vanilla candles for your office staff. Your assistant has provided a few options for mysteries she likes. If you don't have a preference, I suggest this one from the list." Alex led him to a nearby bookcase and picked one off a shelf. "We can gift wrap them for you if you'd like."

"Perfect. I think this whole gift-giving thing is a scam, but what can you do? Once you start, you're expected to do it every year."

Hanna wrapped the purchases while Alex rang them up.

As Joe waited for Hanna to finish wrapping, Alex asked, "Have you always lived here?"

"No. I'm from the West Coast originally."

"It's beautiful there. Where exactly did you live?"

"You know, I think I better take another one of those books from the list for my assistant. I don't want to come across as cheap."

Too late. Alex selected another book and rang it up as well. "I take it from your comment the other morning you weren't a fan of Jane's, the lady that died. You were yelling at her the day before she was murdered."

"That seems to be all anybody in this village is talking about." He clenched his jaw. "She was a real busybody. I can't say I'll miss her. She was always hounding me and my staff, trying to find out personal information. She said she wanted to research my family tree. I told her to mind her own business. If I want to share my family tree with the whole world, I'll do it myself."

"She did love researching people's history." Alex helped put tags on the gifts that had been wrapped. "What were you up to on Monday night?"

"Me?" He snorted. "I was having an office meeting until ten that night and had to pay my staff overtime for it too. I'm starting to think you're as nosy as that other dame was. If I were you, I'd be more worried about your plant there." He pointed at Jane's poinsettia. "It doesn't look like it's doing too good."

Joe's purchases were wrapped, and Alex handed him his bag of gifts. With a muttered "Thanks," he was out the door.

"Friendly guy." Hanna squinted her eyes in disgust.

"He wasn't very helpful, was he? Until his alibi is verified, he definitely stays on our suspect list. He obviously didn't like Jane looking into his background. So I'm asking myself, why?"

Alex told Hanna what she'd discovered about Penelope.

"You know, technically, knowing about her third and fourth marriages doesn't mean she didn't kill Jane."

"I know, but I don't think there's any motive. It looks like she lived in North Carolina until her fourth marriage to the bigamist. I found an Instagram page for her, Southernbelle#1. It dates back a long time. There were lots of pictures of her pouting into the camera. Her past looks fairly benign. She certainly doesn't seem to be hiding from anyone. I suppose it could be something completely unrelated to the true-crime episode, but that seems to stretch the imagination too far. No, as much as I wish she were the killer, I think she's only a divorcée desperately seeking a new husband."

Alex told Hanna how they could search to see if Oliver Robins was a pseudonym. Hanna went to the computer and pulled up Cadastral and narrowed in on Harriston. "What's his address?"

"I'm not sure. His backyard backs onto Jane's."

"Hang on." Hanna narrowed in on Jane's house and then easily found the correct property and tapped on it. "Oliver King."

"Well, having a pseudonym as an author doesn't mean he's trying to hide anything."

Hanna took Alex by the arm. "Let's go have lunch."

"I'll search his real name after I eat and see what I can find."

They quickly threw the fixings for taco salads together and enjoyed a few minutes of quiet as they ate. Alex was putting her dishes in the dishwasher when the door jingled. She went to see who had come in and to tell Maggie to go for lunch.

Eudora was bundled up in a warm coat, hat, and matching fluffy pink scarf that covered her face from the nose down. "I dashed over to do some quick Christmas shopping during my lunch. I was hoping you might have those books I ordered."

Alex went behind the counter and dug three novels out of a drawer. "Would you like me to gift wrap them for you?"

Pushing the scarf down under her chin, Eudora smiled brightly. "That would be wonderful. I'm not very good at wrapping. My gifts always look like a five-year-old bundled them up."

Alex laughed. "I find it hard to believe you do anything poorly."

"You're too kind. You know, after you left, I was thinking about who might want to kill Jane. A year or two ago, the historical society decided to take on a project to do some genealogical research on residents of the village who hadn't already done so on their own. We had hoped to do an update to *The History of Harriston*." Eudora smiled as one of the books was wrapped and placed into a bag.

"We have a couple of copies for sale here. It's one of the few non-mystery books we carry."

"We did a comprehensive one in 1999 to celebrate Harriston's centennial and decided it would be nice to have an update twenty years later. We divided the residents who had moved here since the 1999 version was printed between all the members of the society. Jane happened to get Joe. She tried doing some research online but didn't have any success. In the end, she explained what we were doing and asked him some questions. Things like where he came from, who his parents were, if he had been married, if he had children, that sort of thing. He became quite upset and told her, in no uncertain terms, to mind her own business. You know that was like waving a red flag to Jane. It made her all the more determined to find out why he was so sensitive about the society researching his family roots."

"I think he must have found out she didn't give up. Gary saw him yelling at her Monday morning, and I asked him about it. He said she'd been looking into his family history. Do you know if she ever found anything?"

"I'm not sure. She couldn't believe there would be nothing on the internet about him. So she started wondering if he'd changed his name. She found out he's from Washington State and started sending requests to various county courthouses, trying to find a legal name change for him. I don't think she found anything."

"I'm curious. Do you know how Jane found out he's from Washington?"

"She was a friend of one of his secretaries, who had seen some correspondence that indicated where he was from. I think Jane only discovered that a couple of months ago. I hope that's helpful. I've got to go next door to do some more shopping." She held up her parcel. "Thank you so much for wrapping this."

A little while later, Alex saw Eudora's receipt on the counter. "Hanna, I'm going to run over to the post office for a second. Maggie's still gone for lunch."

Alex hurried across the street and gave Eudora the receipt. She also checked the mail. As she was leaving the post office with a parcel, she ran into Stella, who had been chatting with another woman in front of the post office.

"That was Joe's admin assistant." She nodded at the woman getting into her car a few yards away. "She was telling me she's been dealing with another angry client. Joe managed to hoodwink someone else with one of his misleading contracts. Joe had all his staff in a meeting until ten on Monday night to tell them how to handle those customers."

"Rather sharp business practices. I wonder why he doesn't worry about being sued."

Stella shook her head. "It's people like him that have all the angles covered."

As Alex walked into the shop, Maggie was bringing chocolate samples from the kitchen. "While you were out, Netta stopped by. She said to tell you she remembered hearing something that doesn't make sense and wants to talk to you about it. She also remembered who was in the post office when she told Eudora about Jane's latest true-crime killer. She's on her way to Kalispell now, but she'll try and drop by the shop tomorrow. Otherwise, she'll talk to you at church on Sunday about it."

"This is a day for news. Stella just told me something that confirms Joe's alibi. It's too bad, because he was my top pick among our suspects."

Chapter Seventeen

While Alex and Maggie restocked shelves, Hanna came out of the kitchen with a small plate of chocolates. "Try these, my lovelies. They're made with my new recipe for Salted Cyanide Caramels."

"These are delicious," Maggie finally managed, after savoring the caramel-filled chocolate with her eyes closed.

"You don't think they're too soft? I've been experimenting with the filling. I couldn't decide whether to make these chewy or soft and creamy."

"My vote says they're perfect as is. I love the way the sea salt combines with the sweetness of the caramel and chocolate, and it all just melts in your mouth." Alex grabbed another one from the plate, and Maggie could only nod her agreement as she bit into a second one.

"I'm going to make a chewy caramel that will be part of our seasonal chocolate assortment as well."

Alex wondered if Hanna was genuinely happy at the bookshop. Her skill at making chocolates had been much better utilized at their parents' store. Murder and Mayhem would never achieve the volume of business Hanna had previously been used to, though she did have more creative freedom.

The rest of the afternoon at Murder and Mayhem was mayhem. Alex and Maggie didn't have another quiet moment until Maggie left and Alex closed and locked the door behind her.

By the time Alex and Hanna were ready to leave the shop, Alex was wishing she hadn't committed to going caroling tonight, especially since the temperature was supposed to dip down to minus twenty-five.

"What are you doing tonight?" Alex locked the door behind them as they stepped out into the dark. The icy breath of the wind enveloped her, and she shivered.

"Having a long, hot bath and then heating up a frozen pizza. Followed by gorging on Christmas cookies and drinking hot chocolate in my pajamas in front of the television, watching a Hallmark Christmas movie."

"Sounds lonely. How about coming Christmas caroling with me." Alex had made the commitment at the beginning of the month before she knew she'd be playing detective to solve Jane's murder. Now she wished she could stay home and do more research on her remaining suspects.

"Do I look crazy to you?" Hanna laughed.

Sticking out her tongue and shivering again, Alex moaned, "Please think of me out here in the cold while you soak. I'll barely have time to eat before I have to head out."

At home she made a peanut-butter-and jam sandwich as she put together two boxes of cookies. The carolers were each bringing cookies for two of the homes they would be caroling at. Alex tucked a couple of the chocolates they'd made the other night into each box as well. Tanya had organized the event, so they were meeting at her house and caroling up and down her street.

After a short drive, Alex parked in front of Tanya's, which was just up the street from Jane's. Everyone was prompt, and the carolers started next door, where an elderly couple enjoyed an enthusiastic "We Wish You a Merry Christmas." The group caroled one or two songs at each house, and it wasn't long before Alex's toes were frozen and she wished she'd put on an extra pair of socks. By the time they crossed the street and were working their way back to Tanya's, her fingers were numb. Fortunately, they didn't need to stop at Yvonne's house, as she was one of the carolers.

Alex had been a little surprised when Yvonne joined them, since she was still sporting her cane and limping along, and said as much to Stella.

"Oh, she participates in all the village activities. I think she gets lonely in her little castle."

They stopped at Gary's house, which was sandwiched between Yvonne's and Jane's houses, and sang, "Silent Night, Holy Night." Gary's gruff expression softened as Alex handed him her cookies.

Alex faced Jane's house sadly as they walked by. It was completely dark and reminded her of a corpse, eyes shut, cold, and silent. The door still had crime-scene tape across it, and the house stood in stark contrast to all the brightly lit, warm, inviting homes on the street. A sudden deep sadness washed over Alex, and she dug in her pocket for a tissue. She missed Jane. Other than Hanna, Jane had been the one person she could always confide in.

Alex could understand how Jane's interest in other people's lives might have been misconstrued as meddling or nosiness. After a brief, childless marriage, she'd taken a personal interest in the lives of the children she'd taught over the years, as well as the residents of the village. Her curiosity had led her to find out about people, but she wasn't a scandalmonger. Every person she had erroneously suspected of being from one of her crime shows had been confronted privately. It was the individuals themselves who had shared Jane's accusations with the community, except in Clive's case. Trixie had thought it so hilarious, she'd told everyone in town. Why had Jane shared her concerns with Netta this time, knowing Netta would shout it from the rooftops?

Unless that had been the point. If Jane didn't want to approach the individual directly, then telling Netta would have been the next best thing. But why hadn't Jane approached the killer herself this time?

At the next house, Alex focused on happier thoughts as they sang another Christmas carol. It felt as if the temperature had fallen at least ten degrees since they'd started, and she was grateful to finally return to Tanya's for hot chocolate.

After circling the room packed with cold and weary carolers and chatting briefly with several people, Alex huddled beside Stella, whose freshly colored auburn hair was teased and set with enough hair spray to necessitate a flammable-hazard warning sign. Alex hugged her hot cocoa between her hands and asked Stella about the night Jane was killed.

Stella took a moment to finish chewing the cookie she'd popped into her mouth before responding. "I arrived home shortly before Jane from Sleuth, a bit before eight thirty. My cat had gotten out, and I was trying to get her back in the house. I saw Jane go in and turn on her lights. Before I went to bed at quarter to eleven, I turned off my Christmas lights and looked out the window. Jane still had lights on. I can't believe Jane was being murdered while I was sitting in my living room watching television."

"Did the deputies question you?" Alex asked.

"They questioned all the neighbors. I may have been the last person to see her alive. Aside from the killer, of course."

Zach, Clive, and Trixie had actually been the last people to see Jane alive that night. The killer must have remained at the house well after he killed Jane, if the lights were still on at quarter to eleven. What had he been doing there all that time?

Alex left Tanya's at eight to stop at Tom's and tell him Penelope was no longer a suspect.

Tom's face lit up when he opened the door and saw Alex standing there. "Please come in. Quickly, before Penelope sees you."

"Is Penelope watching for me?"

"I'm not sure, but I've noticed she seems to show up every time you're here."

They went into the family room, where he had the fire going and the television on mute.

"I only stopped by to let you know I've taken Penelope off the suspect list, so you should be safe if she comes over. Unless you eat her cooking, of course."

Tom chuckled. "I'm wiser than that. What made you clear her from your suspect list?"

"I found several mentions of her online from her life before she moved here. She has something in her past she's probably a bit sensitive about, but it's nothing that puts anyone in danger. I won't repeat what it is, because it's not relevant."

"I certainly won't press you on the matter. I respect your desire not to pass along gossip. I wish a few of the other ladies in the village felt that way."

"Would you mind if I looked at another one of those true-crime shows while I'm here?"

Tom handed her the remote and told her which episode to start with. It didn't take her long to realize it wasn't what she was looking for.

"I was meaning to ask you," Tom said as she scrolled to the next episode. "What are you and Hanna doing for Christmas?"

"Maggie invited us over for Christmas dinner. On Christmas Eve, we call our family in Michigan. It's a German tradition to celebrate that night. Are you celebrating with your kids?"

Tom nodded. "I'm going to my daughter's on Christmas morning for a bit. They've invited me to come back for dinner that evening when all my other kids will be there as well. This will be my first Christmas without my wife, and they didn't want me spending the day alone."

Alex sympathized with Tom and blurted out, "Why don't you come over Christmas Eve and spend it with Hanna and me? We usually just play games and have potato salad, schnitzel, and the German cookies we used to bake with our mom. It's not exciting, but it beats being alone."

Without hesitation, Tom said, "I gratefully accept your generous invitation. I was actually—"

Whatever Tom was going to say was cut off by the doorbell. He stiffened, and his eyes went wide. He slowly got up and headed to the door as if he were going to meet the executioner.

Alex also rose and headed to the door in time to see Penelope poking her head in and asking Tom if he'd like some of the cake she'd baked. Alex took one look at it and knew it came from a grocery store—probably safer for Tom that way. Penelope appeared to have dressed up even more than usual for the occasion. She was wearing an extremely low-cut, clingy sweater made of some kind of sparkly red fabric over skintight black leggings with high-heeled black boots. Alex didn't think Tom could miss the implications.

"What a coincidence. I was hoping to run into you, Penelope. Tom was just telling me he needs to make an important phone call, so we'll leave him to it." As she said this, Alex put on her boots. She took Penelope's arm and had her outside before Penelope had even registered what was happening.

Alex continued to lead Penelope across the lawn toward the road. "I just wanted you to know that whatever you have in your past is your business, and I won't be sharing it or discussing it with anyone else. Merry Christmas." She headed back to her house, leaving Penelope staring after her in surprise.

True to her word, Hanna was on the sofa watching a Christmas movie with a warm blanket on her lap. She'd changed into red pajamas covered in white reindeer and snowflakes. On the coffee table sat a giant red holiday mug topped with a mountain of whipped cream.

Watson jumped up and greeted Alex with much tail wagging before flopping down in hopes of a tummy rub. Alex knelt down and accommodated her for a minute before heading upstairs to put on her own festive pajamas. Downstairs again, she made a cup of chamomile tea and sat in a comfortable chair near Hanna. Watson had curled up at Hanna's feet on the sofa and was snoring gently.

"I hope you don't mind—I invited Tom over for Christmas Eve. It didn't sound like he wanted to be alone."

"Not at all. It'll be nice to have a guest. You know if Mom calls while he's here, she's bound to say something embarrassing?"

"I know. We should try and call before Tom comes over."

As briefly as possible, Alex told Hanna about her evening. "We know Jane was alive around nine fifteen. She would have to have gotten into bed and possibly been asleep, and the murderer would have had to get into the house and kill her, all within forty-five minutes to stay within the time frame the ME gave. Doesn't that stretch the imagination a little bit?"

Hanna took a sip of her hot chocolate. "I agree with you. That time frame does seem a bit tight, but how else could it have happened?"

"I'm not sure. There are things that just don't add up. It would make more sense if she'd been killed later. Plus, the killer had to drop off the chocolates laced with a sedative earlier in the day, which suggests it was premeditated, not just a simple robbery." Alex popped one of their Poison Pear Ganache chocolates into her mouth and enjoyed the snap of the chocolate followed by the release of the smooth, creamy center. "On a happier note, I'm going Christmas shopping in Swanson tomorrow afternoon. Do you want to bring Watson to work with us?"

"Didn't you have all your Christmas shopping done weeks ago?"

"I do. I'm looking for some odds and ends and stocking stuffers. You know I always like to go out, once, just before Christmas. I don't expect it will take more than an hour."

"We should definitely bring Watson to the shop. I'm sure she'd like the change of scene."

Finishing her tea, Alex got up. Watson briefly opened one eye before snuggling deeper into the blanket at Hanna's feet.

Alex headed upstairs and called over her shoulder. "I'm going to do a search on Oliver and see what I can find. It looks like Watson is staying with you."

In the spare bedroom they had converted to an office, Alex sat at the desk and researched the new last name she had for Oliver on her laptop. It didn't take her long to come up with several articles. Absent-mindedly, Alex grabbed a chocolate from a small jar on the desk and popped it into her mouth. It didn't look like there was much new information in the articles under Oliver's real name.

After his parents' death, Oliver's godfather had become his guardian, but a year later the godfather had also died. At that point, Oliver had been sent to boarding school in England.

She couldn't find anything after that until he showed up as Oliver Robins a few years later, living in the States. An interesting past, but it didn't seem likely that he left a trail of corpses in England and then waltzed across the ocean and set up life in Montana. His life seemed, more or less, an open book. And yet she was sure he hadn't been completely truthful when she spoke to him at the library.

Later, as she lay in the darkness, trying to sleep, she wondered if Oliver had friends in the village. She'd never had a great many friends. Friendly acquaintances, coworkers, very casual friends, yes, but not close friends, the kind you could tell your innermost thoughts to and who loved you even when you sounded like a nut case.

Since Alex had moved to Harriston, Hanna and Jane had filled those roles for her. Now Jane was gone, and Hanna might be considering a move back to Michigan. Alex didn't believe in self-pity, but she had to admit, losing both of them would leave an aching void in her life.

She had spent years after her divorce building a safe cocoon for her heart. By keeping people at a distance, she'd been safe from hurt and failure. Opening Murder and Mayhem had been more than a fresh start for her business dreams; it had opened her heart to people again. And with that came the potential for failure and personal pain.

Chapter Eighteen

Alex was up and ready for work earlier than usual on Saturday morning. She decided to fill a couple of plates with cookies, thinking they might come in handy if she went to interview some of her suspects again. She had read you created a sense of obligation when you gave a person something. She hoped her little psychological trick would help generate a feeling of reciprocity today.

She'd had a restless night worrying if Hanna was really thinking about leaving Murder and Mayhem. Alex had enjoyed making chocolates the other night, but she couldn't do that and run the bookstore. How would she deal with being alone again?

Shaking off the negativity, she decided to spend the day thinking more about Christmas, since she'd be going shopping later, but first, she'd get scones for herself and her crew.

Unfortunately, Sam didn't have time to talk this morning. It seemed half of Harriston was in Cookies 'n Crumbs, which was unusual so early on a Saturday morning. Maybe people were still discussing Jane's murder. There seemed to be two main camps, one that believed the sheriff had the right person in jail and another that thought there was still a dangerous robber or a psychopath on the loose. Most people had dismissed Jane's true-crime theory as another wild idea from a declining elderly woman.

Alex was able to get some of her bookkeeping done and decided she would go see Oliver again today. She needed to find out exactly where he had been the evening Jane was murdered so she could, once and for all, cross him off the suspect list.

Twenty minutes before opening, Maggie arrived. Two minutes later Hanna arrived with Watson, who was happy and excited to see Maggie. After the dog got some attention from Maggie, Hanna settled her in the conference room. "Do you mind keeping an eye on Watson later when Alex leaves?" she asked Maggie. "I'll be in the kitchen until midafternoon."

"Of course not. She's family. We'll have a great time."

Customers started arriving as soon as the doors were unlocked. It was amazing how many people left their shopping until the last weekend before Christmas. A few people still asked Alex about finding Jane's body and whether Zach had done it. For the most part, Alex remained noncommittal in her responses.

Midmorning, Yvonne walked into the shop and approached Alex. "It's warming up a bit out there. I'd like to get a few novels to keep me busy over the holidays. Jane often mentioned her love for murder mysteries and true crime, though I never really understood the attraction to reading about murder, but I've decided to give it a try. Would you help me find a few novels I might like?"

"Of course. First, we need to figure out the genre you prefer."

After some discussion, Alex suggested Yvonne try a James Patterson novel and a cozy mystery. "Once you've read them, you'll know if you have a preference, and then I can recommend some more."

Maggie approached Alex. "I'm sorry to interrupt. Netta is on the phone and wants to know if you'll be in this afternoon. She'd like to drop by and discuss the matter she mentioned earlier?"

"You can tell her I'll be out for a bit, but I should be back toward the latter part of the afternoon."

Yvonne looked at Alex curiously. "Have you heard any more about Jane's murder? I understand they've arrested Zach. Such a shame. He seemed like such a nice young man."

Alex took the books to the counter to ring them in. "Yes, I'm afraid that's true." She took a deep breath that ended in a sigh. "I hope they keep searching for Jane's killer. I'm not convinced Zach did it."

"That's not realistic though, is it? Certainly they must have some evidence, if they've arrested him."

"They did find something, but it's circumstantial."

"There you have it! I'm sure the sheriff's department knows what they're doing." Before leaving, Yvonne reminded Alex to come visit her again soon.

Alex and Maggie couldn't believe it when ten seniors entered. Alex welcomed them to the store.

"We're from Kalispell," one of them said.

A heavyset woman with gray hair in a bun took charge. "We're members of the Southside Community Center's Victorian Mystery Book Club. We read about your shop in the *Kalispell Living* magazine. Another fifteen of our club will be coming in after us. Some of them went to the bakery first, and the others are at the antique store."

Hanna came out with a tray of chocolates. The woman with the bun looked at Alex and then Hanna. But other than raising her eyebrows, she didn't comment on their looks. Alex and Maggie spent the next hour and a half helping all the members of the club find books and gifts. Watson stayed by the counter watching the activity and seemed to relish the attention she received. A few of the ladies asked what the dog's name was and were absolutely tickled when they found out she was named after Sherlock Holmes's iconic assistant. When the last of them had finally left, Alex sent Maggie home for her lunch. Drew had been missing his wife's presence and looked forward to her noontime visits.

Alex was basking in the store's successful day and giving Watson a little attention when the bell rang and another customer walked in. Alex turned around with a ready smile to welcome the newcomer. Her smile froze when she saw it was Penelope. Watson ran back behind the counter and hid under the desk. The divorcée was sporting her usual skintight jeans and an off-the-shoulder sweater but was wearing more sensible footwear.

"You can put away your fake smile. I won't be staying long. I just wanted you to know I see what you're up to, swooping in on Tom when his wife's barely cold in the ground. I'm going to make sure he sees right through your little tricks. And don't think the sheriff's forgotten about you. She was at my house again yesterday asking more questions about your comings and goings. I've got my eyes on you." Penelope stood with her arms crossed, her gaze flinty and her nostrils flaring.

Alex had been so surprised by the divorcée's entrance, she hadn't yet been able to form a coherent response. She finally snapped, "For the record, I'm not *swooping* in on anyone. I bring treats to lots of people in the village. If you want to report my comings and goings to the sheriff, feel free. I have nothing to hide. And if you want to try and snap up Tom as your next conquest, then go to your destiny. But please don't bother me with your wild and ridiculous accusations." Alex walked past

Penelope into the hall and held the door open. She struggled to keep a straight face and waited for her to leave.

Penelope left with a final, "I never!"

Alex shook her head and snorted with merriment.

Hanna poked her head out of the kitchen, laughing. "Is it safe to come out?"

"Did you catch all that?"

"Every word. You've really raised her dander."

Watson had quietly sneaked into the hall and was rubbing her body against Alex's leg, in need of some reassurance.

Alex gave the dog a pat. "I guess I'd better watch my back around Penelope from now on."

"She obviously thinks you're a threat to her and Tom's future happiness together." Hanna giggled. "Kitty's got her claws out."

Chapter Nineteen

Alex was restocking chocolates in the display cases when Maggie returned from lunch.

"It's warmed up some. I left the car at home and walked back," Maggie said.

"Maggie, you missed all the excitement." Alex filled her in on Penelope's visit. "I'm leaving in a few minutes. I shouldn't be more than a couple of hours."

At the last minute, Alex grabbed Hanna. "Come with me to Oliver's. I'll bring you back to the shop as soon as we're done talking before I head to Swanson."

Hanna was reluctant. "I don't want to leave Maggie alone on a Saturday."

Alex called out, "Maggie, do you mind if Hanna and I leave you alone for about thirty minutes?"

Maggie assured them she'd be fine, so amid Hanna's protests, Alex dragged her out to the car. To Alex's satisfaction, the weather had turned, and the sun shone through the ragged clouds. Clumps of snow were falling from the trees and roofs.

Oliver's house was directly behind Jane's. It was a newer ranch home that had been renovated to a midcentury modern style. There were lots of clean angles, no adornment, and it was done in cedar with some kind of stone-and-black trim. While it didn't appeal to Alex, she had to admit it looked attractive, though in complete contrast to Jane's and the other neighbors' homes.

Alex knew the back of Oliver's house had large windows overlooking Jane's backyard. The front had fewer windows and was well kept, though it didn't look like the snow had been shoveled after the last snowfall. It was beginning to melt under the sun's rays.

As Alex and Hanna walked to the front door, they had to pass directly by the garbage bin. Alex didn't feel she could let the opportunity pass, so, after a quick glance around to ensure no one was watching her, she lifted the lid and had a good look inside. *Aha!* There were two empty vodka bottles that she could see, and she pointed them out to Hanna, who was keeping a lookout in case anyone walked past. Score one for Stella. The rest of the garbage was bagged, and Alex didn't think she could get away with opening the bags in broad daylight.

Oliver was surprised by their presence but welcomed them in as Alex presented him with a plate of their homemade *Vanillekipferl* and *Zimtsterne* cookies.

"I know you're into healthy eating, but hopefully you indulge a bit at Christmas. We have a few questions we hope you can answer."

Alex quickly took off her boots to ensure she got an invitation to sit down and nudged Hanna to do the same. Looking around, she noted the house was fairly clean, though a little untidy. The midcentury modern look had been carried inside the house as well and looked a bit stiff. Alex preferred furniture that provided comfort for lounging. To their right was a small formal living room.

Oliver led them through the hall and kitchen into what was obviously meant to be a family room but was more of an office with a meditation area. Closest to the kitchen was an area on the floor with cushions, a yoga mat, and a large, beautiful mandala wall hanging. Next to the mat was a low table with an aroma diffuser and a small Himalayan salt lamp. In the middle of the room were two relatively comfortable-looking leather chairs, with a small wood-and-metal table between them. They faced a wall of windows and a set of sliding glass doors that led out onto a deck and the backyard beyond. In the far corner, in front of the wall of windows, was a telescope.

Oliver indicated they should sit in the two leather chairs as he sat in his desk chair. From that vantage point, Alex had a full view of the back of Jane's house and her yard.

The village of Harriston occupied one square mile of land near the southwest shore of Echo Lake. It was a flat section with one corner edging the lake. The village was laid out in a grid of wide streets, and each ten-acre block had been divided into eight large lots. While some had since been subdivided, many were still the original size, thus allowing for particularly large back-yards with dirt alleys between them.

Oliver's block had been subdivided, so there wasn't an alley between the properties. It was, nonetheless, a long backyard, with Jane's house at least fifty or sixty yards away, though there was no fence separating the two properties.

"This is quite a view. I'm sure it must be beautiful in the summer. You must enjoy the sunsets in the evenings." Alex took in her surroundings.

"I do. That's why I had the windows enlarged when I did the renovation. I'm afraid I don't do much in my yard. Jane's yard is quite something, though. She spent a lot of hours on it. There are

157

gardens bordering the north and south sides that curve partially around the dividing line between our properties. I couldn't tell you any of the things that grow in her garden, though. I'm afraid my knowledge extends to differentiating between dandelions and flowers." Oliver gave a self-deprecating laugh. His manner had changed from sullen to almost hospitable since Alex had last seen him at the library. Perhaps it had something to do with the appreciative glances Hanna was getting from him.

"I don't think there are too many people as dedicated to their garden as Jane was," Alex agreed.

"Except maybe Yvonne, on the corner. Her backyard is on the other side of Gary's, and she has quite the garden oasis as well. Gary's is nice too, but much simpler." Oliver casually scooted his chair a little closer to Hanna. "A few years ago, the horticultural society organized a garden tour and awarded trophies and ribbons for first, second, and third place. They did a little award presentation in Jane's backyard. Jane got first place and Yvonne got second. It looked like Yvonne was going to throw her trophy at the judges. She spent the rest of the summer making major changes. It's worthy of a magazine spread now." Oliver pointed in the direction of Yvonne's garden.

Oliver offered to make them some tea, and Hanna jumped up to help. As they walked into the kitchen, he said to Hanna, "My favorite is one from the Black Currant. It's a blend of chamomile and mint, good for stress and anxiety."

Hanna started talking about the teas she usually preferred, and Oliver seemed completely wrapped up in what she was saying.

Alex took the opportunity to glance around the room. There was an empty glass on the table beside her. She picked it up, then quickly put it back. While they said vodka had no scent, she'd bet her bookshop the slight odor in the glass was vodka. A few photographs on the bookshelf looked like Oliver when he was younger—with his family, perhaps?

Several minutes later Oliver set a mug beside Alex and drew his desk chair even closer to Hanna.

"Is that you in the picture?" Alex pointed to a frame.

He glanced to see where she was pointing. "That was me with my parents, a long time ago. What was it you wanted to ask me about?"

"You said you weren't home until ten Monday night, the night Jane was murdered, but did you perhaps see anything after that? Did you notice if the lights were on in the house, for example?"

"Now that you mention it, there were lights on in the kitchen when I first got home."

"Did you notice when the lights went off, by any chance?"

Oliver began to fidget with his mug; he took a sip of his tea and then stared into its depths like he might find the answer there. "No, I don't think I noticed anything else that night. I'm sorry. I don't mean to hurry you, but I've got a call in ten minutes with my editor, and I still need to prepare a few things."

"Just one other question. Where were you Monday night?"

His face was pale and tight despite his tan. He stood abruptly. "Not that it's any of your business, but I was in Kalispell with a friend." The warmth Oliver had shown earlier in their visit cooled by several degrees as he headed to the door.

Alex and Hanna had no choice but to follow and left without getting any more information.

"Did you get the feeling he wasn't telling the truth?" Alex looked at Hanna.

"He's definitely being secretive."

"But he seemed to enjoy talking to you, and you certainly appeared to enjoy spending time with him."

"I was just trying to make him feel comfortable around us in hopes he'd open up." Hanna got into the car.

After dropping Hanna off, Alex spent an hour and a half focused on Christmas shopping. She played Christmas music in the car, singing along to Michael Bublé's "Let It Snow" and a classic version of "Silent Night."

Wandering through locally owned and festively decorated boutiques, she purchased a few generic gifts, as their Christmas plans had changed. She wasn't sure what would be an appropriate gift for Tom, but since she and Hanna always exchanged one gift on Christmas Eve, she wanted to ensure they had a gift for him.

Before Hanna moved to Montana, Alex had spent many of her adult Christmases alone watching Hallmark Christmas movies. She'd never worried about it, with all her hobbies to keep her busy over the holidays. She'd even taken fencing lessons one year. But she imagined it would be difficult for Tom after so many years with his wife. Could Hanna be right? Was the widower showing more than friendly interest? There had to be some baggage there, and Alex had always run from any kind of drama. Even in her first marriage, she'd preferred divorce to constant arguments with her husband over his rare appearances at home. Since her childhood, she'd used her sense of humor to deflect and laugh things off whenever she could. Humor was a shield to prevent others from getting too close, and she still wasn't sure she was ready to let anyone else in. Especially after what had happened to Jane. When you cared about people, there was so much more risk of getting hurt. Hopefully, Hanna was wrong about Tom's intentions, and then she wouldn't have to make a decision one way or the other.

In a small, exclusive accessories boutique, Alex found a beautiful silk scarf in blues and yellows that had been marked down to a price she could afford. She knew it would be perfect for Maggie. She also saw a tie clip in the shape of handcuffs that would be perfect for Tom, since he so enjoyed his true-crime shows. After finding several other gifts that would suit both men and women, she made her way to a specialty coffee store to get a hot chocolate covered in whipped cream.

Arriving back at the shop an hour before closing, she was surprised to hear Everett had come by again and left a message for her to call him as soon as she came in. He and his wife had been among the carolers last night, but he hadn't mentioned anything new. With a quick call, it was arranged for Everett to come by just after closing to give her an update regarding Jane's house.

There wasn't much time to think about the reason for Everett's visit. Maggie was leaving shortly, and there were a number of last-minute shoppers in the store.

Maggie slipped on her coat and told Alex that Netta had stopped by again. "She seemed quite anxious to talk to you and said she'd see you at church tomorrow."

"Thanks. My shopping took a little longer than I expected. I'll stop by and see her tonight."

Everett arrived on time, and though Hanna was just as curious as Alex, she tidied the store while Alex went to the conference room with Everett.

Everett handed Alex an envelope with her name on it in Jane's handwriting. "Jane wanted you to have this when you got the keys to the house." He dropped the keys into her palm. "The sheriff's department has finished with it as a crime scene, so you're free to go inside whenever you wish. I'll take care of all practical matters. I've arranged for a trauma-scene cleanup company to clean the house next week. Just keep me in the loop when you do the estate sale."

"Who's taking care of the funeral?"

"That would be me as well. Jane didn't especially care for most of her extended relations, and her cousin, who she did like, has dementia, so he's not capable of arranging it. She left instructions for everything. Her body still hasn't been released, so the funeral probably won't happen until after Christmas."

After Everett left, Alex filled Hanna in on the things she hadn't been able to overhear while getting the shop tidied up.

"So what does the letter say?" Hanna asked curiously.

"I haven't opened it yet." Alex took the single handwritten sheet out of the envelope and read it aloud.

My Dear Alex,

I hope this hasn't taken you too much by surprise. With the passing of my brother, I really don't have anyone else I want to leave my estate to, aside from those bequests I've made in my will. You and I have become such good friends, and I certainly like you better than my brother's progenitors. If they give you any trouble, refer them to Everett.

I've had such fun solving mysteries with you. I hope you'll continue to do so for a long time. Please don't be sad at my passing. I've had a good life and have no regrets.

There are a few things in the house I really hope you will keep. The silver tea set we used so many times is meant for you, as are the antique teacups. Hopefully they'll remind you of our little chats. There are some old family albums and antique dolls that can be donated to Harriston's Historical Society. There is a small collection of jewelry that belonged to my mother. Just go to my special spot to find it, along with my journal. No tears. Just remember, I may be pushing up daisies, but you aren't.

I don't want to burden you with things you may not want, so the remainder is for your discretion.

I'll see you on the other side, but not too soon, I hope.

Your Friend,

Jane

They stared at each other when Alex finished. Even though Alex had known about the inheritance for a few days, it still seemed so impossible.

"I'm going to go to Jane's. Do you want to come?"

"Yes, but I can't." Hanna looked crestfallen as she checked her watch. "I made plans to have dinner with Duncan in Swanson to see if I can find out anything new about the investigation. Maybe I can see who they've gotten alibis for. I want to make sure my sister isn't about to be arrested, especially after what Penelope said."

Chapter Twenty

Fifteen minutes later, Alex stood in the hall of Jane's house, listening to the utter and complete silence. It was as if the house sensed its owner's passing and was quietly mourning her. The only illumination in the hall was from the Christmas lights strung around the porch that Alex had just turned on. Was it less than a week ago she had come in this very door, only to discover Jane's body upstairs?

Feeling very guilty and saying a silent apology to Jane, she left her boots on. Once the house had been cleaned, she'd go back to respecting Jane's rule; her friend would understand. Walking to the back of the house, she turned on the light in the kitchen.

It appeared much the same as when she had led Sheriff Summers and Duncan through. Alex was careful not to touch too many things because of fingerprint powder everywhere. After looking through the kitchen and living room, she went upstairs to look in the murder room for Jane's journal.

The letter had referred to Jane's "special spot," and that was definitely the murder room. It was possible Jane had left a clue to her murderer's identity in her journal. Alex rifled through drawers and files, which were messier than she'd expected, but she supposed the sheriff's deputies had searched them as well.

She checked for false bottoms in the drawers to no avail. Maybe Jane's murderer had taken the jewelry and journal.

As she contemplated where else to look, a sound came from the back of the house. Alex raced down the stairs as quietly as she could, her car keys clutched in her hand. She'd taken a basic self-defense class a few years ago, and her instructors had pointed out that many everyday objects could be used as a weapon in an emergency. When she got to the bottom, she carefully peered around the staircase and down the hall into the kitchen. It sounded like someone was coming in the back door.

She hesitated for a split second and then, without considering the wisdom of her next move, sneaked out the front door and ran around to the back of the house. The back door was ajar. She positioned her finger next to the emergency button on her cell. "Stop where you are! I've got the police on the phone."

"It's just me, Gary," he intruder shrieked as he whirled around, putting his hands in the air. "I saw the lights on, and I knew no one was supposed to be in here. It's a crime scene."

She lowered her phone but kept her finger near the emergency button. "It's me, Alex." She climbed the stairs to the deck. She walked into the kitchen and looked suspiciously at Gary. "How did you get in here?"

He held up a key.

"Where did you get that?"

"From under the flowerpot." He pointed at a large planter beside the door into the kitchen.

"I thought the deputies would have taken that into evidence."

"Obviously not. How did you get in here? And what are you doing?"

"I have a key." She patted her pocket. "And it's no longer a crime scene as of today."

"Okay, so what are you doing here? Maybe I should be calling the sheriff's department." He returned Alex's suspicious look.

"I got the key from Jane's lawyer. Jane left me half the house and all its contents. So how do you know where Jane keeps her spare key?"

Gary lowered his gaze to the floor. "Actually, I've seen Jane's handyman get it from under the flowerpot. I tend to keep an eye out for Jane, or rather I kept an eye out for her. Clearly, I didn't do a very good job."

"You weren't even home when Jane was murdered, so you couldn't have done anything." *Unless you're the murderer.* It was too bad he had an alibi. "Do you know if anyone else knew where she kept this key?"

"I don't think it was a huge secret. A flowerpot isn't the greatest hiding spot."

"True enough. I'm going to lock up now, so I'll take that key from you."

He seemed reluctant to hand it over, but she waited with an outstretched hand until he finally dropped it in her palm. "Next time, just knock if you want to see who's here. And I'd really appreciate it if you didn't mention my inheritance from Jane to anyone."

What on earth had possessed her to rush out and confront Gary like that? Alex wasn't usually that impetuous. She tended to carefully weigh the pros and cons of every decision, making multiple lists before proceeding on any course of action.

Alex drove by Netta's house on her way home, but all was dark. At home she tried calling the older woman, but there was no answer. Grabbing a meal-size container of turkey chili out of the freezer, she popped it into the microwave and let Watson outside. After putting the purchases from her shopping excursion into her bedroom, she went back to the kitchen to eat her dinner before heading over to Tom's with Watson and another plate of cookies.

"Watson, we're going through the backyard so that nasty Penelope doesn't see us and spoil the evening."

Alex knocked on Tom's sliding glass door. He smiled when he saw who was standing on his deck. "This is a surprise." He cocked his head to one side. "Are you afraid the neighbors will talk if they see us visiting?"

She laughed. "I'm only concerned about one neighbor who seems to watch my every move. Do you mind me bringing Watson over? Hanna's out, and I didn't want to leave the dog alone." Alex handed him the cookies. "All yours."

"Please come in. You're both welcome." He opened the door wider and gestured them in, leading them into the family room, where a football game was playing on the television.

"I'm sorry. I'm interrupting your evening." She nodded toward the television. Watson had settled herself beside the recliner where Tom had been sitting.

Tom grabbed the remote and turned it off. "Not at all. I'd much rather have you here to talk to."

He must be lonely after living with someone for so many years. Once Alex had adjusted to living alone, she had enjoyed her single life. But now—and she hated to admit it—it would crush her if Hanna moved back to Frankenmuth. "I wanted to update you on what's been happening. I wasn't sure how much Maggie has been telling you. Want to guess where I was just before coming here?"

"At the bakery picking up these cookies so you could pass them off as your own?" Tom smiled. "I'm just kidding. Maggie says my sense of humor is going to get me into trouble."

Alex chuckled. "You're quick, I'll give you that. I was in Jane's house."

"Did Duncan need you again?"

"No. The sheriff's department is done with it. It's not officially a crime scene anymore. I was there after meeting with Everett, Jane's lawyer."

Tom looked confused. "I'm not sure I understand."

"I've inherited half of Jane's house and her possessions. That's why the sheriff considers me a top suspect. She thinks I have a financial motive. But I had no idea Jane had made me a beneficiary. She never said a word."

Tom's eyes widened. "Did Everett tell you why Jane made you her beneficiary?"

She handed him the letter from Jane.

He read it. "That's incredible. I'm happy for you. I guess if I were to start courting you now that I know your anticipated financial position, it would make me look like a scoundrel." He was smiling, but Alex wasn't sure if he was joking.

"That's not all, though." She decided to ignore his attempt at humor and told him about finding Gary with a key. "If he didn't have an alibi for Jane's murder, he'd be at the top of my suspect list, because he obviously had a way into the house."

Tom looked concerned. "There's a murderer out there. What were you thinking, confronting an unknown intruder? I worked with murderers for a long time, and if you're right about your theory, then this person wouldn't think twice about killing you if you get in their way. I'd be devastated if something happened to you. Where would I get my cookies from then? I'd be at the mercy of Mrs. Matthews and have to hear all about her bodily functions forever."

She wasn't sure if he was serious or not, but he had a point. She wasn't sure what had come over her in that moment; she would have to try to be more careful in the future.

"Hanna and I went to see Oliver today. I'm certain he's hiding something." She snapped her fingers. "If Gary saw where Jane's key was hidden, there's a better than good chance Oliver did too. Remember? Zach even mentioned it. I wonder how I can find out if Oliver's alibi is legitimate."

"Don't you think you should share this with Duncan?"

She sat straight up and leaned forward. "What's the point? They're determined to pin this on Zach or me. They aren't buying into the theory Jane identified a killer from a television show or any other motive, for that matter. Maybe we should watch another one of those true-crime episodes."

They quickly went through another episode with no success. Alex knew Tom might not even have taped the episode that Jane had watched. There were literally dozens of true-crime shows on television each day. They might never find the right show with so little to go on.

"Netta has been trying to get hold of me to tell me something, but we keep missing each other. She said she'll talk to me at church tomorrow if she doesn't see me sooner."

"She never misses church. I'm sure you'll see her there."

"I'm just stumped. The only people with no alibi are Zach and Louise. Maybe it's one of them. I wish I could see that episode. The murderer must have deleted it. If only I could recover it."

"You can." Tom looked up from the television.

Alex leaned forward and directed all her attention at him.

Tom shrugged his shoulders and gave Alex a sheepish look. "It never occurred to me that you didn't know that was an option."

Turning the remote toward the television, he showed her how to do it on his own television's DVR.

"You're wonderful! I'm going over to Jane's to recover those episodes right now."

"I'm coming with you. After what happened earlier, I think it's best if you're not alone there."

They drove over to Jane's house after Alex took Watson home again. Jane's Christmas lights were still on, winking cheerfully at passersby, belying the fact that the house's owner had been murdered less than a week ago. Alex would have to remember to turn off the lights when she left.

Inside, Tom turned on the television and went through the same process he had at his house a few minutes ago. Going to the recently deleted list, he found a long list of true-crime shows.

"You'd better resave them all, since we don't have any idea which one it is."

He finished. "These are going to take you quite a while to watch."

In the end, they resaved nineteen shows. Two she had already watched at Tom's, but she didn't want to take any chances, so she had him resave them anyway.

"Maybe tomorrow after church I'll be able to watch some."

A few minutes later, as they were pulling back into the driveway at Tom's house, Alex saw a figure in a dark hooded coat running from her porch and around the corner of her house.

"Stop the car!" Alex got out and ran after the person, but by the time she struggled through the snow piled beside the driveway and got to the other side of her house, she couldn't see anyone. She stood there silently, listening for any sound and looking for boot prints in the snow, but there were too many places someone could be hiding. If only she'd had Watson with her. She headed back to the porch.

Tom was already there, pointing at a small basket in front of her door. "It looks like you've been elfed! They've left you some goodies."

She felt silly. She'd thought it had been the murderer breaking into her house, but instead it was some kind soul who'd left her some Christmas treats. This whole business was making her far too suspicious.

"Now I feel foolish. Do you want to come inside and see what they left?"

"I'd better not. I'm sure I saw Penelope at her window. She'll be over momentarily if I hang around here any longer." Tom left with a rueful smile.

Alex took the basket into the house. There was a festive tea towel in the bottom of the basket, wrapped around the contents. There were half a dozen scones, a container of whipped butter, and a small jar of raspberry-blueberry jam. A tag was tucked inside that said *Merry Christmas*. She was tempted to have a scone with butter and jam, but it was too late, not to mention it was high time she started saying no to all the sugar she'd been consuming. Better to wait until breakfast.

Getting ready for bed, she wondered if the sheriff's office had gotten the alibis of people they'd questioned in Jane's neighborhood after her murder. Hanna was going to ask Duncan some of those questions. She looked at her watch. Where was Hanna?

A little concerned, Alex dialed Hanna's cell. "Where are you? Are you okay?"

"I'm fine. I'm just pulling onto our street. I'll see you in a minute."

Alex put on her slippers and headed for the kitchen to get the water boiling for some herbal tea. Watson scrambled to greet Hanna as she came in.

The two came into the kitchen a moment later. Hanna was carrying a cardboard container. "Leftovers." She put the container in the fridge. "Sorry for not calling. After dinner Duncan let me do a ride-along, and I found out a few things. How was your night?"

She told Hanna about her fruitless search of Jane's office. "Next time I go over, I'll make sure I'm not interrupted."

"You're lucky it was just Gary at the back door."

Alex picked up her narrative again, filling Hanna in on Tom's recovery of the missing true-crime episodes and her surprise Christmas visitor. "I felt like an idiot when I realized it was just someone from the village leaving a treat. Do you want some scones and jam?" Alex held up the basket that had been left.

"No, thanks. I'm still stuffed from dinner. I can't believe how much Duncan eats."

They went into the living room and sat on the sofa, the dog between them.

"Tell me what you found out from Duncan." Alex tried to take a sip of her tea, but it was still too hot.

"Oliver has an alibi. He was at an AA meeting with his mentor, and he definitely didn't get home until after ten. Duncan said anything he told me was not for sharing, you excepted. Zach says he went to his girlfriend's after he left the Sleuth meeting, and she didn't react favorably to his revelation and asked him to leave at about nine. From there he went to Jane's to confront her. We know Clive and Trixie saw that, but it still gave him plenty of time to go back and kill Jane in the window the ME gave."

Alex frowned but refrained from saying anything.

Hanna glanced at Alex. "I walked Watson for half an hour, and they said that was technically enough time for you to get to Jane's and back, though it would be tight if you were on foot.

Most of the other neighbors were with their spouses or have an alibi, and the sheriff hasn't found anyone else with a motive."

Alex shook her head. "I'd have to be an Olympic runner to have made it to Jane's and back in half an hour, let alone had time to kill her and ransack downstairs. We have to remember what happened to Jane was premeditated. I can't stop wondering if we were meant to fall under suspicion because of those chocolates. Zach didn't know ahead of time how his girlfriend would react to his news. If he had planned to steal from Jane, that would explain the doctored chocolates. They would ensure Jane didn't wake up. But then why kill her? The thing that makes the most sense is that someone who wanted Jane dead gave her the chocolates to ensure she'd be asleep when they snuck into the house and killed her. No struggle, easy peasy. We know two people who knew about her spare key, Zack and Gary. And maybe Oliver."

"But Oliver and Gary have alibis."

"I know. That's why it doesn't make sense."

Later in bed, Alex wondered if she would know who the killer was once she watched the true-crime episode. And how she'd know which episode it was. Jane had said the picture wasn't much help. It was the details of the episode and how it related to the character of the individual that had made the connection for her. Would Alex know this person well enough to make that same connection?

Chapter
Twenty-One

A t church the next morning, Alex sat beside Hanna, in the
same pew as Maggie and Drew, at the back of the chapel.
Alex and Hanna had slept in and had barely had enough time
to shower and dress. There'd been no time for breakfast, and
Alex's stomach was growling. She had been watching for Netta
but didn't see her anywhere. The service was lovely. The children
sang a few Christmas carols, and Tom gave a sermon on the
miracle of peace that could be had even in the midst of great personal loss, tragedy, and continuing trials. Even though Tom had
lost his wife of many years only six months ago, Alex had never
seen him feeling sorry for himself or even angry at his circumstances. Instead, he spent much of his time helping and serving
others. Alex would do her best to remember the message from
today's Christmas program.

After the service, Alex ran into Everett as she searched the
halls for Netta.

"Do you have a second?" she asked him. "I have a kind of
strange question to ask you."

"Sure, shoot," Everett said good-naturedly.

"Someone mentioned Joe built your house."

"That's right."

"They also said you had a few minor issues and he fixed them for you. I heard someone else had a similar issue but, because of a clause in the contract, Joe didn't have to fix the problems with their house. Does that make any sense to you?"

Everett frowned. "Joe's a pretty sharp businessman. I read that contract over very carefully from beginning to end before I signed it, and I found that clause. I told him there was no way I'd sign it as is. He took it out and fixed the few minor things that came up after construction without a problem."

"Interesting. Is it legal for him to do that?"

"Absolutely. The wording was carefully written. It's unethical but not illegal. Before anyone signs a contract, they should read it over thoroughly."

Alex thanked Everett for answering her questions and continued her search for Netta.

She found Hanna talking to Maggie in the foyer. "Have you seen Netta anywhere?"

Hanna shook her head. "No, but I just saw Trixie head into the kitchen. She might know."

"You go ahead to Sunday school. I'm going to ask Trixie if she's seen Netta, and if not, I'm going to head over to her house. She wanted to talk to me about something."

Alex found Trixie in the kitchen gathering up dishes from last weekend's church social that needed to be returned to people.

"Have you seen Netta this morning? I didn't see her here, and I tried calling her last night but didn't get an answer."

Trixie turned around with several bowls in her arms. "She was shopping with me in Swanson yesterday. We got back around quarter to five. She was complaining about a headache. Maybe she didn't feel well this morning. If you're planning to go see her, can you take this pan and return it to her?" Trixie handed Alex a baking sheet. "I was at the gym on Friday with Louise. She mentioned your visit earlier this week and seemed touched by your thoughtfulness in bringing her chocolates."

"I didn't know Louise went to the gym. In fact, I don't really know much about her. She seemed in rough shape when I saw her."

"She goes to the gym to strengthen her heart. In the summer she even goes hiking with Clive and me, when she's not working. She has bad days here and there, but she's in good shape, all things considered."

Alex had been feeling rather guilty for judging Louise so harshly ever since she'd discovered the woman had a heart condition. It had never occurred to her she might have a legitimate reason for being absent from work so often. She'd have to remember to give people the benefit of the doubt in the future.

"Yvonne mentioned she was going to ask Netta to help with the flowers for Jane's funeral. Have you found out when the funeral will be?" Trixie picked up another pan.

"I don't think there's a definite date, since the medical examiner hasn't released the body yet. I'm certain they won't have the funeral until after Christmas."

"Well, that's good. I'm not sure how we would have managed a funeral this week."

Alex stood in the kitchen awkwardly. She finally blurted out, "Someone mentioned Clive had an argument with Jane a few days before she died."

Trixie looked up at Alex and laughed. "Clive told her to stop watching those true-crime shows and accusing innocent people of being serial killers. Jane told him to mind his own business. He thought that was rich, coming from her. But that was about the extent of it. Like I said before, small towns."

It was already halfway through the Sunday school class when Alex headed to Netta's. She wished she had brought chocolates; she'd have to come back again later with some.

At Netta's door, there was no answer to her knocking. Alex didn't want to take the pan home and decided she would put it inside the door, if it was unlocked. She'd try calling Netta later from home.

The door readily opened. In Harriston, few people locked their doors during the day. Probably most of the homes of those at church right now would be unlocked if she checked. Then again, since Jane's murder, maybe that had changed. Alex called out quietly but didn't get a response. She would just put the baking sheet on the closest table and leave.

A few steps from the front door, Alex knew she wouldn't need to return with any chocolates. She had discovered why Netta hadn't come to church. The elderly woman was lying at the bottom of the stairs, in an awkward position. Alex knew it was futile, but she checked for a pulse anyway. Netta was dead.

At least there wasn't any blood. Looking around, Alex couldn't see anything out of place. It looked as if Netta had fallen down the stairs and perhaps hit her head, but was such a coincidence possible?

Alex knew she should call Duncan right away, but instead, she went into the kitchen.

There was an empty mug on the counter, and beside it was a plate with a chocolate on it. The chocolate looked distinctly like one of Murder and Mayhem's Strychnine Strawberrys, and her stomach clenched.

Knowing she couldn't delay any longer, she pulled out her phone and called Duncan.

Sitting in her car waiting for Duncan to arrive was like déjà vu. Could this be happening again? Poor Netta. Maybe this really was an unfortunate accident rather than something more sinister.

When Duncan arrived, he asked her what had happened. She explained about Netta trying to get ahold of her during the week. "Since she wasn't at church, I decided to stop here on my way home. Trixie asked me to drop off a baking pan. When Netta didn't answer the door, I stepped in to put it on a table by the door. That's when I found her."

Duncan told her to wait in her car and went inside. When he came out, he told her to go home; he'd come get her statement later. "I'm not saying anything for sure, but at first glance, this looks like an accidental death."

When Alex started to argue, Duncan held up his hand, and a shadow of annoyance crossed his face. "I'll do a thorough investigation, just as I would in any unattended death. I'll let you know once we have a cause of death. Just remember, sometimes an accident really is an accident."

Alex sent a text to Hanna before making tea. Hanna was home in record time and joined her sister on the sofa.

As they sipped their tea, Alex explained how she'd come upon Netta.

"You do seem to have developed a penchant for finding bodies," Hanna said wonderingly.

"Do you think this could just be an accident? Doesn't that stretch the imagination a little too far?" Alex knew there was a hint of sarcasm in her voice.

"Isn't there a saying about the simplest answer being the one that's usually right?"

"Occam's razor. I'm just finding it hard to believe Jane's friend dies less than a week after Jane and it's not related. She's been trying to talk to me about something she remembered or discovered, and suddenly she's dead. An accident? I don't think so."

"Until we find out how Netta died, I think we should assume it was from the fall."

"You're certainly welcome to think that, but I disagree. She must have died yesterday. Trixie dropped her off at home before five and I stopped at her house at about six, and everything was dark; it didn't look like anyone was home."

The doorbell rang, and Alex answered it. "No Sheriff Summers?"

"I'm deputy coroner, so I usually handle accidental deaths and report back to her, and this looks like it's an accident. The medical investigator came at my insistence, but it looks like the trauma from the fall caused her death sometime yesterday evening." Duncan sat down and prepared to write down Alex's statement. "Tell me exactly what happened."

Alex recited everything one more time. She looked at Duncan expectantly. "Now what?"

"I've asked for an autopsy and full toxicology screening to make sure there's nothing suspicious, but for now, it looks like an unfortunate accident. She was seventy-nine, and those stairs at her place are pretty steep. A surprising number of seniors die from falls each year. Nothing appears to be missing. We found her purse in her bedroom with several hundred dollars in it as well as her credit cards."

"Doesn't it seem strange to you that Netta dies six days after Jane is murdered?"

"Honestly, no. It seems like an unfortunate coincidence." Duncan got up to go. "Before I head out, one more thing." Duncan stared at Alex and Hanna shrewdly. "It's come to my attention you two are actually questioning people in Jane's murder. Is that true?"

Hanna and Alex looked at each other uncomfortably.

Alex needed to speak up. "Well, since I'm a suspect, we decided it would be prudent to ask a few questions. That's all—it's really just listening to gossip."

"And that's all it better be. You know, you can get into serious trouble for interfering in an investigation."

Alex avoided Hanna's gaze. "Of course." She raised her shoulder in a shrug and shot Duncan her best attempt at an innocent look. "We're just doing what everybody else in the village is doing."

"Will you still let us know when the ME has a time and cause of death?" Hanna lowered her chin and looked at Duncan with pleading eyes.

Duncan sighed. "I suppose. But right now, I have to go make sure everything gets locked up, and then I have to call her family. I really hate that part."

After Duncan left, Alex quoted her favorite author. "'Any coincidence is always worth noticing. You can throw it away later if it is only a coincidence.' Miss Marple said that in Agatha Christie's *Nemesis*. Well, it appears we have another suspect cleared."

"Who?" Hanna sipped her tea.

"If the two deaths are related, Zach. He couldn't have killed Netta because he's still in jail. We need to check who has an alibi for Netta's death, once we know when she died."

Hanna's eyes brightened. "I talked to Eudora at church. On Friday morning, Netta asked Eudora if she remembered who was in the post office when Netta told her about Jane's latest true-crime killer. When Eudora told her she couldn't remember,

Netta stood there for a moment with her head down, then looked at Eudora with a surprised expression and said, 'Oh, dear.' And left. Eudora thinks Netta remembered who it was, but she never said another word to her. Isn't that strange?"

"I wonder what it was that she remembered, aside from the identity of that person. It's very unlike Netta not to have said anything more. I'm going to have to ask Eudora again if she can remember who was in the post office."

Chapter
Twenty-Two

The next morning, after showering and dressing in a pair of blue jeans, a chunky crew-neck sweater, and a red scarf that Hanna would probably fix later, Alex put on her coat and stopped at Cookies 'n Crumbs on her way to work. She needed a cream-cheese-filled cranberry muffin and a cinnamon-plum tea.

While she waited for Sam to fill her order, Alex sidled over to Louise, who was clearing a table. Louise was as surly as ever, so Alex decided not to mince words. "Did you hear about Netta's death?"

Louise didn't respond immediately but put down the cloth she had been wiping the table with and looked at Alex for a moment. "Can't ya tell I'm working? I'm not here to yak at people, but seeing as how you've already disturbed my work, yeah, I did hear about it. You gotta hand it to the town gossips. They make sure everyone knows what's going on."

"Were you and Netta friends?"

"Not hardly. I knew her, though. That woman was a worse gossip than Jane. Jane was just plain nosy, sticking her nose in other people's business, but she didn't go around repeating it. Netta couldn't keep a secret if her life depended on it. The woman couldn't get to a phone fast enough if she had some bit of news. Can't stand people like that. Mind your own business, that's my motto. Now, if ya don't mind . . ."

"Please, just one more thing. What were you doing Saturday afternoon and evening?"

"Not that it's any of your business, but I was here on Saturday until closing and at home the rest of the weekend. Minding my own business." Louise glared at Alex.

As Alex paid for her purchase, Sam leaned in. "Louise is a good worker, when she's here, but she's not much for conversation. She was actually nicer to you than most. She must like you."

Alex wondered how Louise spoke to people she didn't like.

At Murder and Mayhem, Alex turned on the lights and jacked up the heat; it was chilly in the store. In the kitchen, she lit a sugar-cookie-scented candle and looked at the calendar. Monday, December twenty-first. She had only three more days to solve the murders if she was going to meet her self-imposed deadline. She started adding to the murder board. First, another victim. Then Alex added her suspects and their alibis as far as she knew them. As she filled in everything she could think of, Hanna arrived, looking festive in a white sweater with red snowflakes over black faux-leather leggings.

"I was just reviewing our suspects' motives and alibis. We seem to have alibis for everyone but Zach and Louise for Jane's death. I talked to Louise this morning, and she liked Netta even less than Jane because of her gossiping." Alex rubbed her face.

Hanna grabbed Alex's hand. "We don't rub our faces. It creates wrinkles. You don't want to be known as the wrinkly twin."

Alex scrunched up her nose. "Since you think I'm dating material for the seniors, I'll fit right in."

Hanna continued, "It looks like Louise doesn't have an alibi for either murder and didn't like either of our victims. Do you think she could be the killer? Duncan said he'd press for a quick autopsy on Netta today. Even though he won't acknowledge it, I think he's keeping our theory as a possibility, however remote it might be."

Alex sighed. "That's one bright spot this morning. As is the fact that Zach couldn't have murdered Netta. After what Trixie told me about Louise's exercising, I definitely think she could have done it. Gary has an alibi for Jane's murder, so does it even matter if he has an alibi for this one? Oliver has an alibi for Jane, so once again, I'm not sure it matters for Netta. The same goes for Joe, who we know nothing about from before he moved here, by the way."

"We'd better get ready for opening. That poinsettia of Jane's is looking pretty sad. Do you still want to keep it?" Hanna picked up a few more leaves that had landed on the desk.

"I do. I know it looks awful, but it reminds me of Jane and that her killer may still be out there. I'm feeling like we aren't getting anywhere with this investigation."

Hanna gave her a sympathetic look.

"I need to get some magnesium supplements I ran out of last night," Alex said. "I'm going over to the Black Currant and won't be long."

The health food store stocked various vitamins, teas, gluten-free products, and environmentally friendly cleaning products as well as fair-trade chocolate and other things. Alex was perusing the supplements in the far corner of the store when she heard a customer come in. As the customer exchanged pleasantries with the clerk, Alex recognized the voice. *Mist!* Alex often reasoned that a mild curse in German wasn't as bad as the English version—in this case, *crap*. She decided to stay where she was in hopes she wouldn't have to talk to Yvonne. Alex found Yvonne's conversation, not to mention her patronizing tone, trying and hoped to avoid running into her. The clerk was helping her find a few items and asked if she'd always lived in Harriston.

Alex tried to tune out the conversation.

"Florida. We were married over thirty years, but we were in our own little world. We had so few friends, and with no family, it wasn't the same after my Ernest died. It was funny—I happened to see an ad in a magazine that featured the historic railway station in Harriston."

Blah, blah, blah; would it never end? *I just listened to all this the other day.* After the clerk shared her story of moving to Harriston the previous year and mentioned grandparents who had moved to Florida, the two finally wound up their conversation, and Yvonne left.

Alex took her supplements to the counter and paid for them, then hurried back to Murder and Mayhem. Trixie and Alex arrived at the walkway to the store at the same time.

"It looks like you're ready to go hiking," Alex said.

Trixie was dressed in layers and wore hiking boots. "Clive and I are going to Glacier this morning for a little hike, since the weather has warmed up a bit. We hoped to take Louise with us on the weekend after Christmas, but the weather isn't looking very promising, so the two of us are going alone today."

Alex wondered what Trixie considered a "little" hike. A two-mile climb up a scree-covered trail? "You seem to know Louise fairly well."

"As well as anyone, I suppose. She likes the outdoors, and since we're always looking for additional hikers, we've had the pleasure of taking her with us occasionally."

"She doesn't seem all that friendly to me."

"Louise isn't very trusting. It takes a while to get to know her, though she doesn't talk about her past very much. I think she had a bad marriage and it left her a little bitter. Once she trusts you, she opens up and is quite funny. We enjoy her company."

In the store, Alex asked, "Are you looking for anything in particular?"

"I want a Christmas-themed mystery. I read aloud while Clive drives. We don't find we have as much to talk about after almost forty years of marriage. This way we're both trying to pick out the clues as I read and be the first to figure out who the killer is. It makes the drive go by quickly." Trixie paused in front of a display of chocolates. "Thank you again for the chocolate-making lesson last week. I managed to make a batch of chocolates that turned out quite well."

After Trixie left, there were hardly any customers. Hanna was busy in the kitchen making chocolates; they were dangerously low on several varieties. Maggie was filling online orders, so Alex helped the only remaining shoppers, two women who looked to be in their forties and had come to buy several boxes of Killer Chocolates. The two worked for a company in Kalispell and planned to give them to their bosses and coworkers, whom they couldn't stand. As Alex wrapped the boxes, they confessed to imagining they were giving away real poisoned chocolates. Alex joked that the ladies had her wrapping the chocolates so only her fingerprints would be on each box. The ladies promised to visit Alex in prison.

After her customers left, Alex stood at the counter and stared into space. "Maggie, I'm heading over to the post office." She grabbed the keys to their post office box. "I'll be back in a few minutes."

All morning, ideas had ricocheted through Alex's mind. She would fasten on a thought only to discard it moments later. She needed more information.

* * *

"I'm so sorry you were the one to find Netta. It must have been awful for you." Eudora came around the post office counter and gave Alex a hug.

"I've had better weeks, for sure. Hanna said Netta was here on Friday to see if you could recall who was here the day she told you Jane's latest suspicion."

"She was. I'm sorry to say, I still can't recall who was here with us that morning. I must be getting old." Eudora gazed at the door. "It seems the harder I try, the vaguer the memory becomes."

"Did Netta give you any idea what she remembered?"

"I got the impression Netta was perplexed about something when she came in. As she stood here, I think she remembered who was here that day. If it's possible, she seemed even more disconcerted and wandered out without even saying good-bye."

Alex was angry at herself for not making more of an effort to follow up with Netta. And now it was too late. "Let me know if you remember anything else. She told Maggie she remembered hearing something from someone that didn't make sense. I think that's connected with who was in here that day."

At lunch, Hanna got a call from Duncan. The ME had provided his preliminary findings from Netta's autopsy.

Chapter
Twenty-Three

I n the conference room, Hanna put Duncan on speaker so they could both hear him.

"The injuries were consistent with a fall down the stairs, and she would have died very quickly, if not instantly. Toxicology results will take a few days. Since it looks like death was accidental, they aren't putting a priority on them, and they're a little backed up right now. The ME estimated Netta died between five and seven on Saturday. I'll let you know when I hear anything more."

Alex looked uncertainly at Hanna. Regardless of what Duncan said, she didn't believe Netta's death had been an accident. It looked like Louise alone had no alibi for either death.

"Hanna, Oliver has an alibi for Jane's death, but he was hiding something when I talked to him. I'm going to go over there after lunch to see if I can get him to tell me what it is."

"Are you going to lean on him, Alex?" Hanna spoke like a wisecracking gangster and laughed. "Say hi to him for me."

Alex wasn't sure how she was going to get Oliver to tell her whatever it was he was hiding. She was counting on an idea to come to her in the moment.

After lunch, it looked like her first challenge would be getting into the house to talk to Oliver. When he saw who was at the door, he seemed reluctant to invite her in.

"There's something important I need to ask you. It won't take long," Alex promised.

Oliver glanced beyond her shoulder. "You didn't bring your sister?"

"She was busy at the store, but she said to say hi." Oliver's expression showed his disappointment before he turned away to lead Alex down the hall.

Seated in the same chair she'd occupied on her last visit, Alex probed the room with one sweeping glance. Things weren't quite as neat as last time. A collection of dirty dishes sat on the counter, clothes had been draped over furniture, and Alex was fairly certain she saw the edge of a vodka bottle sticking out from behind a stack of books on the bookshelf. Oliver was also looking a little rougher today; his jaw was covered in stubble, and his eyes were red.

"I can't believe a week ago I was talking to Jane at our book club meeting for the last time. I'm really going to miss her." Alex gazed out the expansive windows and doors at Jane's house.

"I miss her too. She usually came over at least once a week to see how I was doing. I was teaching her how to meditate." Oliver slumped in his chair.

Alex cleared her throat. "I'm going to be honest with you. I've been looking into Jane's death because I'm not convinced the sheriff has the right person in jail, and I don't think you killed her either. I do think you know something. What aren't you saying? If you were Jane's friend, don't you think you owe it to her to be honest?"

Oliver stiffened. He gazed at Jane's house and then looked at the picture of his family on the bookshelf. He sat up straighter and tapped his fingers on the armrest. Finally, he stopped tapping and leaned forward. "I'm going to tell you something, and I hope you'll be discreet about who you share it with."

Alex nodded her agreement.

"My father owned a company that made pharmaceuticals. When I was sixteen, my parents were killed in a car crash. They were driving on a winding road through the mountains and went over the edge of a cliff. They'd gone that way dozens of times before. It was daylight, and my father was a good driver. It didn't make sense. But nobody questioned it, and my godfather inherited me, along with control of the company. He was my dad's business partner and had been his best friend since they were kids."

Alex was sympathetic. Jane was the first person she was close to who had died.

"Six months after my parent's death, my godfather got a note in the mail that insinuated that if he didn't vote a certain way at the next board meeting, he should be careful when he went out driving. He didn't want to show me the note, but I was there when he opened it and saw the expression on his face. I told him to give it to the police, since it was proof my parents' crash wasn't an accident. He told me he would handle it. A couple months later, he was dead too. The police called the accident suspicious, but they never found evidence to tie it to anyone. I didn't see the point of saying anything. No one was going to believe an emotional teenager about threatening letters that had disappeared. All these years, I've regretted not saying something to the police when that note came."

"That must have been terribly difficult. You were only a teenager then, so don't be too hard on yourself." Alex couldn't imagine what it would be like to lose both parents and a guardian in less than a year.

"I got sent to live with my aunt in England, and she packed me off to boarding school, and that's when I began to drink." He smiled ruefully. "I saw you look at the bottle of vodka on the bookshelf. Anyway, a few years later at uni, I was still drinking. I'd become an alcoholic. As a trust-fund baby, I've never had to work a day in my life if I didn't want to."

Oliver stared out the window as if he could see the scene replaying in his mind. "One night, I drove home after being at the pub all night. I almost hit another car, but instead I crashed into a wall. When I got home, I took some medications that don't mix well with alcohol and almost died. That sobered me up, and I checked into rehab a week later."

Oliver looked at Alex, perhaps expecting to see some kind of judgment. He seemed to be satisfied with what he saw. "After rehab, I carried on with meditation, eating right, and exercise. I got involved in volunteer work and basically changed my life. Soon after I was approached to tell my story. Eventually, I had a book deal, but when I handed in my first draft, they thought it was going to be a lost cause.

"Long story short, they hired a ghostwriter, who took my experiences and turned it into a book. It was a best seller. Unfortunately, not everything in the book was one hundred percent accurate. It made me sound a lot better than I was, and suddenly I had people writing to me, asking for advice, and I was hardly the person to give it." Oliver stopped and was quiet for a moment.

Alex spoke tentatively. "I think that happens a lot. People only see the after, when you've got your act together, and they want to know what the secret sauce is, the magic that made it all happen. Social media pages are covered with pictures of perfection.

The golden tan, the gleaming smile, the happy family, and they think that's real. People forget life is far from perfect, no matter who you are."

Oliver nodded. "Exactly. I felt like such a fraud. I started to have anxiety attacks and started thinking about going back to the bottle. I talked to my shrink about it, and we decided I should get away from the whole London scene. I literally looked for a place as far from my life there as possible, where I could almost start over.

"I was on the hook for two more books, so, with the help of another ghostwriter, we got a second one published. Number three is due next year, and I was determined to write it on my own. Instead, I've been buying vodka and staring out my windows. Somehow Jane figured most of that out and helped me commit to going to AA. She even found a group for me. Last Monday was my first meeting." There was self-loathing in his voice. "When I got home last week around ten, I saw lights on at Jane's. I sat down at my desk and tried to write but couldn't seem to get my ideas together. I had a partial bottle of vodka hidden away, and I started to think maybe if I had one little drink, it would help relax me. I managed to convince myself that I could have just one drink. In the end, I sat here having one drink and then another and another, watching Jane's house, thinking how disappointed she would be in me.

"I saw her moving around in her kitchen, and then, about eleven, she started turning off her lights."

Alex was shocked. "You're certain Jane was still alive at eleven?"

"One hundred percent. But this is where it gets a bit unclear, because I was getting drunk. I think it was about quarter to twelve when I saw someone on Jane's deck. They must have had a flashlight, because it looked like a little speck of light dancing around. They paused—I assumed they were unlocking the door—and went inside. No lights actually went on in the house, though, so I was wondering what was happening."

Alex leaned forward. She couldn't believe what she was hearing.

Oliver continued. "I went to my telescope and zoomed in on Jane's back door. I kept watching on and off, and about thirty minutes later, someone came out, and this is the crazy part—they moved the planter Jane kept her key under and propped open the screen door.

"I'd finished drinking at this point, and I was just sitting in my chair watching, though I may have dozed off, I'm not sure, but at about four AM, I was awake but still not completely sober. I saw someone on Jane's deck again. I went back to the telescope, and I watched them put the planter back in place and go inside. It couldn't have been more than two minutes and they came back, closed the door, and left.

"I was thinking I was crazy or so drunk I was hallucinating. Until the next day when the sheriff's deputies knocked on my door and wanted to know if I saw or heard anything the night before at Jane's house. What was I going to say? I wasn't even one hundred percent sure I didn't dream it all. I couldn't admit I'd been drinking, though I was pretty sure they suspected I was hungover. I must have smelled like a distillery. Would they even have taken me seriously?"

Alex was elated. Finally, the information she needed to make all the pieces fit together. "What does it matter if they believe you or not? Isn't it better to give them the information and let them decide?"

"I have a clause in my contract that says I can't drink or take drugs and a bunch of other things. Do you see my problem? If

I tell the deputies what I saw, are they even going to believe me? And then I may be ruining my career to boot. I don't need the money, but I need a purpose. We all need a purpose, responsibility, and accountability. Now you know. What are you going to do?"

Alex didn't know what to say. Her brain was going crazy trying to assimilate the new information. "Can you tell me anything about the person you saw? Height, coloring, anything?"

Oliver shook his head. "It was too dark and too far away to make out any details. They wore a dark jacket with a hood. I got the impression it wasn't a tall guy, smaller build, shorter, but I couldn't even swear to that. I was pretty hammered."

"I'm curious. How did you know Jane had a key under that planter?"

Oliver flushed. "I often sit here when I'm working, or trying to work, and I've seen Jane's handyman get the key from under that pot. It's not like he tries to hide what he's doing. Anybody with a view of Jane's deck could see him."

Alex nodded. It made sense. Any number of people might have known about that key. "You're right. Sometimes I forget how small this town is. I really appreciate your honesty. I'll do what I can to keep things confidential, but you know the sheriff's department has to be told what you saw."

Oliver gave silent assent.

"Unfortunately, I don't think there's any way to keep your name out of it. Now that you've made a clean breast of it to me, maybe this can be your new beginning. I'm sure Jane was trying to help when she set you up with AA, but I realize you have to make that decision. I'm hardly in a position to give you advice, but just because you stumbled doesn't mean you can't pick yourself up again."

They talked for a few more minutes before Alex said good-bye and headed back to the shop.

Alex was reeling with the information Oliver had given her. She knew much of what Oliver had told her was private. She had been entrusted with a secret from Oliver's past as well as more recent events. As much as she would like to keep everything to herself, she couldn't. Duncan would have to be told about what Oliver had seen. Even though he hadn't recognized the individual at Jane's house, this changed everything.

When she got back to the store, there were a few people who needed her help, so it was almost closing before she had a chance to talk to Hanna.

She shared what Oliver had seen the other night. "Oliver may not be able to identify the intruder, but it means Jane was still alive after ten PM."

Chapter
Twenty-Four

"**D**o you know what this means?" Alex paced back and forth in front of the counter. "Jane's killer could be anyone. She was seen alive as late as eleven. If Oliver saw the killer going into the house at eleven forty-five, then they're all suspects." Alex paused and looked thoughtfully at the desk behind the counter.

"What are you staring at?" Hanna looked at her sister curiously.

"I think I just figured out what happened to Jane's poinsettia." Alex pointed at the pitiful plant on the desk. "Poinsettias are extremely sensitive to cold. If that door was left open for four hours on a night that was so cold—remember Monday night last week was about minus thirty?—that would easily account for the condition it's in. Why would someone do that?"

They looked at each other and said at the same moment, "Time of death!"

Alex grabbed Hanna's arm. "By cooling the house down dramatically, the killer was trying to mess with the body temperature. The ME would have assumed the body was cooling at whatever the ambient temperature was when the police arrived. By cooling the house down, the body would have cooled more quickly. I bet that's why they came back to close the doors and, no doubt, turn up the thermostat to normal, making it look like the time of death was earlier than it actually was, thereby giving the murderer an alibi."

Hanna said, "Louise and Zach never had an alibi. Both of them said they were home alone."

"True, but Zach did have an argument with Jane, and Louise disliked her, and we don't know anything about her past. I don't think we can completely rule them out."

"What if Oliver told you that story just to put you off the track, in case you suspected him? His alibi is gone too, because he was home around ten."

"Oliver had a solid alibi without telling me what he saw. The sheriff's department bought it, and they were focused on Zach. It doesn't make sense for Oliver to lie. He could have kept his mouth shut."

"That makes sense. How do we narrow down the rest of the suspects?"

Alex sighed and looked at the ceiling. "We need to find out who had an alibi for Netta's death. If we believe the two are connected, then maybe we can cancel someone out. Based on that reasoning, Zach is out as a suspect, because he couldn't have been involved in her death. Louise already told me she was home alone on Saturday evening, so she doesn't have an alibi. I guess we have suspects to question again. We also need to decide whether to tell Duncan what Oliver saw."

"Alex! We don't really have a choice. Duncan needs to know."

Alex's cell phone began to play "It's The Most Wonderful Time of the Year." "Everett's calling, hang on." She answered the call and listened, then thanked him and disconnected. "The trauma-scene cleanup company was at Jane's today, so it's all cleaned up. Do you want to come with me tonight to watch some of those true-crime shows Jane taped?"

"Of course."

"The answer to this could be on one of them. Let's think about what to tell Duncan overnight. I'm not sure if it will make much difference to the sheriff's department. They may think the information is too unreliable because he was drunk, or they may take it as confirmation Zach was at the house multiple times stealing things."

"You're on. But we call Duncan first thing in the morning."

*　*　*

When the sisters entered their house, the aroma of a roast, potatoes, carrots, and peas that had been simmering all day greeted them. Alex wasn't a fan of cooking after work. On the other hand, she wasn't terribly fond of cooking before work either, but necessity occasionally demanded it. The Crock-Pot had been an able assistant in ensuring a ready-to-eat meal for dinner.

"Do you ever miss home?" Hanna looked at Alex curiously.

"Sometimes, especially Mom's cooking. I wish we didn't live quite so far. It would be nice to visit more often, but if I lived too close, Mom would drive me completely nuts. How about you?"

Hanna was nodding. "I miss everyone, but I needed a new start. After the divorce, moving here was the right thing to do. Not that I want you to keep finding bodies, but this past week has been really exciting. I'm glad we're here together."

"You're not tempted to go back and work with Mom again?" Alex hadn't been able to get it out of her head that Hanna might be regretting her impulsive move.

"Absolutely not. I love Mom, but working with her all those years was murder. Not literally, but you know. She was so controlling. Anytime I had a new idea, she told me when I had my own store, I could do it my way, but in her store, it was her way. I could never go back."

Alex wasn't sure if Hanna meant what she said or if she just didn't want her sister to worry. Which was exactly what Alex would continue to do.

After they had eaten and tidied up, Alex said, "I'll drive. I'm just going to grab something for us to snack on while we're at Jane's. We might as well be comfortable while we do this." She grabbed some cookies and a couple of water bottles.

"I'm bringing Watson. She's been alone all day."

The dog trotted to the door as soon as Hanna grabbed the leash and sat down obediently to wait for it to be attached.

Once parked in Jane's driveway, Alex turned to Hanna. "Why don't you go unlock the door and take Watson in? I'll be there in a minute. Oh, and maybe wave to Stella. I saw her peering out her window as I pulled into the driveway."

Alex walked around to the other side of the car and got her notebook and pen out of her bag on the back seat. As she backed out of the car and straightened up, she nudged into something solid behind her and let out a cry.

"I'm sorry, dear. I didn't mean to startle you." Yvonne was bundled up, wearing a hat and scarf as well as warm winter boots. "I was out for a walk, and I saw the lights on in Jane's house and wondered what was going on."

Alex didn't want anyone else to know about her inheritance from Jane. What could she say?

"Everett asked me to check on some things. He's Jane's lawyer and is looking after the estate. Do you often go out walking in the evenings? Aren't you worried about slipping with that injured foot?" It was amazing how easily lies slipped off her tongue yet again.

"I walk almost every day. I wear these unattractive"—Yvonne pointed to her feet with her cane—"but very practical boots. I'm a little slow at the moment with this injury, but I can manage a short walk to the end of the block and back."

Alex glanced over Yvonne's shoulder to Gary's house and saw him looking out his front window at them. When he saw Alex return his stare, he quickly stepped behind his drapes.

"That's wonderful, but I'd better get in the house. Hanna is helping me check on things. Have a good night." Alex smiled and hurried to the house, leaving Yvonne standing in the driveway, watching her go.

"What took you so long?" Hanna asked when Alex ran into the house.

"Yvonne practically scared the pants off me. She was standing right behind me when I got the stuff from the back seat. She wanted to know what we're doing, so I told her we're checking on some things for Everett."

"You lied?" Hanna pretended to look stern.

Alex scrunched up her face. "No, I didn't. We can look at a few things and list what's going to be auctioned. Gary was watching us out of his window. He seems very interested in the comings and goings of this house. Why is it so cold in here?" Alex rubbed her arms.

"The cleaning company must have turned down the heat when they left. I've turned it up, so it'll be warm in here soon. In the meantime, we can watch those shows."

Sitting with Hanna on the sofa, Alex noticed the umbrella stand from the hall had been moved into the living room by the television; she'd have to move that back to the hall later.

"Let's start with the oldest ones first and work our way forward in time." Alex grabbed the remote and selected the first show.

Before starting the second episode, Alex went in search of a bowl for Watson so they could all have some water.

The cleaning company had really done a marvelous job. The house was spotless; even so, she gave the bowl a good rinse before filling it. As she did, she looked across the backyard to Oliver's house. She could just make him out, sitting in one of his chairs, facing Jane's house. Was he watching her right now?

The second episode wasn't helpful either, other than by making Alex realize how often people committed horrible crimes and tried to get away with it.

"You keep watching the shows. I'm going to look for Jane's journal upstairs. I'll be right back."

She checked behind the books on Jane's bookshelf and looked under and behind Jane's desk, but still nothing. She tried to pull off baseboards and checked under the chair in the office. Finally giving up, she decided she'd bring the letter with her next time and see if the precise wording was more help.

Chapter
Twenty-Five

December twenty-second—where was the time going! Alex was up extra early again to get a head start on the day. Christmas Eve was closing in fast, and she still had no idea who had killed Jane.

After emptying the dishwasher and starting a load of laundry, she quickly did a little cleaning and tidying. She tossed the now rock-hard scones left by the Christmas elf into the garbage. While she waited for the washing machine to finish, she whipped up a batch of scones she could put in the oven at Murder and Mayhem. She grabbed the jam and butter that had been left by the elf and popped them into her bag. That would be perfect to go with the fresh scones.

She stopped at the bakery. She needed something to give Duncan as an apology for keeping Oliver's information to herself overnight. She'd decided it was only fair for her to take any heat for not telling Duncan last night.

"Sam, what's a good treat to use as an apology gift?" Alex almost drooled as she looked at the pastries in the display case.

"If this is really serious, then I suggest the Gingerbread Eggnog Sandwich Cookies or the Marshmallow Hot Chocolate Cookies. If they don't help, nothing will."

"I'd better take a half dozen of each, but could you wrap them in packages of four? And I'll also take a peppermint hot chocolate with whipped topping."

"Ooooooh, this must be serious. Wanna dish on what's bothering you?"

"Maybe later. I don't have much time right now." Alex lowered her voice. "And I'd rather not talk about it publicly."

Sam winked. "Gotcha! Get your errands done early. It's supposed to start snowing tonight or tomorrow, maybe even turn into a blizzard."

Alex had heard the forecast as well, but she was hoping the snow would hold off until Christmas Eve at least. When Hanna arrived at work, Alex suggested they call Duncan right away and hoped he'd forgive them. Later, they could go see Gary with some cookies in hopes it would get him talking. His past was still a complete blank, and since he was a suspect again, Alex wanted to know more about him.

Hanna chewed her lip. "I hope Duncan's not too mad."

"Me too. I don't want him thinking we're interfering in the investigation." Alex got her backpack from behind the counter. "I can't imagine where Jane's jewelry and journal are. I need to look at the letter again and see exactly what she wrote."

Alex pulled it out of her bag and read the relevant section: . . . *go to my special spot to find it, along with my journal.* The only special spot Alex knew of was the chair in Jane's murder room where she liked to read and puzzle out her mysteries.

Hearing the knock at the front door made Alex's stomach drop, and she dragged her feet to answer it. She brought Duncan into the kitchen and indicated a stool for him, then offered him one of her fresh scones with the jam she'd brought from home.

"That looks delicious, but I've only got a minute." He took a plain scone. "Mmm, warm. I was going to call Hanna later. The only prints on that ice pick we found are Zach's. Unfortunately, we couldn't find any traces of blood on it. I figured you two would want to know. So, what's up? You said you had some information on Jane's murder." Duncan looked from Hanna to Alex.

"Don't get angry with Hanna. She would have called you last night, but I'm not even sure if you'll take this information seriously."

Duncan nodded and took another bite of his scone.

"I happened to be chatting with Oliver yesterday, and he mentioned he may have seen something the night of the murder. He said it was late, and he was tired, but he's certain he saw someone—he assumed it was Jane—moving around in the house up until eleven PM, when the lights went off."

Without mentioning the drinking, Alex told Duncan what Oliver had seen. "Hanna and I think Jane was actually still alive until after eleven and the murderer entered the house before midnight and then left the door to the kitchen open until early the next morning to make the time of death appear earlier than it really was, so they would have an alibi."

Duncan covered his face with his hands. "Why didn't Oliver tell us this when we were questioning all the neighbors?"

"I think he was afraid you might not believe him. It was late and dark . . ." Alex avoided looking Duncan in the eye.

"Why do I get the feeling you're not telling me everything?" Duncan looked from Alex to Hanna through narrowed eyes. "If you know anything else, you need to tell me. This is serious."

Alex cringed slightly. "Oliver had been drinking, and he figured you might question the accuracy of what he saw. He's not allowed to have alcohol. There's a clause in his book contract. He didn't want to risk word of his drinking getting out when you might not believe him anyway."

Duncan put both hands on his head and closed his eyes. "Alex, you can't withhold information like that."

"I only found out late yesterday afternoon. It's not like I withheld it. I just didn't have a chance to tell you until now."

Duncan looked at her skeptically. "This will make the ME happy. He was having a heck of a time justifying the time of death. He said there were a number of contradictory issues with body temperature and digestion he couldn't reconcile. If someone left the door open for about four hours on such a cold night, and assuming they may also have lowered the thermostat, then that would definitely throw off the time of death. Didn't I tell you not to interfere in the investigation? That's it for you two." He looked from Alex to Hanna. "As of right now, you will cease and desist any activity involving the questioning of a person who could even remotely be considered a suspect. Is that clear?"

Alex and Hanna nodded, trying to look contrite.

"I'll have to call Sheriff Summers, and I guess we'll be interviewing Oliver again today."

"Does this help clear Zach?" Hanna asked.

"Not necessarily. We don't know the person Oliver saw wasn't Zach. Maybe he was trying to throw us off completely by leaving the door open. He had an alibi until after nine that night. Maybe he thought it would keep the suspicion off of him. Remember, he had a prescription for the same kind of sedative used in those chocolates left on Jane's doorstep."

"What about the possibility of another murderer? There are other people who may have had a motive to kill Jane," Alex pointed out. "I researched eszopiclone, and it's a commonly prescribed drug. I saw it in someone else's house just last week."

"We've been investigating this, and as far as the sheriff's department is concerned, there is no evidence connecting anyone to Jane's death except you and Zach." He looked at Alex. "In fact, Penelope called me yesterday and told me she overheard you claim that if you were going to kill someone, you'd make it look like an accident. When she found out about Netta's death, she thought we should know that." Duncan smiled at Alex. "What have you done to her? She's determined to see you go down for one of these deaths."

"Long story. I hope this doesn't mean I'm now a suspect in Netta's death too?"

"No. Her cause of death hasn't changed. She died of injuries consistent with a fall down those stairs. But, with this new information about Jane, I might push to get the toxicology results sooner rather than later. Not that I think you did it, but where were you between five and seven on Saturday night?"

Alex stiffened. "You said you don't think I did it."

"At this point, Netta's death is assumed accidental. I'm just covering the bases. You're not the only one I'll be asking."

"I suppose I can understand that. I was here with Hanna until about five thirty and went straight to Jane's. Gary Jenkins can vouch for my being there until about six. I drove by Netta's on my way home, but the house was dark, so I didn't even stop. I was with your uncle a little while after that."

Duncan finished writing everything down in his notebook. "I hope you know I don't think you had anything to do with these deaths. But I have to do my job."

"I understand."

"At any rate, Zach had the opportunity, he had the means, and we found Jane's property in his apartment, so he is and remains our prime suspect in Jane's death. We'll talk to Oliver, but I wouldn't count on this exonerating Zach. Just out of curiosity, you mentioned other motives. What were you talking about?"

Alex mentioned Joe's anger at Jane's interest in his family history.

"I think that's a stretch. If being nosy was a criteria for murder in Harriston, half the town would be dead."

Alex let it drop. She had been feeling a little guilty for not sharing most of the information she and Hanna had gathered, but now she felt justified, since Duncan probably wouldn't take it seriously anyway.

Alex handed Duncan the cookies she'd purchased that morning. "I really am sorry I didn't tell you sooner about Oliver." She kept her fingers crossed.

"I meant what I said. No more amateur sleuthing. No more questioning suspects. And I'm assuming these cookies aren't a bribe, just a kind gesture between friends."

After following Duncan to the door and watching him leave, Alex stood there, deflated. "Great. So now if they find out Netta's death wasn't an accident, I'll be under suspicion because of Penelope."

Hanna flipped their sign to OPEN. "I don't remember you saying you'd make someone's death look like an accident."

"I do. It was here in the shop. There were customers browsing, and when one of them left, I thought it looked like Penelope. She must have been in the other room listening to our conversation."

"It doesn't matter anyway. You didn't have an opportunity. I guess it's a good thing Gary tried to sneak into Jane's house that day."

"Why don't we pay him a visit as soon as Maggie gets here? We'll bring him the cookies and question him again."

"Didn't Duncan just tell us not to question anyone?"

"No. He said not to question *suspects*. He also made it clear Zach and I are the only suspects. Since Gary isn't even remotely considered a suspect, we can talk to him."

"Aren't you twisting the intent of what Duncan said?"

Alex shrugged one shoulder and raised her eyebrows in response. After so many years as a scrupulously honest banker, here she was, flouting the law like a juvenile delinquent.

At Harriston Blooms, Gary was alone and invited them to join him as he continued to water the plants. Alex presented their little package of cookies. "We wanted to let you know how happy we are with the poinsettia. It's flourishing. Unfortunately, Jane's is still dropping leaves and looking quite dismal, but we've determined it suffered exposure to several hours of cold. Should we be fertilizing it?"

Gary put down the sprayer and turned his full attention to them. "Thank you for the treats. You really didn't have to do that. Why don't you sit down?" He pointed to a wrought-iron garden set for sale as he placed the cookies on the table. "As for the damaged poinsettia, I wouldn't fertilize it. If it's suffered a cold shock, it's stressed enough already. Encouraging growth will stress it more. Prune any obviously damaged parts, but otherwise, just water it gently. Overwatering can also stress it. It may come back eventually."

"We can do that," Alex said. "Did you hear about Netta? I can't believe you've lost two members of the horticultural society in less than a week."

"Since the average age has to be over seventy, maybe not quite so surprising."

"Were you home Saturday night, or have you been involved in Christmas celebrations?" Alex asked.

"Actually, I was here. I've been doing some planting and preparation for post-Christmas seedlings. Some varieties take a long time to grow, so I start them right around the holiday. Eudora and Yvonne grow some interesting plants in their greenhouses, and they suggested I try some new varieties." He pointed to a workbench that had soil and trays on it. "I was just working with deadly nightshade, which is also known as *Atropa belladonna* or, more commonly, belladonna. It's especially dangerous for children, because the berries can be mistaken for black currants or blueberries, and they have a sweet taste." He opened the box of cookies and tried one. "These are delicious." He gestured for Alex and Hanna to have one.

"No, thanks. We already indulged at the shop this morning." Alex smiled. "If I'm not careful, I'm going to start expanding around the middle."

Gary laughed and patted his stomach. "It's not so bad, and it beats exercising. I know it's good for you, but I can't seem to make myself do it, not like Joe."

Alex and Hanna looked inquiringly at Gary.

"Joe, the contractor. I saw him again on Saturday night running past the greenhouse. I can't believe someone would be out running in the dark on such a cold night. That's dedication, I guess."

"Really? I know he's a runner. What time was it when you saw him?" Alex asked.

Gary rubbed his chin for a second. "It must have been past five thirty. It was already dark. I was looking out and getting ready to close. That's how I happened to see him."

Alex and Hanna looked at each other meaningfully.

"I was telling Hanna about your career change ten years ago. I used to be a banker, but after twenty years in a career I never especially liked and the constant stress, I was thrilled to open the bookshop."

"What was your job before you opened Harriston Blooms? I heard you left a stressful career." Hanna used every bit of her pretty, innocent-eyed charm, and she had plenty. Most men bowed down and gave her what she wanted without a struggle.

Gary stood and looked at his watch. "I'm afraid my job wasn't very exciting. Much of my work was done in an office, but depending on who you work with, that can be stressful too. I should get back to watering those plants. Wouldn't want them to die on me." He laughed hollowly. "Thanks again for the cookies." He didn't wait for them to leave before he grabbed the sprayer and started watering the plants again.

Alex looked at Hanna and shrugged. They got up and left. It seemed any attempt to talk about Gary's past ended in a quick and resounding dismissal.

Chapter
Twenty-Six

Walking back to the car after their dismal failure to get more information from Gary, Alex said, "It's pretty obvious he doesn't want to talk about his past. Why be so secretive? When we get back to the shop, we need to see if we can find out anything about him online. He's one giant question mark before he showed up in Harriston, and he's purposely trying to stay off the radar. Do you want to go back to the shop and check on Maggie and I'll go see Yvonne? She's been telling me to see her again, and I can ask her about Gary's alibi."

"Sure. I'll check the mail too."

"Why don't you drop me off at Yvonne's and take the car back. I'll walk back to the shop from there. I really need to try and get some exercise." Alex got into the passenger seat and handed Hanna the keys. "I think I might have to start going to the gym or eat fewer sweets. I've gained almost five pounds since the end of summer."

"Maybe you can start running with Joe." Hanna playfully punched Alex in the arm. "You can question him at the same time."

Alex glared at her sister.

* * *

Standing on Yvonne's doorstep again, Alex wondered what the elderly lady's garden looked like. There were trees and shrubs strategically placed to hide most of it from the street, and the garage blocked her view from the doorstep. Next time she went to Jane's, she'd have to take a closer look from the deck, where she would have a much better vantage point.

Elegant in a dark-green velour lounge outfit, Yvonne answered the door.

"Hello. I hope you don't mind my dropping by unannounced," Alex said. "Do you have time for a visit?"

"Of course. Please come in. It's so nice to have a visitor. I was just drying some of the herbs from my greenhouse." Yvonne moved carefully along with her cane. "Were you able to finish your work at Jane's last night?"

"Unfortunately not. I'll have to go back another time."

"What is it you're doing for Jane's attorney?"

"Nothing, really. I'm looking to see what can be sold at auction. Most of Jane's belongings will be auctioned off and the money given to certain organizations. I guess you know about Netta?"

"Dead now, the poor thing. Fell down the stairs. Terrible, just terrible."

"Did you see Netta on Saturday? I heard you were hoping she would help with the flowers for Jane's funeral." Alex sat on one of the kitchen chairs at the table where Yvonne had been working.

Yvonne carefully sat down, leaning her cane against the wall. "No. Tanya came here and did my hair at five. I'm not sure when Netta came home, but by the time Tanya left at seven, it was too late to visit. I tried calling, but there was no answer. I'd also hoped to talk to Netta about electing a new president of the horticultural society. Of course, I expected to be Jane's successor.

I suppose now that's certain. I was told you were the one that found her. It's become quite a habit with you."

"Yes. Trixie asked me to return a baking sheet. It's a good thing too, or it may have been even longer before she was found."

"Yes. So fortunate you were on hand. One shudders to think of something like that happening. It's terrible getting old. Especially when you live alone."

Alex decided it was time for a change of subject. "Do you know if Jane had been threatened or had any difficulties with Joe?"

Yvonne was silent for a moment. "Not Joe, but I know Gary was quite upset with her. She was petitioning the village council to change a bylaw, and the change would have required him to make some extensive changes to his greenhouse. It would have been expensive for him, and he was quite angry about it. It was one of the things we discussed after the horticultural meeting last week. He was fit to be tied."

"Was this public knowledge? I didn't know anything about it until now."

"The information about the bylaw change was certainly public. Anyone can attend the village council meetings. I don't suppose many knew how angry he was about it. He needed to be discreet, since Jane was so popular. You know how it is here in the village."

Alex certainly did. Disagreements became public knowledge almost instantly, and there was inevitably a division as people took sides. "Did you see if Gary went straight home after the horticulture meeting that night?"

"We left at the same time, and he followed me home. I saw him pull into his driveway."

Alex would have to talk to Gary and Joe again. Jane had certainly stirred up some acrimonious feelings before she died.

After walking briskly back to the shop, Alex went straight to work helping wrap up customers' purchases while Maggie rang them into the register.

Later, with the store almost empty, Alex eagerly told her two companions what she'd learned from Yvonne.

"Let me get this straight," Hanna said. "According to Gary, Joe had an argument with Jane the morning of her death. That same day, Gary was talking to Yvonne about how angry he was with Jane over a possible bylaw change? Both of them were angry with Jane, and neither have alibis for either death."

Alex made a check mark in the air with her finger. "Did you find anything about Gary online?"

"Nothing. It's like he's a ghost." Hanna shook her head.

"I suppose Gary Jenkins is a fairly common name. If we don't have any idea where he came from . . . Why don't you try searching Cadastral? Try the greenhouse and his home and see if it has his name on the properties."

After a few minutes, Hanna looked up from the computer. "The greenhouse is owned by Harriston Blooms LLC, and his home says it's owned by Gary Jenkins. Dead end."

"I thought it was Alaska that everyone moved to when they don't want to be found," Maggie said.

"I just read an article that said there are tens of thousands of felons that don't get prosecuted because they cross state lines and no one is willing to go to the expense and trouble of extraditing them to bring them back for trial." Alex started tidying up as she talked.

"Wow. That's not very comforting. I guess we'd better figure out who killed Jane and Netta before they decide to skip town and get away." Hanna popped the last chocolate from their sample tray into her mouth.

"Careful how you put that, Hanna. Remember, we can't interfere in the investigation." Alex waggled her finger in Hanna's direction. Alex hoped Maggie wouldn't let anything slip around Duncan about their continued efforts to find Jane's killer.

"I'm going to the post office." Maggie picked up a parcel for mailing, and Alex opened the door for her.

Less than a minute after Maggie's departure, the door jingled, and Drew came in. "I'm here to pick up Maggie. I thought I'd take her into Swanson for dinner."

"That's so sweet of you," Alex said. "Maggie's mailing a parcel. She'll be back in a few minutes."

Hanna smiled at Drew and headed down the hall. "I've got to go tidy up the kitchen." She returned almost immediately, carrying a tray with the scones Alex had baked that morning and jam and butter. "Why don't you have one of these to tide you over?"

"Oh, well, do you think? Does this have gluten? I probably shouldn't. But they do look good. Maybe just a piece to taste it." Drew cut a generous piece from a scone, slathered butter and jam on it, and popped it into his mouth.

A few minutes later, Maggie returned, and the two left for Swanson. Alex continued tidying up. She grabbed the books sitting on the counter that needed to be reshelved. The first belonged on the shelf for authors whose names began with *B*. As she slid it into place, she slapped her forehead. "Hanna! I figured it out!"

Hanna came running from the kitchen. "What did you figure out? Who killed Jane?"

"No. But it might be almost as good. I figured out where Jane's journal must be. I kept thinking the phrase "pushing up daisies" sounded familiar. Jane's favorite books were M. C. Beaton's Agatha Raisin series. *Pushing Up Daisies* is one of those books. When I was looking behind the books on the bookshelf, she had a large-print edition of *Pushing Up Daisies*. I bet there's a clue tucked inside it."

When the shop was almost ready for the next day, Alex asked, "Do you think you can get Duncan to tell you how the interview went with Oliver?"

"Pretty sure. I'll talk to him after my yoga class. I'll probably be home late, so I'll try and be here early tomorrow so we can update the murder board with everything we know."

Alex knew this was a sacrifice for Hanna, as she wasn't a morning person and usually liked to sleep in as long as she could.

"By the way, when I spoke to Oliver, he seemed disappointed you weren't with me."

Hanna looked pleased. "Did he now? I almost forgot to mention, Eudora has some mail for Jane. Everett asked if you could get Jane's mail and let him know if there's anything requiring his attention, and then he'll pick it up from the shop."

"I'll get it tomorrow." Alex started shutting off the lights. "Let's go home."

Hanna took Watson out for a walk while Alex surveyed the kitchen for inspiration. She hadn't planned anything for supper.

She was startled by a knock at the back door. Tom was standing there with his arms full.

"I hope I'm not being too presumptuous. I prepared all the ingredients for lasagna and hoped you could put them together and then update me on what's been happening with your investigation. It seems to be way beyond a theoretical discussion at this point." He smiled.

"That's so kind. Thank you. I was looking in the fridge to see what I could whip up for supper. Hanna will be back shortly from walking the dog. And, just to be clear, we're not investigating anything. Duncan warned us to stay out of it, so we're merely being neighborly, delivering cookies to a few people, and having a nice old chat."

Alex quickly assembled the lasagna and put it in the oven. She fixed a green salad from the things he had brought, and then they sat down in the family room to wait for the lasagna to bake.

"It's comforting to know you're taking his advice to heart." There was no missing the sarcasm in Tom's voice. Despite that, he seemed anxious to hear about the day's events.

Alex started with the extraordinary news that Oliver had seen Jane's killer and that this changed the time of death.

"You have been busy, haven't you? Has it occurred to you that if the person who killed Jane figures out you're looking into her death, he or she might target you? If Netta was killed because of something she remembered, the killer may be getting nervous." Concern was evident in his voice.

"Possibly. I'd like to know how the killer found out Netta remembered something." Alex paused for a moment, finally giving her head a slight shake. "I'm sure I'll be fine. Not that many people know what I'm doing. Besides, I need to find that true-crime episode, and that should solve this. So, what have you been up to today?"

Tom ignored Alex's attempt to change the subject. "The whole village probably knows what you're up to. If the killer doesn't, it's because they've left town or they're in a coma. I went to see Zach today at the jail in Swanson."

"How's he doing?" Alex drew her eyebrows together.

"Not well. He's depressed and swears he didn't hurt Jane. I believe him. All the evidence against him is circumstantial. The coins Jane gave him were a gift for work he did over the summer he didn't charge her for. She knew he wouldn't take money from her, so she gave him the coins as a Christmas gift. She had wrapped them up, but he said he was curious, so he opened them when he got home. If he'd kept the wrapping paper and tag, he could have proven it was a gift. They set his bail, but it seems like he just doesn't care about getting out of jail."

"I need to solve this so I can get him out. Where's his girl-friend? Has she tried to contact him?"

"No. He hasn't heard from her since the night he told her about his criminal record."

"Someone needs to tell her what's going on. I wonder where she went."

The timer rang, and Alex checked the lasagna. As she tossed the salad, Hanna came in with Watson.

"Hi, Tom. It's nice to see you." Hanna gave him one of her brightest smiles as she took off her gloves. She cast a sideways glance at Alex and raised her brows.

"Tom brought dinner for us. Wasn't that sweet?" Alex returned Hanna's raised brows with a glare.

Hanna gave Alex one of her *I told you so* looks and went about preparing Watson's dinner.

Alex almost stuck her tongue out at Hanna. As far as Alex was concerned, the fact that Tom had brought them dinner didn't indicate anything other than his curiosity in the investigation.

As they enjoyed their meal, Alex said, "I'm going back over to Jane's after dinner. I need to try and find her journal. It might have information that will help us."

Hanna and Tom both said, "I'll come with you."

Alex frowned. She hardly needed a babysitter. Before she could tell them she was going alone, Tom's cell phone rang. They watched his face dissolve into concern as he spoke to whoever was on the other end.

"Do you want me to come over?" He paused as the caller spoke. "I'll be right there."

Alex and Hanna looked at Tom with a mixture of apprehension and curiosity.

"That was Maggie. Drew is sick. He started feeling ill at dinner and quickly got worse. Initially, she thought he was just exaggerating. You know how he's been. She drove him home, but she's quite worried now."

"What are his symptoms?" Alex asked.

"Maggie said he's flushed, his mouth is dry, nausea and diarrhea, and now he seems to be hallucinating. She's wondering if he caught some kind of really bad twenty-four-hour flu."

A terrible thought flashed through Alex's mind. "I don't want to cause unnecessary alarm, but those are also symptoms of belladonna poisoning. She should check to see if his pupils are dilated." She spoke as she did a search of other belladonna symptoms on her phone.

Hanna turned to Alex. "Where would he have consumed belladonna?"

"Just before Maggie came back from the post office, he had a bite of the scone with some jam. That was the jam left on the doorstep the other day. It was meant for us. What if the killer left it?"

"I'd better go over to Maggie's. She needs to call the poison control center." Tom headed for the door. "Sorry to eat and run, ladies. I'll call you later and let you know what's going on."

Hanna was already getting up and heading to the closet. "I'll run to the shop and get that jar of jam and call Duncan."

"Do you want me to come with you?" Alex asked.

"No. You go to Jane's and find that diary. Maybe it will give us a clue who's behind all of this."

Chapter Twenty-Seven

Jane's house was dark, in sharp contrast to the other festively adorned homes with their lawn ornaments and twinkling lights. The evening was frosty, and the air was heavy with unshed moisture; it would snow soon, though it was holding off for now. Alex was getting chilled standing in the driveway looking at the lonely shell of what was so recently a warm and inviting home. All this sentimentality had to stop; she had a job to do, though she hoped Drew was going to be all right. Even though he'd only eaten a small quantity, that was all it took with some poisons.

She squared her shoulders and marched up the front steps, unlocked the door, and turned on the hall lights. Just to be cautious, she locked the front door behind her and checked to ensure the back door was also locked. She went through the downstairs, flipped lights on, and turned up the heat.

Alex went upstairs and sat in Jane's chair. Turning her head, she discovered the book she sought was right there at eye level. She glanced at Jane's desk and saw several things that she thought had been in a drawer sitting on top of the desk. She thought back to last night; she was sure those things weren't on the desk yesterday. She had only checked behind and under it; she hadn't actually gone into the drawers. Had she?

She didn't think she was losing her mind. Those things definitely hadn't been there last night. No one else would be in here except maybe Everett, and she didn't think he'd be going through Jane's things. She'd have to ask him about it tomorrow. The spare key was tucked inside her backpack, so it was impossible anyone could have been in here.

Alex opened the letter Jane had given her and reread it. *Just go to my special spot to find it, along with my journal. . . . Just remember, I may be pushing up daisies, but you aren't.* How could she not have clued in sooner! Jane had had an incredible sense of humor.

She pulled the book off the shelf. The large-print edition of the novel was far heavier than she'd expected. Upon opening the book, she saw the interior had been cut out and there was a journal inside, along with a slender velvet box. Inside the box were several rings with diamonds, emeralds, and rubies in their settings. There was also a heavy gold chain and matching bracelet, as well as three antique gold broaches. One was made in a sort of figure-eight pattern, another in the shape of a wreath was inlaid with pearl, and the other looked like a flower with rubies. There was also a long gold necklace with a gold coin hanging from it. Alex had seen Jane wearing some of these pieces from time to time.

Though she was tempted to read the journal immediately, she decided to watch more of the true-crime shows. Hanna knew where she was, and she had her phone if anyone needed her. She would fast-forward through each show, getting enough of the story to see if it might have merit.

Her new strategy allowed her to quickly get through two episodes that definitely weren't what she was looking for.

Another two uneventful episodes later, she heard a noise on the front porch. She quietly crept to the front door, tore it open, and sprinted outside. Alex wasn't sure who was more surprised; Gary jumped a foot in the air before turning to her. He was standing a few feet away and had obviously been peeking in the front window.

"Can I help you?" Alex managed to muster a bewildered look for Gary's benefit.

"You scared the crap out of me! The forecast is calling for snow starting tomorrow afternoon. I saw your car and was just checking to see if you were inside. I was going to offer to shovel the sidewalk and driveway when it snows. I think I almost had a heart attack." He clutched his chest.

"Sorry. I thought you were Hanna trying to scare me. She does that sometimes. I would very much appreciate it if you'd shovel the snow, but not if it will give you a heart attack."

"If I can survive the shock you just gave me, I should be okay to do a little shoveling. See you later." He spoke through gritted teeth and quickly walked past Alex and down the stairs, avoiding her gaze.

Alex went back into the house, satisfied. That should teach him to peek in windows. It was getting late, and she wanted to know what had happened with Drew and the jam. Looking at her watch, she wondered why no one had tried calling her yet.

She was spending all this time trying to find the show Jane had watched without even knowing if it would help. Alex had lived in Harriston only three years. It was conceivable she wouldn't even recognize the individual Jane had identified in her mind. Alex hated to admit it, but was it possible that Jane, after several erroneous guesses, had been mistaken again? There was no denying she'd been murdered, but did it have anything to do with the true-crime show? Perhaps it was just a coincidence. There seemed to be no shortage of people who had been annoyed with her. And one thing Alex had learned watching all these true-crime shows was that people killed for seemingly trite reasons.

As she went through the house turning out lights, she wondered if Gary really wanted to offer his shoveling services or if that had been an excuse. He was one of the people Jane had upset prior to her death. But would any of those petty grievances have been enough to trigger her murder? And what about Netta? Was her death only an accident, as Duncan believed, or was there something more sinister involved? There were too many coincidences for Alex to accept the sheriff's theories. Especially since she was still considered a suspect.

Hanna was on the phone with Duncan when she got home. As soon as the call was done, they both spoke at once.

"What happened?" Alex asked again.

"Duncan was already on his way home when I called him on my way to the shop. He called an ambulance, and they've taken Drew to the hospital and are treating him. I got the jam, and Duncan took it with him to the hospital. They'll get it tested and see if it has belladonna in it. Duncan called back just before you got home. It looks like Drew will be okay, though he'll have an unpleasant night. He should be back to normal in a few days. Maggie is going to stay with him at the hospital overnight. Tom is already on his way home. I feel terrible. If I hadn't offered that food to Drew . . ."

"Then it would have been you or me or even Maggie that ended up eating it. And we probably would have eaten far more, and the outcome might not have been as positive. I offered Duncan a scone with that jam this morning. Thankfully, he only took the scone, or he could be in the hospital right now."

"If you hadn't recognized the symptoms, Drew's fate could have been worse."

"It's that poster in the shop. I was looking at belladonna today because Gary said he was working with it; otherwise I might not have recognized the symptoms so quickly." Alex went to the kitchen and made a pot of chamomile tea.

"I'm going to let Watson out, and then I'm going to have a soak in the tub." Hanna opened the door to the backyard.

"I'll be down here. I'm going to start reading Jane's journal. I skipped through several more episodes at Jane's and saw nothing that remotely resembles what she described."

Alex let the dog back in and gave Watson a pat as the dog followed Hanna upstairs. Taking her tea and the journal to a chair by the lamp, Alex sat down and started reading the last entry. It was so sad reading Jane's final thoughts. The entry had been written the night she died. She recounted the events that Alex already knew about: her deliveries of the poinsettias and Joe's fury at finding out she was still trying to find out about his history. Jane wrote poignantly about her evening at Sleuth and how she felt Alex was like a daughter. Alex was getting teary eyed and took a sip of her tea. Jane briefly mentioned Zach's anger at his disclosure of his past to Jennifer. Apparently, Jane had called Jennifer later that night and told her not to be too hasty in making a decision about Zach. She'd suggested Jennifer take some time to think about the relationship before making any decision. That certainly proved Jane had still been alive well past ten that night.

Alex's ringtone startled her, and she fumbled trying to answer her phone.

"I'm sorry to call so late, but I promised I'd give you an update on Drew," Tom said apologetically.

"Thank you. I hope he's going to be okay."

"He's not feeling great right now, but they expect him to make a full recovery. Your presence of mind may have saved him.

Maggie said she won't be in tomorrow morning, but she'll be there in the afternoon if Drew is feeling better."

"Oh, she doesn't need to come in. She should be with Drew or getting some sleep."

"They've given her a cot beside him, so she'll get some rest tonight. I have a feeling once Drew starts to feel better, Maggie will need to have some time away from him. I'm going over later in the morning so she can go home if she wants to."

They spoke a few more minutes, and Alex went back to reading Jane's journal. Unfortunately, the entries for the Sunday before her death were largely about her interactions at church and didn't contribute anything to who the killer might be. Alex was starting to fall asleep and finally closed the journal. She'd have to continue tomorrow; it was well past her bedtime.

Chapter
Twenty-Eight

The world was still in darkness when Alex awoke, tangled in her blankets and breathing heavily. She'd been dreaming Hanna had moved away and she was trying to make chocolates. She'd burned them all and was surrounded by smoldering chocolate. It was obvious what her dream meant, and there was no point worrying about that now. She grabbed Jane's journal from her nightstand and flipped through the entries without reading them in their entirety. The word *coins* jumped out at her, and she stopped to read an entry from a couple of weeks earlier. Jane wrote about her intent to give Zach the coins. It was exactly as Zach had said. When he had stubbornly refused to take any payment last summer, she'd decided to give him the coins collected by her father. They had some value, and Zach could sell them or not, but since she had no immediate heirs, she didn't have a sentimental attachment to them.

There was another entry the day she gave them to Zach; Jane expressed her pleasure that he'd accepted her gift after she had extracted a promise not to return it. This was proof that Zach hadn't stolen the coin collection from Jane's house. Alex was thrilled. This should certainly be enough to get him out of jail.

The journal needed to be handed over to Duncan today, but she would read as much as she could first. Jane had made a brief reference to the person she'd recognized on the night of the true-crime show. Unfortunately, she hadn't named them. At least now Alex knew the date the show had aired and could hopefully narrow down the episodes she needed to watch.

Jane also wrote of Gary's reaction when she told him of her proposal to amend the bylaw that would impact him. Jane said he'd stood there as his face reddened and spoken in a tight, quiet voice, suggesting she might consider knitting as a more appropriate pastime for a woman her age instead of interfering in other people's business. Alex would have to read through the entry more carefully to see what other nuggets might be there.

After completing her morning ritual, she went downstairs and put the journal and everything else she needed into her backpack. She left a note on the counter to remind Hanna they needed to make the German potato salad today for Christmas Eve. The salad, made with potatoes, eggs, pickles, onions, mayonnaise, and their secret ingredient—pickle juice—always tasted best if it was made a day ahead.

There was a timid knock on the door as she was zipping up her coat. She wasn't in the habit of having callers at six thirty AM, and after her scare the night before at Jane's, she was jumpy. She grabbed a wooden nutcracker from the table in the entry hall and held it like a club. The window of her door was frosted for privacy, so she asked through the door who was there.

"It's Oliver. I'm sorry I'm here so early, but I saw your lights on."

Alex let out her breath and opened the door. "Come in. What are you doing up so early, hanging out in front of my house?"

Oliver looked at the nutcracker still clutched in Alex's hand.

Alex wiped an imaginary spot. "Dusting."

"I was taking my morning walk. The sheriff and a deputy talked to me last night, and I told them everything I saw the night of Jane's murder. The sheriff asked me point-blank if I'd been drinking. She said the deputy that questioned me the morning after Jane's murder had noted I appeared to be hungover. I told them the truth. I didn't think lying to them would be a good idea."

"You're definitely right about that. Did they tell you anything?"

"Just that I could be called on to testify if there was a trial." Oliver had a pained expression. "Unless I have to testify, it's unlikely anyone will ever find out about my drinking that night. But I'm going to tell my editor about everything. I'm tired of keeping secrets. Anyway, there's something I didn't mention to you. When the person I saw left, they headed over to Gary's backyard. I can't say where they went after that, though. It was too dark.

"The sheriff said they found tracks, but there were so many different boot treads between Jane's, Gary's, and Yvonne's back-yards, they said it was like a party of toddlers had played all over the yards. Plus, it was difficult to say when the tracks were made."

Alex digested that for a moment. "You said you were going for your morning walk. Isn't this a bit early for you?"

"I have you to thank for that." Oliver beamed. "After you left the other day, I poured out the rest of the vodka and decided to take my own advice. I've been doing lots of walking and meditating. Whenever I feel like having a drink, I either go for a walk or do some yoga or weights. It seems to be helping. I went back to the AA meeting Monday night as well. I feel like I owe it to Jane to get my life back together. If I'd been sober, I might have gone over to Jane's to see what was happening and been able to stop whoever killed her."

"Or more likely, you would have been in bed asleep and wouldn't have seen anything. I don't think it's a good idea to spend a lot of time thinking about what would have or could have been. Make the most of the present. Learn from your mistakes to make the future better, but don't live in the past."

"I might just use that quote in my next book—which I've started, by the way." Oliver smiled shyly. "I'm going to try and write it without a ghostwriter, as I told you, but I'm not going to stress about it if I decide I need help. We'll see how it goes."

Alex followed Oliver out the door, scooping up her bag. She asked if he wanted a ride home, but he declined, saying he wanted more time outside. She was happy he seemed to be getting his life back on track. She'd never struggled with addiction, unless you counted chocolate. Her parents had taught their children not to start a habit they might need to quit one day. Alex had taken that advice to heart, but she'd watched friends struggle with various addictions and knew how destructive they could be.

At the shop, she got a cup of tea and sat down on the bench by the window to read some more of the journal. In moments, she was lost in Jane's thoughts and musings. Jane wrote about Yvonne's obsession with being president of the horticultural society several times. In an earlier entry, Jane mentioned Gary had become angry when she pressed the issue of what he had done prior to coming to Harriston. Jane had tried to find out what she could but had come to the same dead end as Alex.

Alex looked for an entry from last December. She found a brief mention of the picture they had wanted to take of Gary with his poinsettias and his vehement denial of permission to publish any photos of him. Jane wrote he had actually threatened legal action if they mentioned his name or used his picture in the article.

The sound of the door opening had Alex checking the time. She had been so immersed in Jane's world, she'd completely lost track. It was still forty-five minutes before opening. Alex was surprised but delighted to see Hanna with muffins from the bakery and Watson beside her.

"Louise was working this morning, but they were crazy busy. I waited over ten minutes to get these. Have you learned anything helpful from Jane's journal?" Hanna took the muffins to the kitchen and set about making more tea.

Alex followed her, putting Watson in the conference room. The dog wasn't allowed in the kitchen.

Once they both had butter spread on their muffins and steaming cups of tea in front of them at the conference room table, Hanna started talking.

"Duncan called me a while ago and woke me up. That's why I'm here so early. He said the ME is putting Jane's time of death between eleven thirty PM and one AM, though Oliver's information seems to narrow that down even further. They went and talked to Zach at the jail after talking to Oliver. Zach maintains he wasn't at Jane's until a few minutes before you saw him leaving. Duncan says they're probably going to release him because they don't have enough evidence to charge him with murder, and the robbery isn't strong enough to keep him in jail."

"I think I may have the proof he needs to have the robbery charges dropped." Alex handed over Jane's journal. "Check the entry December eighth."

After flipping a few pages, Hanna read the entry. "This is proof he didn't steal those coins, but I bet they'll still be looking at him as a suspect for the murder. Duncan says Sheriff Summers is determined to make a case against him."

"I guess she has a problem with being wrong. That means we need to find the real murderer before she starts focusing on me again."

Alex told her of Oliver's visit that morning, as well as about her experience with Gary the night before. "I swear he jumped about a foot into the air when I rushed out the door."

Hanna laughed. "I wish I'd been there to see that. What do you think he was really doing?"

Alex shrugged. "I have no idea. Every time I'm over there, he seems to pop up. Literally."

She went to stand in front of the murder board. "We're down to three suspects: Joe, Louise, and Gary."

Hanna's phone rang, and she looked at the display. "It's Duncan." She raised her eyebrows and connected the call. She listened for a few minutes. "Thanks." She ended the call.

"They've tested the jam and it's conclusive. The berries in it are a combination of belladonna, raspberry, and blueberry. Drew's lucky they knew what to look for at the hospital because of you. An entire scone covered with the jam would likely have been enough to kill someone. He's pushed to have them do the toxicology screening from Netta's autopsy right away. He's going to go and canvass Netta's neighbors to see if anyone saw someone at her house after Trixie dropped her off. He says he's going to take another look at everyone Jane was close to."

Chapter
Twenty-Nine

A lex was pleased Duncan had finally decided to probe other theories, but she wasn't going to relinquish her efforts. She sensed they were getting closer to the answer. "Can you handle things for a bit?" Alex asked Hanna, grabbing her coat. "I want to pay Louise a visit."

Things didn't seem too busy at Cookies 'n Crumbs. Alex had to wait only a minute to order a hot chocolate from Sam. "Do you mind if I ask Louise to join me for a second? I need to talk to her."

Sam looked curious but didn't ask any questions. "Sure. I'll get her to bring your hot chocolate to you. You can go sit back in the corner. There's a table free."

Alex sat and looked around. The bakery was full of villagers. Many were retired and often came here to while away their days. There were a couple of younger women at another table, intent on their discussion. Were any of these people still talking about the murder, or had the excitement of Christmas and the pressures of daily life superseded that moment of tragedy?

When Louise approached with her hot chocolate, Alex gestured to the chair on the opposite side of the table. "Will you please have a seat? I want to ask you something. I already checked with Sam, and she said it's fine for you to take a break and talk to me."

Louise sat and eyed Alex suspiciously. "Go ahead, then. Talk."

"I'm not sure if you know, but I'm trying to find out who killed Jane and Netta."

"Didn't Netta fall down her stairs?"

"She did, but that doesn't mean someone didn't push her. I respect your desire for privacy, I really do, but I think the person responsible for Jane and Netta's death may have moved to Harriston in the last ten years. You're one of a few people who that could be."

Louise stiffened, and her mouth fell open. "You think I killed them?"

"To be completely honest, I don't. Unfortunately, you don't have an alibi, and I can't find out anything about your past. So maybe you've left a trail of bodies wherever you came from and Jane found out and you killed her. You yelled at her and said something about letting sleeping dogs lie."

Louise blanched but was silent, her lips pinched together. Then one corner of her mouth turned up. "Bless your heart. You're as dumb as a box of rocks." She shook her head. "Why can't you just mind your own business!"

Alex lowered her voice. "Because I'm certain Jane was killed because of something she found out about someone. Maybe she shouldn't have been so nosy, but she was a good person and didn't deserve to die. I'm going to dig and dig until I figure out what it was that got her killed."

Perched on the edge of her chair, her shoulders rigid, Louise made a small choking noise in her throat. "You'd best keep this to yourself, if you know what's good for you. The only thing in my past is an ex-husband that's lower than a snake's belly in a wagon rut. When I won a bit of money in the lottery, I picked up and left, but I knew he'd come looking for me if he ever found out I had a bit of something put by. I can't even tell my kids where I'm living 'cause he'd wear them down till they told him. Jane found one of my kids on the internet and sent them a message. She wanted to tell them where I'm living so they could visit me, but she had no idea the can of worms she'd be opening. I go see my kids and grandkids every once in a while. It ain't nobody else's business." Louise stood. "Well, I better get back to work. You mind what I said and keep it to yourself."

Alex sat at the table, stunned. Whatever she had expected, it wasn't that. Grabbing her untouched hot chocolate, she headed to the door with a wave to Louise and Sam. Louise just glared.

Hanna was rushing around reorganizing one of their displays when Alex got back to the store. A few customers were milling about. "I just checked the store's email. We had one yesterday from the activity coordinator at the seniors' home in Swanson, letting us know a bunch of them are coming by this morning to shop in Harriston. She wanted to make sure we had a heads-up because at least twenty will be coming."

"Let's set up a display of the cozy mysteries that use quilting and knitting as a theme. Look for Christmas-themed ones too. I suspect a lot of the women still enjoy those activities." Alex pulled some books out of a bookcase.

"Okay. I'll find some with embroidery themes as well. I hate to stereotype, but maybe some that prominently feature cats."

"That sounds purr-fect."

Hanna groaned.

"I'll add some jams and candles to the displays as well. That's something I can see them purchasing to go with the books." Alex started moving things around.

Hanna turned to Alex. "What did you find out from Louise?"

Pausing, Alex looked at Hanna and shook her head. "I'm not sure you'll believe it." As they worked, she told Hanna what had happened at the bakery.

"Do you believe her?"

"I think so. When I was at her house, I saw pictures of what were probably her kids and grandkids. But maybe we can't completely eliminate her from our list."

"We need to find a way to narrow down our suspects."

Several customers came in, taking their attention, with a steady stream thereafter making it impossible to discuss the murders or anything else.

Hanna brought samples of their chocolates out for the customers, including one of their Christmas offerings. Fruitcake Fluorine was a cranberry and cherry puree with a hint of rum, layered with a chocolate ganache in a milk-chocolate shell. More than a few sales were made after people tasted the samples.

When the store was almost empty, Hanna asked to see Jane's journal again. "How much of it have you read?"

"Not even half. I've been skipping around and skimming a good deal. I'm going to start copying it right now, and I'll have to take time later today to read it more thoroughly. I'm hoping there will be more clues in there as to who killed her."

Two customers came from the other room and headed to the counter with their purchases.

Yvonne held up a book. "I enjoyed the cozy mystery novel and wanted to try another one."

"I'm glad to hear it. Cozies are my favorite."

"Are you still working at Jane's, or have you finished until after the holidays?"

"I'll probably be there tonight. Hopefully I'll finish soon. Have a merry Christmas."

Yvonne took her book and left.

Hanna rang in the sale for the other customer while Alex ran across the street. She'd remembered there was mail for Jane at the post office. Just ahead of her, Joe entered the building. Alex stood behind him as he checked his box. "Can I bother you for a minute?"

"Sure. What's up?" Joe retrieved his mail.

"I was talking to someone, and they mentioned they saw you running near Harriston Blooms on Saturday evening around five thirty?"

"Yeah. That sounds about right. I go running most evenings after work. What of it?" He turned to give Alex his full attention, crossing his arms and squinting at her.

"That was around the time a lady across the street from there died. She fell down her stairs. I was wondering if you saw anything . . . strange?"

Joe's body relaxed. "I heard about that second lady dying. Pretty odd all these old ladies dropping dead all of a sudden. I don't know if it's strange, but I saw someone walking down the lane behind the dead lady's house as I ran by."

"Could you tell anything about them? Height? Male or female?"

"Nah. It was too dark, and I was running, so I needed to watch where I was going."

"Did anyone else see you on your run?"

"Maybe. You never know who's watching out of their windows around here. If that's all?"

After saying good-bye, Alex checked her box and went into the post office proper. While she waited for Eudora to get off the phone, she started thinking about what Joe had said.

Perhaps the person Joe had seen had nothing to do with Netta's death. Maybe Jane's death was unrelated to the true-crime show and Netta's death really had been just an accident?

Eudora hung up and waved Alex to the counter. "Merry Christmas."

"Merry Christmas to you too. Can you believe tomorrow is Christmas Eve? Where does the time go?"

"I know. It seems we look forward to it for so long, and then suddenly it's here."

"Hanna said I needed to come by and pick up Jane's mail?"

"Yes. Let me get it. You'll need to sign for it."

A moment later, Eudora handed Alex a small stack of mail as well as a clipboard and pointed to where she had to sign. "My sources tell me they released Zach. It's about time. I'm glad he's home before Christmas. It seems his girlfriend is back as well."

"Don't you mean former girlfriend?"

"From what I hear, a reconciliation may be in the air."

Alex was so pleased to hear some good news for a change, she almost skipped back to the store. The bus from the seniors' home was parked out front, and a collection of ladies, thin, stout, tall, and short, were shuffling out of the bus and into the store. Alex dropped the mail behind the counter as several elderly ladies approached her and Hanna.

Alex's customer was a petite lady with grayish-mauve hair and little half-glasses dangling from a chain around her neck. After introducing herself as Thelma, she said in a surprisingly strong voice, "I see you've got all these completely unbelievable cozy mysteries set up in your displays. That may be what my friends are looking for, but I want some hard-core stuff. I don't care if there's bad language and sex. Just find me a good, scary thriller. Something that will keep my heart beating over the holidays."

Alex was a little taken back but smiled. "I think I may have some books you'd like." She led the older lady to bookshelves in the east room, pointing out some popular thrillers. When Alex left her, she was happily perusing a best seller.

Hanna was handing out more of the chocolate samples. The older ladies definitely favored Strychnine Strawberry, Gingerbread Gelsemine, and the Ricin Raspberry Creams. Apparently, those with dentures were less likely to try the varieties with nuts. Many grabbed a box of the chocolates once they'd sampled a couple.

Some of the ladies were milling around the displays with the mysteries Hanna and Alex had put out that morning, and a few had jars of jam in their hands as well. As the ladies were leaving, Alex watched them go and wondered if that would be her one day—no one to spend Christmas with, just a bunch of mystery novels and a box of chocolates. Maybe she'd even have mauve hair. At least she wouldn't have a cat.

Alex and Hanna redid the now-decimated displays, restocking the items the ladies from the seniors' home had purchased. When they were done, Hanna offered to go buy lunch from the General Store. While she was gone, Alex sat down and went through the mail.

After sorting through her own and throwing out the junk, she sorted Jane's. There were a number of Christmas cards; she would write to those people and let them know Jane had passed away. There was also the usual assortment of bills and junk mail. Junk mail went in the trash, and bills would go to Everett. There was one mystery magazine, which Alex would keep at the store, and a large brown envelope with a return address for the county clerk in Spokane County in Washington.

Chapter Thirty

Using a letter opener, Alex slit open the envelope from the county clerk in Spokane. The envelope contained only two sheets of paper and a receipt. The first paper was a brief letter indicating that a copy of the requested legal name change document was enclosed, along with a receipt for services. Alex looked at the second paper, which showed that one Joe Cameron used to be Jeremy Camalleri. Jane hadn't given up but had obviously continued to dig to find out where Joe had come from and who he really was.

Alex immediately went to her computer and looked up Jeremy Camalleri from Spokane, Washington, on her search engine. In seconds, she had multiple hits for his name. Several were articles in online newspapers. She clicked on one and eagerly started reading.

The gist of the article, written twelve years ago, was that Jeremy had been sued by a homeowner after shoddy construction caused leaking and moisture issues, resulting in extensive mold in the home. The couple's daughter had asthma and had suffered repeated serious asthma attacks in the months after they moved into the house, the final one resulting in her death.

Unfortunately, the jury didn't agree with the homeowners that Jeremy was to blame for their daughter's death. Jeremy won the lawsuit, but it was a shallow victory, as his wife left him shortly thereafter, taking their two children with her. Her name was Laura Camalleri. Alex checked the other articles she'd found, but they all said essentially the same thing. There was a picture of Jeremy and Laura in one of the articles. Jeremy and Joe were definitely the same person.

She did a quick social media search and found a Laura Camalleri from Spokane who matched the pictures in the article. On a whim, Alex typed a direct message, explaining why she wanted to talk to Laura in person. After deliberating for about two seconds, she pressed send. *Worst case, the ex-wife doesn't respond.*

Hanna came in about a minute later.

"Take a look at this." Alex showed Hanna the name change documents and the online article. "I sent Joe's ex-wife a message asking for her phone number so we can call her."

"You didn't!"

Alex nodded. "I want to know if there's more to it than what they say in the article. If this is his big secret, then it explains why he didn't want Jane poking around in his past."

As they were looking at the screen, a notification popped up, telling them there was a message. Laura had replied with her phone number.

Alex called her right away. After the preliminary greetings were out of the way, she told Laura about Jane's murder and why they were trying to find out what had happened.

"Do you know why Joe—I mean Jeremy—changed his name and moved here?" Alex asked. "He's very protective of his past."

Laura laughed. "That's good to know. He did that mainly at my request—well, not the name change, but moving away. I told

240

him I didn't want him around and I was willing to give up any claims to his business in the divorce if he agreed to move far away and leave the kids and me alone."

"Was that because of the lawsuit?"

"That was part of it. Jeremy wasn't a nice person to do business with. He liked to put clauses into the fine print that basically left the homeowners high and dry. He was always taking shortcuts. Nothing that was outright illegal, but he was always skating a fine line. I got tired of the threats and dirty looks people gave me, like I was part of it. So when that girl died, it was the final straw. I made it too good for him not to leave. He's allowed to call the kids and take them for a couple holidays a year. I know it may sound harsh, but I've remarried, and the kids have a stepfather who's really good to them. They don't need any more scandal hanging over their heads."

"Do you think he would resort to violence to keep his past quiet?"

"I can't imagine it. Jeremy had a temper, but he was never violent with anyone. He didn't even believe in spanking the kids. What day was your friend killed?"

"She was killed around midnight, Monday night the fourteenth."

Laura was quiet for a second. "According to my calendar, Jeremy was talking to our kids that night from about ten our time to almost eleven thirty; that would be eleven o'clock until twelve thirty your time. I remember I was annoyed it was so late, but we had made last-minute plans to go away for the next day until after Christmas, and Jeremy said he had a meeting earlier. As it turned out, we had to cancel our trip because my husband had an emergency at work. He's a surgeon, so there's no putting off some things. I'm not sure if that helps."

"It does. I really appreciate your letting me call. I'm sorry I asked so many personal questions."

"It's fine, but I've got to go. We rescheduled that trip, and we're leaving tomorrow, so I've got lots to get done. Hopefully, we'll actually get to go this time."

When they'd disconnected the call, Hanna and Alex stared at each other in silence.

"Is there any way Joe could get off the phone after midnight and still get to Jane's and kill her?" Hanna asked.

"Not if we believe the person Oliver saw and the killer are one and the same person. There couldn't be two people breaking into Jane's. And another question: would Joe have known where the spare key was?" Alex tapped her chin. "It wouldn't have been hard to find the key under the planter, but I don't believe there were two people. I think we have to take Joe off our suspect list."

"Hallelujah! That only leaves Gary, and maybe Louise, since you've eliminated the others."

"He's definitely hiding something. He wouldn't even allow his picture to be taken last year, remember? If he's wanted for murder somewhere, I can imagine he would avoid any kind of publicity. It all fits. He also knew where the key was. Jane was jeopardizing his business with the bylaw changes she was proposing. Yvonne said Gary was 'fit to be tied' over it the night of Jane's murder."

"Maybe he didn't even know about Jane suspecting him of being wanted for murders elsewhere? Maybe he was so angry with Jane over the bylaw thing he killed her. Jane said it went back to character. If Gary murdered in the past, why wouldn't he kill again?" Hanna asked.

"I don't think there's any way he didn't know about Jane's suspicions. Netta told him about it at the horticultural society meeting."

A young boy and girl came in at that moment, and Hanna greeted them. The boy looked to be about twelve, and the girl was maybe nine or ten. They were sizzling with excitement to be shopping on their own.

"We need a present for our mom. Dad gave us some money and told us to get her a book for Christmas. Can you please help us find one from our list?" The girl handed Hanna a crumpled piece of paper.

Absently smiling at the children, Alex reflected that the evidence was stacking up against Gary. He was hiding something, but, if she was honest, she liked him. Of course, people often liked serial killers. She stared at Jane's sorry-looking poinsettia and recalled her conversations with Netta. Something had been niggling at her since the morning after Jane's murder. Netta had wanted to know all about Jane being stabbed. But that morning, the only people who knew Jane had been stabbed were Duncan, whoever was there from the sheriff's office, Hanna, Alex, and the killer. How had Netta known? She obviously wasn't the killer, so the only way she could have known was if the killer had told her. *I wonder if that's what she wanted to tell me.* That morning, Alex had told Netta she'd been asked not to discuss the murder. Netta must have figured out that whoever had told her Jane had been stabbed knew something that perhaps they shouldn't have.

While Hanna was helping their junior customers, Maggie walked in, interrupting Alex's thoughts.

Alex gave her a hug. "How's Drew?"

"He's doing well. The worst of the symptoms seem to have passed overnight. He was busy telling the doctors everything that was wrong with him this morning, so I think he'll be back to normal soon. They expect he'll be able to come home tomorrow.

I think they would have let him go today, but Drew is insisting on more tests."

"Thank goodness. We were so worried. I can't apologize enough for giving him that jam."

"Pish. It's not your fault. The killer is to blame. Have you gotten any further on narrowing down the suspects? Duncan told us Zach has been released from jail."

Alex brought Maggie to the kitchen and let her know what she'd found out so far. "I need to copy Jane's journal so we can give it to Duncan."

"Why don't I do that now and you go find that murderer."

Alex looked at the murder board. Jane had said it was about character. Did Gary have the character of a killer? He was very protective about his past, shutting down any attempt to discuss it. He was also angry about Jane's interference with the local bylaws, and he didn't have an alibi for either murder. It was possible he had spoken to Netta the morning Jane's body was discovered, when many of Jane's neighbors had gathered on the street. He could inadvertently have said Jane had been stabbed. Also, every time Alex went near Jane's house, he popped up. If she knew the details of the true-crime episode Jane had seen, maybe she'd be able to make the connection the same way Jane had. Could Gary have been the one in the post office the Friday Netta revealed Jane's suspicions?

Chapter
Thirty-One

Alex was reading the pages of Jane's journal that Maggie had already copied when the phone rang. Waving Maggie off, she picked up the phone.

"Alex, this is Yvonne. Would you join me at my home for afternoon tea? As tomorrow is Christmas Eve, it would be nice to have someone celebrate with me. I'm doing a proper English tea. It's a bit of a tradition. I usually invite Netta, but of course, that's not possible anymore."

The last thing Alex wanted to do was go to Yvonne's. She needed to focus on reading Jane's journal, but Yvonne sounded so sad and lonely. Ugh. She gently pounded her forehead with her fist. She didn't know how she could refuse. "I'd love to." She shook her head.

"Wonderful. I'll see you at four sharp."

"Hanna, do you mind if I take off at four? Yvonne invited me to tea, and she sounded so lonely, I didn't have the heart to say no."

"Of course not. Try to enjoy yourself. We're going to figure this out."

"Can you call Duncan and let him know about Jane's journal? I think Maggie's almost done copying it."

At five minutes to four, despite her reluctance, Alex drove to Yvonne's house. She got out of her car and looked up to see banners of dark gray blanketing the sky. It would snow soon. She hoped it would hold off for a few more hours. Why would Yvonne invite her over? Didn't she have any other friends her own age? Thinking about Yvonne's somewhat conceited and superior air, Alex figured it was quite possible the older woman didn't have many close friends.

In the formal living room, a beautiful, white damask table-cloth covered the coffee table. Alex was impressed. It was obvious considerable effort had gone into preparing the meal. Yvonne had put out exquisite white dishes with a border of holly and berries that had a scarlet ribbon running throughout, and in the center of each plate was a beautiful green wreath intertwined with more scarlet berries.

She had two white teapots decorated with the same motif and matching teacups and saucers. In the middle of the table was a magnificent three-tiered tray. The bottom tier was filled with tiny, perfectly cut finger sandwiches, the middle tier had freshly baked scones, and the top tier held an assortment of little cakes and pastries. There was jam and clotted cream on the table as well.

"Please have a seat." Yvonne gestured to the sofa.

Alex placed a white napkin embroidered along the edge in scarlet on her lap. "This is beautiful, and it's so festive. Have you had these dishes long?"

"They were my mother's. She was English, so we had after-noon tea quite often, but only during Christmas with this set. I looked forward to it for months. Would you like Earl Grey or peppermint tea?"

"Peppermint, please."

"Oh dear, I forgot the sugar on the kitchen counter." Yvonne poured Alex's tea.

"No problem. I'll get it." Alex jumped up and went to the kitchen.

"I can get it," Yvonne called after her.

A sugar bowl that matched the tea set was sitting on the counter. As Alex grabbed the sugar bowl, she glanced around and admired the beautiful kitchen and family room. Everything was certainly in perfect order. Yvonne kept an immaculate and organized home.

Once Alex was seated again, Yvonne pointed out the different sandwich fillings. There was egg salad, a smoked salmon filling, cucumber with watercress, and chicken salad with cranberries. They all looked delicious, but Alex really wasn't very hungry after all that had happened. She took a square each of the smoked salmon and chicken salad sandwiches. Her hostess put one of each kind on her own plate and pressed cucumber and egg salad sandwiches on Alex. She relented, as Yvonne seemed eager to have her try a bit of everything. The older woman reminded Alex of her mother. At her mother's table, you would have food urged on you until you were ready to burst. It was a wonder their whole family hadn't been obese.

Once they were settled with their plates and cups filled, Yvonne seemed to relax. "What are your plans for the next few days?"

"Well, the store is open until two tomorrow. Hanna and I are having Tom Kennedy over for dinner. I'm still not certain what my plans are for Christmas Day. We were planning to go to Maggie and Drew's, but Drew became ill yesterday and had to go to the hospital. I'm not sure he'll be up to having company. What will you be doing?"

"I'll spend the holiday reading and listening to Christmas music. I don't have any close relations, so the day is quiet, much like every other day. Please don't look so sad. I'm quite content on my own." Yvonne took a dainty bite of a chicken salad sandwich.

"I assumed everyone likes to be around family at Christmas."

"I was an only child, and both my parents were only children. There really isn't any family to speak of. I do miss my parents, but generally, I prefer to be by myself. When my husband passed away, a great sense of relief filled me, though I do miss him, of course. But I found it rather trying to always be on call for someone else's whims and fancies. Now I do as I please, and I'm quite happy. Perhaps even more so than when I was married."

Yvonne took a scone and encouraged Alex to have one as well. "I made the jam myself. Black currant."

Alex definitely didn't feel like eating jam after what had happened to Drew, but she took a scone anyway to be polite and ladled a bit of jam on one half. She also took one of the petit fours and took a bite. "These are delicious. Do you make them yourself?"

"I made everything, except the Earl Grey tea, of course. Look, you haven't even touched your tea, and it's probably cold."

Yvonne made quite a fuss about getting her some more hot tea. While the older woman was in the kitchen, Alex quickly put a couple of her sandwiches and her scone in some tissues and slipped them into her purse. Yvonne had been so gracious; Alex didn't want her to be offended. Despite how good everything looked, Alex was too worried to enjoy it, as she kept thinking about the time she was wasting having tea instead of proving Gary was their killer.

When Yvonne returned, she seemed pleased to see Alex had eaten most of her food. "Please have some more."

Alex cautiously bit into a small piece of fruitcake, and it almost made her eyes water. The rum was so strong, the fumes alone might put her over the legal driving limit.

"That's one of my mother's recipes. The secret to the fruitcake is soaking the fruit in good-quality rum. I remember one year when I was a bit older, I kept eating the fruit that was soaking in the rum, and it wasn't long before I was quite tipsy. I thought Mother would be angry with me, but she just laughed. My parents were very good to me and gave me everything I wanted." Yvonne sighed.

Alex got up and went to a side table, where there was a small silver frame holding a photo of two adults and a young girl next to the picture she'd been shown previously. "Is this you with your parents?"

Yvonne smiled and had a faraway look in her eyes. "Yes. I was only about eight in that picture. It was taken on a sabbatical in Switzerland."

"You all look very happy. What was your maiden name?"

Yvonne upset her cup and spilled some of her tea in her saucer. "Oh, I'm so clumsy. I'll go get something to clean that up with."

While she went to the kitchen, Alex was curious if there was a date on the back of the photograph and quickly slid it out of the frame. On the back, it said, "Dad, Mum, and Vi, July 1952."

When Yvonne returned, Alex put the picture frame back on the table. "Actually, I must get going. Maggie came in this afternoon to help out, but I'm sure she wants to leave early and return to the hospital, so I should help Hanna close the store. Thank you so much for inviting me. This has been lovely." Alex grabbed her purse and got up from the sofa.

"Of course. Thank you for coming on such short notice. I'm sorry to hear about Mr. Fletcher. I hope he'll be all right. I'll wish you a merry Christmas, since it's unlikely we'll see each other again before tomorrow."

"Merry Christmas to you too."

The air was thick and heavy with the precipitation that had been promising to fall. The cold stung Alex's cheeks, and when she looked up at the sky, a few flakes of snow fell on her face. It was already getting dark, and Alex had to turn her car lights on. As she walked into the shop, she heard Hanna on the phone.

"She's here. I've got to go."

Alex walked into the main room to find Hanna sitting behind the counter. Watson was sleeping on her doggy bed on the floor at the end of the counter and opened one eye.

Hanna looked up from her phone. "How did that go?"

Alex raised her brows and looked around the store.

Hanna assured her, "There's no one here. It's been quiet the last half hour. I sent Maggie home a few minutes ago."

Alex took her coat off and put it over the back of a chair behind the counter. "It was interesting. First, let me take this out of my purse." She carefully pulled out the tissue containing the sandwiches and scone with jam.

"You didn't bring that back for me, did you?" Hanna had a horrified look on her face.

Alex laughed. "No, these are a bit squashed. But Yvonne wanted me to try everything. She's as bad as Mom. When she left the room for a minute, I put them in my purse so she'd think I ate them. The food looked delicious, but I wasn't that hungry, and I didn't want to offend her. She went to an awful lot of trouble." Alex recounted the last part of her visit and told Hanna about looking at the back of the picture of Yvonne with her parents.

"So the picture said Vi, not Yvonne?"

Alex nodded.

"What do you think that means?"

"I'm not sure. Maybe that was a nickname, or maybe she uses her middle name now. It's not that uncommon for someone to use a different first name than the one they used in childhood. No one calls me Alexandra except Mom."

"True. Duncan uses his middle name. His parents named him after one of Drew's brothers who died as a boy, Percy. Duncan made his family stop calling him Percy when he was seven or eight, right after he punched another boy at school for making fun of his name."

"Can I tease him about that?" Alex's lips twitched.

"I wouldn't if I were you. He's still pretty sensitive about it, and he might start writing speeding tickets on me if he finds out I told you."

Hanna had a heavy foot and would surely have lost her license if Duncan had written out a ticket every time he stopped her.

"Fair enough." Alex smiled.

"He stopped by shortly before you came back, and I gave him the journal. I pointed out the pages where Jane said she gave Zach the coins. He thinks all the charges will likely be dropped. Sheriff Summers won't be very happy about it, though."

"Good. I hope it wipes that smug expression off her face. Let's close up. I want to have a quick supper and then head over to Jane's. I'm determined to watch the rest of those true-crime shows tonight."

"Will you have time?"

"I'm going to try and find the ones from the night she wrote about it in her journal. If I fast-forward through all of them, then I might be able to. I'll stay up as late as I have to. But really, I'm not even sure it will help. Jane could have been as wrong this time as she was every other time."

Alex locked the door to the shop. "I think I'll go have a chat with Gary before I start watching those shows."

Hanna looked concerned. "Do you think that's a good idea? He could very well be a murderer. A serial killer, in fact."

"I'll make sure to tell him people know where I am. I have you in my contacts. If I feel in any danger, I can reach you with the press of a couple of buttons. If I don't respond, you can call Duncan to come check on me."

"I don't have a good feeling about this. Why don't I come with you? I was just going to help Maggie with her preparations for Christmas Day and then go home and make potato salad."

"That's silly. I'll be fine. It's not the first time I've spoken to him. I want to ask him about the bylaw thing and see if he seems really angry about it." Alex slapped her forehead. "I almost forgot to tell you. I think I might have figured out what Netta wanted to tell me." She explained her deductions after remembering Netta's words on the day Alex found Jane's body. "That could have been Gary who told her Jane was stabbed. He told me he was one of the neighbors gathered out on the street that morning."

"That does make sense. But now I'm even more sure you shouldn't go there alone." Hanna snapped her fingers. "I have an idea. Why don't you take Watson with you? I know she's a coward, but she looks fairly intimidating to anyone who doesn't know her."

Alex looked at the dog standing between them. The dog wore an adoring gaze. "Yeah, until she whimpers, runs away, and hides. But sure, I'll take her."

As Alex drove home, a light snow began to fall, like little frozen tears shed by all the angels in heaven. Inside, she turned on the Christmas lights and went upstairs to change into comfortable clothes.

Feeling much better in jeans and a sweater, Alex looked in her freezer for two individual containers of lasagna from the other night. She grabbed two slices of French bread and slathered them with butter and garlic and wrapped them in foil. She gathered everything up and put it in a basket.

While the dog was in the yard, she put fresh water and food in Watson's bowls. Her thoughts drifted back to Hanna hanging up the phone abruptly when she returned to the store after tea with Yvonne. Who had Hanna been talking to? And why did she need to hang up before Alex walked into the room? Maybe Hanna was still discussing a move back to Michigan and didn't want to upset Alex before the holiday.

She called the dog back inside and left her to eat while she headed out the back door.

Chapter
Thirty-Two

When Tom opened his sliding back door, Alex held out a basket with the containers of food. "I come bearing gifts."

Surprised, he took the food and stepped aside. "Bearers of food are always welcome. Well, maybe not all bearers of food."

Taking off her boots and coat, Alex focused on how wonderful it would be when the weather warmed up and they didn't have to wear all these heavy clothes.

"You'll need to supply the vegetables and the dessert. I only brought the main course, and a few cookies."

"Vegetables are not my favorite, but I have some carrot sticks in the fridge and apple crisp, courtesy of Mrs. Matthews. I'm definitely thinking of proposing to that woman. I could put up with the recital of her health issues in exchange for her cooking. The apple crisp cost me a discussion about bunions. Hers, not mine."

"I don't have bunions, though I did have a wart as a child, but I don't feel compelled to discuss it with you. Perhaps I should just tell you about my conversation with Louise."

Tom put the containers of lasagna into the microwave. "I'm sure it was far more interesting than any conversations I've had today."

As they ate dinner, Alex explained about her visit to the bakery. "Suffice it to say, Louise's past isn't littered with bodies, only a useless husband."

Tom seemed satisfied. "I never really thought she was a serial killer."

"Apparently, neither is Joe." Alex ran through her discovery of Joe's real name and his alibi for the evening of Jane's death. "I'm still assuming Netta's death wasn't an accident and is tied to Jane's, so if a suspect has an alibi for one, then they're cleared for both. Though I am willing to concede it's possible, however unlikely, that Netta's death was an accident. Hopefully, I'll find something in Jane's journal that points me in the right direction."

"Where is Hanna tonight?" Tom asked. "I hope you didn't leave her at home to fend for herself."

"She's at Maggie's helping with some of the preparations for Christmas. Hanna and I feel awful it was the jam that made Drew sick. That night you and I came back from Jane's, I actually saw the killer. I wish I'd gotten a better look. Of course, Gary's the only person left on our suspect list. It must have been him. It all fits. You know, he was telling me he's starting seedlings for deadly nightshade. I imagine it would be quite easy for him to have access to berries from that plant. He must be pure evil to have left that jam. Anyone could have eaten from it."

"If Gary was going to start seedlings, then he wouldn't have any berries yet. It takes a while to get to that stage; even I know that."

"Yes, but what if he has a mature plant? He does have a greenhouse, after all. He could even have the berries in his freezer. Who knows what's in his past."

The doorbell rang as Alex cleared the table. She looked at Tom. "I'm sure Penelope didn't see me come over."

Alex stayed in the kitchen until she heard Hanna's voice. "Maggie wanted me to run a plate over to you. She didn't know if you'd eaten yet. We've been making apple pies and prepping everything for the stuffing. Hi, Alex. I didn't know you were here." Hanna arched an eyebrow as Alex walked down the hall.

"Since I was eating alone, I decided Tom might want to have dinner with me. I've been telling him we're down to one suspect. In fact, we just finished dinner and I was going to head over to Jane's. Do you want to come?"

"We still aren't done over there." Hanna turned to Tom. "Maggie was wondering if you wanted to go visit Drew this evening, since we're busy with preparations. Duncan is planning to stop by the hospital as well, if he has time."

"I can do that, but is it a good idea that Alex goes to Jane's alone? There's still a killer out there."

"I know my sister, and she's going to do as she pleases."

"Hello. Your sister is standing right here. I'm an adult, and I'm not going to be chaperoned like a child who can't be left on her own."

"See? I told you." Hanna looked at Tom despairingly.

"There's a killer with no compunction about killing innocent bystanders," Alex said. "If it takes all night, I'm going to figure out who killed Jane and Netta. I'll have my phone with me, so please don't worry."

The snow was falling harder as Alex put an excited Watson in her car. There was already almost an inch on the driveway. Upon her return from Tom's, she'd taken Watson on a short walk. The dog had frolicked and played in the snow like a puppy. She would be ready for a nice, quiet evening, lying by Alex's feet on the sofa.

Pulling into Jane's driveway, Alex decided to take the bull by the horns and question Gary to see if she could get any more information from him.

With Watson's leash grasped firmly in her hand, Alex rang Gary's doorbell and wondered if she was going into a murderer's lair. At least Hanna and Tom knew where she was. If anything happened, it might be a while before anyone figured out something was wrong, but there was no question as to her plans for the evening.

"I'm counting on you to protect me, Watson." Alex looked into the quizzical stare of what amounted to a fifty-pound toddler.

Gary opened the door promptly and looked displeased to see Alex standing there. He glanced from dog to Alex. "What can I do for you?"

"I wanted to chat with you for a few minutes. Can I come in? This is Miss Watson, though we just call her Watson. She's very friendly."

Gary seemed to have dropped his usual cheerful veneer. He stepped aside, indicating she should enter. "I wasn't expecting visitors, so please excuse the mess."

She looked around the comfortable house. It wasn't messy; it just looked like Gary was in the middle of doing some transplanting on the kitchen counter. There were a couple of plants, gloves, a bag of potting soil, a beautiful blue-and-white ceramic planter, and a small spade laid out. Gary led the way to the living room adjoining the kitchen. As Alex sat on a chair, she glanced at the coffee table. On it was a book: *Death in the Garden: Poisonous Plants & Their Use throughout History* by Michael Brown.

Gary bent over to pet Watson. "I didn't know you have a dog."

Watson flopped down so Gary could rub her belly.

"She does seem very friendly."

So much for bringing Watson as a form of intimidation. If Gary offered her a treat, she'd probably help bury Alex's body in the backyard. Alex was suddenly questioning the wisdom of her decision to come here alone. "Hanna and I got her from a rescue shelter a couple years ago. When I told Hanna I was heading over here, she wanted me to tell you how lovely the poinsettia is looking." *There. Now he knows my whereabouts are known.* "Thank you again for offering to shovel Jane's walk. It looks like it's going to snow for a while."

"The forecast says it'll be snowing until tomorrow morning sometime. They're saying five to ten inches by the time it's done. But don't worry, the greenhouse is closed tomorrow, so I'll be looking for something to do." Gary got up and headed to the kitchen, Watson following close behind.

"It looks like you've got lots to do." Alex pointed to the plants on the counter.

"It's a peace lily I'm repotting for Yvonne. She admired them this past summer, so I'm giving her one for Christmas. I'm afraid I'm not much for baking cookies and such." Gary gave a self-deprecating laugh. "Can I get you some coffee? Would Watson like a cookie?"

Fat chance I'll take anything to eat or drink from you. "No, thank you. I'm fine, but I bet Watson would accept a small piece of cookie. Nothing chocolate, though." *He won't poison my dog, will he?* "What I really came to ask you about was the bylaw change Jane had proposed to the village council. Someone mentioned you were really upset about it, and I wondered if it would still go ahead now Jane's gone?"

Gary's jaw clenched, as though he was trying to conceal his impatience. "I'm not sure if the council will move forward or not.

Jane raised the issue, so without her here to pursue it, I'll make a case against it. I doubt anyone else has the interest to carry it forward."

"Do you mind telling me what exactly the issue was?"

"In a nutshell, Jane suggested the shed I'm using to store pesticides and fertilizer can be accessed by almost anyone because the door and lock are so flimsy. She said if a child ever got in there, it could be a dangerous situation. She suggested I build a more stable structure that can be properly secured. She was right to an extent, but it would take a fairly determined child to get in there."

"So you were angry about her interfering, then?"

"I was. It would be a significant expense, where there's relatively small risk. I may have been a little hard on her, and I feel bad about that now."

"You sound as if you have experience with the law. What did you do before you moved here?"

"You don't give up, do you?" His eyes were like chips of ice. "I prefer not to talk about my life before I moved here. I left it behind for a reason, and quite frankly, it's none of your business." Gary's response was curt, and he abruptly headed toward the door, Watson following.

Alex was beginning to notice she was quickly wearing out her welcomes in the village. "That looks like an interesting book." She pointed to the one on the coffee table.

"Yvonne lent it to me, and what I've read so far is very interesting." Gary scowled and was obviously waiting for her to leave. "I'll make sure Jane's snow is shoveled in the morning. The snow seems to be falling even harder now."

As she headed to the door, she glanced over at the kitchen counter again. Sitting off to the side, slightly obscured by the bag of potting soil, if she wasn't mistaken, was a deadly nightshade plant. She recognized it from the sketches on the poison poster at the shop. When she turned back toward the door, Gary was watching her; he had probably seen her glance at the plant.

Outside, the large, fat flakes were coming down quickly, obscuring her view across the street except for pinpoints of blurry colored lights. If the wind picked up, this would be a full-fledged blizzard.

Watson had been reluctant to leave Gary's and was definitely skittish entering Jane's dark house. Alex locked the door behind them. She stomped her feet on the entryway rug and tried to shake off the worst of the snow that had accumulated on her hair as Watson did her own burst of shaking. Pausing to turn up the heat, Alex went to the kitchen to start the kettle boiling for tea. She got a bowl from the cupboard and put water out for Watson. In the living room, Alex turned on the television. As she was heading back to the kitchen, her cell rang. Alex frowned. Hanna was checking up on her.

"Hi there, I'm putting you on speaker. I'm making tea." Alex set her phone on the counter. "Have you seen the snow? We're going to be buried by tomorrow morning."

"I know. I just got home from Maggie's. We were done, and she was going to call Tom and tell him to head home. I wanted to make sure you were safe. How's Watson doing?"

"She's listening to every word, so don't accidentally mention what you got her for Christmas." Alex smiled at the dog, who cocked her head as if she understood what they were saying. "Listen, I have some news. I went to see Gary, and he wasn't particularly friendly." Alex quickly apprised Hanna of the conversation she'd had with Gary. "Why would he be so reticent about his background if he isn't the killer? And he's obviously very interested in poisonous plants. There was a deadly night-shade plant on his kitchen counter, and he didn't seem pleased when I saw it. How do we prove he's the killer?"

"More to the point, how do we keep you safe? Gary's behavior is very suspicious, and he's our only suspect now. Plus, Duncan called. He got Netta's toxicology results. She ate a chocolate containing powdered foxglove before she fell down the stairs. The one on the counter was filled with the same mixture as what they found in Netta's stomach. Even if she hadn't fallen down the stairs, she probably would have died. Someone wanted her dead."

Alex poured her tea. "Great. Now I'll be a suspect in her murder as well. Don't worry about me. I'll be fine. I've got Watson here." She gave the dog a pat. "The doors are locked, and there's no spare key floating around anymore. I'm going through all of those true-crime episodes. Better that one of us stays home."

When Hanna tried to argue, Alex interrupted, "I'll be fine. I can call you with a couple of taps to my phone. Don't worry. Nothing is going to happen."

Alex hung up and had a thought. She quickly dialed Tom's number, but it went straight to voice mail. He was probably driving. When the beep sounded, she left a message. She put her phone down and got her tea. In the living room, she grabbed a blanket that was lying across the end of the sofa and put it over her legs. Watson snuggled into it and promptly fell asleep. There were a number of things niggling at Alex's mind.

Looking at her watch, she knew it was time to start watching those shows. She turned on an episode taped the day Jane recognized a murderer living in the village. As Alex watched, paying attention to the beginning of each show to see if it held promise and then fast-forwarding if not, she got out the copied pages of Jane's journal and started reading.

Chapter
Thirty-Three

On Saturday, December fifth, nine days before her death, Jane wrote: *Gary is obviously still annoyed with me. I brought him a freshly baked loaf of bread with some of my herb butter as a peace offering, but he barely opened the door and was quite abrupt with me.*

On Wednesday, December ninth, Jane wrote a short entry: *Told Netta my suspicion that a murderer I'd seen on a true-crime episode was living in Harriston. She laughed and said I was being ridiculous. She insisted I tell her who it was, but I told her that after she laughed at me, there was no way I'd tell her my suspicions. Knowing Netta, I'm certain she'll share that with everyone. Then, if I'm right, the killer will have to do something and I'll know. I'll have to stay sharp. I'll talk to Alex on Monday at the book club meeting about it.*

Jane had been playing a dangerous game, hoping to taunt a killer into exposing himself. *Oh, Jane. If only you'd confided in me sooner.*

Later that week, on Friday, December eleventh, Jane wrote: *Yvonne invited me over for tea this afternoon. I declined. Instead, she gave me a tin of tea she'd made. She has always been extremely boastful of her skills with herbs and plants. If I hear one more time how her sainted mother taught her all about the plants in their woods and their garden. . . . It must drive her absolutely mad I was voted president of the horticultural society. I'm sure it was her that cut off the heads of all my flowers the summer I was voted president, though I have no proof.*

Jane's final entry on Monday, December fourteenth, read: *I know I'm right about my suspicions. It all fits. Alex will confirm it tomorrow when she watches the true-crime episode.*

As Watson snored, Alex turned things over in her mind. Whoever had killed Jane had to have known where the spare key was hidden. Gary had certainly known.

Gary had tried sneaking into Jane's house on at least one occasion, and Alex had found him peeking into the window. Then there was the deadly nightshade plant on his kitchen counter. Could he have made the jam? Alex remembered she'd seen Gary with an ice pick at the greenhouse. Could that be the murder weapon?

They knew the murderer had to have moved to Harriston in the past ten years or so. Yvonne had implied she had lived in Harriston a very long time, but after hearing her recount her history to the clerk, Alex wondered what the truth was.

Alex thought back to her visits to Yvonne's home and her feeling last time that something was off. Thinking back over each room, it dawned on her there weren't any pictures of Yvonne's husband anywhere. All the pictures were of her or her parents. Yvonne had a close bond with her mother in particular. Jane had implied that Yvonne spoke about her mother ad nauseam, the mother who had taught her about plants and herbs.

Gary had said Yvonne grew a number of poisonous plants in her greenhouse. She also made jam. She had tried to get Alex to eat her black-currant jam earlier today. Had been quite insistent about it.

Things were starting to click in Alex's mind. The Tuesday Alex found Jane's body, Yvonne had said she was going to Lavish Locks. Later that day, Netta had come in and said she'd been to Lavish Locks. What if they'd been there together and it was Yvonne who had told Netta that Jane had been stabbed?

On Friday Alex had her hair done, and Tanya said she and her family were leaving for the cabin in Whitefish right after she closed the next day. The day Netta died.

Tanya couldn't have been doing Yvonne's hair Saturday evening. That meant Yvonne had lied.

When all these things were put together, what made the most sense? Could Yvonne have been physically capable of killing Jane and Netta?

Character. It had to be Yvonne. Didn't it?

Alex hoped Tom would call her back with the answer to her question.

Alex turned to the television. The reenactment showed an actor portraying an older man, Larry Huston, who had been diagnosed with cancer. Though the prognosis had been excellent and he was in good health, he declined rapidly and, despite the doctors' efforts, died quickly.

The husband's adult children from an earlier marriage were suspicious, as the wife was quite a bit younger and there was a substantial amount of money involved.

It was discovered the victim had been poisoned with a plant found in the wife's greenhouse. Unfortunately, the wife had fled at the first hint of trouble. Upon further investigation, they discovered three previous marriages and three sudden deaths, though all had been attributed to natural causes.

The investigators were eventually able to get exhumation orders, and autopsies were performed. Many months later, it was confirmed that all three men had been poisoned with a variety of deadly plants. There had been significant financial gain involved with the death of each husband.

With no luck finding the wife, the investigators had decided to put out an appeal on the true-crime show, hoping someone would recognize her from the one picture they had obtained. She had always claimed to be camera shy.

A very out-of-focus picture of the real wife was on the screen, taken when she was fifty-nine. She would be in her seventies now. The usual cautions were issued that she could be dangerous and not to approach her but to call the number on the screen, or the FBI.

Alex looked at the coffee table to grab her phone and remembered she had left it in the kitchen when she was making tea. Gently dislodging Watson, Alex swung her legs off the sofa and was about to stand up when she got a shock that sent her heart racing.

Dressed in a parka and heavy boots, Yvonne was standing in the dining room, staring at the television.

Looking at the older woman, Alex understood how accurate the warning was. While the picture on the television was an extremely poor likeness, there was no doubt in Alex's mind that the woman in the photograph and the woman standing in Jane's dining room were one and the same.

"Not a very good picture. You really can't even tell it's me. It was one of the very few taken during my marriage to Larry. I destroyed most of them, but those darn children of his had that one. I really hated those children," Yvonne said as calmly as if she were offering tea.

Alex thought she heard a sound on the front porch, but it was probably the wind that had picked up and was now howling outside, no doubt creating blizzard-like conditions. "How did you get in here? I'm sure the door was locked."

"It was, but I happen to have a key." Yvonne held up a shiny, silver key. "I had this cut a week and a half ago. It's come in quite handy."

"You were in here this week. The things on Jane's desk were moved. I noticed it the next day."

"Yes. I had a nasty surprise when I found you going into Jane's house Monday evening. I thought I would have lots of time to look for Jane's journal. I had no idea her attorney was going to give you a key, and I needed to find the journal before you did. I searched for it the night I killed Jane, but I had no idea where she kept it. Is that how you found out it was me?" Yvonne's quiet voice was full of hatred.

"To be honest, I wasn't sure you were the killer until tonight. Jane never said who she suspected in her journal." A surge of anger coursed through her veins. "When I realized you couldn't have gotten your hair done the night Netta was killed, I suspected it was you. After all, you had your hair done earlier that week. I remembered you had been off to a hair appointment when you stopped in the book shop the day I found Jane's body."

"You must have known. The fact you're still alive tells me you figured out I'd poisoned the cucumber sandwiches and jam at tea this afternoon. You should be dead by now. How did you dispose of them?" Yvonne snapped.

"I didn't know they were poisoned. I just wasn't hungry but I didn't want to offend you, so I wrapped them in a tissue and put them in my purse while you got more tea."

"Aren't you lucky?" she sneered. "I knew I was taking a risk, inviting you to tea on such short notice, but I overheard you'd found Jane's journal. I was afraid she might have mentioned me, so I needed to act quickly. Not my best work, obviously."

A Christmas Candy Killing

"You left the gift basket on my doorstep with jam and scones. Poisoned jam." Alex clenched her fists.

Yvonne stood motionless, her hand wrapped tightly around the cap of her walking stick. "Yes. You were asking too many questions, so I decided to give you a merry little surprise. But it was taking too long. I needed you out of the way. The sheriff's department had Zach locked up, and even if they couldn't prove he murdered Jane, they would always have suspected him."

Alex's eyes flashed. "An innocent man ended up being poisoned by that jam. He's in the hospital right now because of you."

"Collateral damage. If that meddlesome woman had minded her own business, none of this would have happened. But Jane was always looking to be the best, to find out everyone's secrets. She watched those true-crime shows in the hopes of catching a real murderer. I could have just poisoned her with the chocolates I left on her doorstep, but I wanted the satisfaction of watching her die. It was her own fault I had to kill her. It's really Jane's fault you have to die as well."

"What about Netta? Why did she have to die?"

"That halfwit was worse than Jane. She actually thought she should be the next president of the horticultural society. Can you imagine? I am obviously the most knowledgeable person in this village about plants. I should have been president all along.

"That twit couldn't stop laughing at the absurdity of Jane suspecting another person from a true-crime show at the post office. When I was at Lavish Locks the morning you found Jane, Netta was there as well. We were talking about Jane's death, and I inadvertently said Jane had been stabbed. But you and the sheriff's department were the only ones aware of that. A few days later, Netta recognized my mistake. She asked me how I'd known, and I made up an excuse. I think she believed me, but I knew

267

I had to keep her from telling you. I was there at the bookshop when Maggie said Netta wanted you to come by so she could tell you something. Saturday, shortly after she came home, I brought her a couple of the chocolates you'd given me, only I'd replaced some of the filling with a mixture of powdered foxglove. She said it tasted bitter, but she ate it anyway, the fool. The poison took effect more quickly than I expected. I had a terrible time getting her up the stairs so I could push her down. Even if the fall hadn't killed her, the poison would have before anyone found her. Better to tie off loose ends." Yvonne looked at Alex pointedly.

Chapter
Thirty-Four

Yvonne was holding her cane and lightly tapping it on the floor. Alex had never really looked at it closely. It was quite attractive, with a black tapered hardwood shaft and topped with a hammered silver cap.

Yvonne unscrewed the cap of her cane and brandished a very dangerous-looking stiletto knife. The type of knife the ME said would have created the stab wounds in Jane. "Unfortunately, you too are a loose end."

Alex stood rigid. "Why did you have to kill her? You could have just left. You've done that before."

Yvonne's face grew tight, and her lips stretched into a snarl. "Because I hated her! That woman is to blame for all of this." She made a sweeping gesture with the knife. "I enjoyed keeping this with me as a reminder, even while the deputies questioned me." She gently stroked the blade.

"You wanted to poison her first, didn't you? She wrote in her journal that you invited her to tea a few days before you killed her." Alex tried to take tiny sideways steps around the coffee table, moving surreptitiously toward the front door.

Yvonne pointed at Watson sleeping quietly on the sofa. "Don't do anything stupid, dear. You wouldn't want something unfortunate to happen to your dog."

"You better be careful. She's a vicious animal," Alex warned, at the same moment Watson chose to awaken.

Watson took one look at Yvonne, whimpered, and buried her head under the blanket she had been lying on.

"Very vicious, obviously." Yvonne slowly walked in front of the living room door, preventing Alex from moving any farther. "Yes, if Jane had accepted my invitation to tea, I could have given her one of my special tea blends, but she refused to come to my home. It would have been much simpler that way, but Mother taught me you need to improvise when things don't work out the way you want them to. I knew where that spare key was kept. I'd watched Zach get it several times while I worked in my greenhouse. All I had to do was retrieve it Saturday night and take it into Kalispell to have a copy made early on Sunday and return it Sunday night."

"You made a mistake, though. One I'm surprised someone as knowledgeable as you would make. Jane's poinsettia was sitting right there." Alex pointed to the coffee table. "You wanted to have an alibi, so you left the door to the house open for several hours. It cooled the house and Jane's body faster, making it seem she died earlier in the evening while you were at the horticultural meeting. But poinsettias are sensitive to the cold, and so it began to lose its leaves. That bothered me all along. You also didn't realize Oliver, Jane's neighbor in the back, was watching you come and go that night. He's already told the police, by the way. You'll be arrested anytime."

Yvonne looked tense, ready to spring, as she paced back and forth. "Thanks to you and your meddlesome friend, I'm going to have to move again. I'd really gotten to like this little village. I was happy here, and frankly, I'm getting too old to keep moving."

"Why was the front door unlocked the morning after you killed Jane?"

"I knew that would make it seem the killer came and went that way. I hoped it would make them think it was a robbery. It turned out wonderfully when they suspected Zach. His showing up the next morning was fortunate and entirely unplanned. You should have stayed out of it."

As the older woman paced, Alex moved closer to the living room door again.

Yvonne stopped pacing. "Don't bother. You're not getting away this time. I'm a lot stronger and faster than I look. I never needed this cane." She leaned the shaft against the wall. "I just wanted people to think I was a weak, old lady. No one ever suspects people my age are capable of something like this. Now, I'm going to give you a choice. You may drink my special tea, or I can stab you with this knife. Personally, I'd prefer you drink the tea. Stabbings are so messy."

Alex knew she wasn't going to get any closer to the door. Her eyes searched for something she could use as a weapon and landed on the umbrella stand the trauma cleanup company had left beside the television. Thankfully, Alex had forgotten to put it back in the hall, and now several sturdy umbrellas were within grasp. "You know, given the choice, I think I'll take the tea. Shall I sit here while you prepare it?"

"You're amusing. Let's go in the kitchen, and I'll tell you how to make it." Yvonne gestured for Alex to go ahead of her as she brandished the knife.

Before she could move, Alex's phone rang in the kitchen. Alex froze. "That will be Duncan. I called him earlier and told him my suspicions. If I don't answer, he'll be here in minutes. You should run. You might even get away."

Yvonne laughed derisively. "What do you take me for? I don't think you really had any idea I was behind all this. If it wasn't for sheer dumb luck, you'd be dead from those poisons I served at tea."

Alex ignored the intended insult and, with mounting courage, said, "You've obviously been poisoning people for a long time. Why did you kill your husbands? Was it for the money?"

Yvonne looked intently at Alex, perhaps to judge whether Alex was putting off the inevitable or genuinely wanted to know. Yvonne's narcissistic side won out, and she finally answered. "My first husband didn't treat me well. He expected me to be little more than a slave, looking after him, cooking and cleaning. Then one day he had the nerve to tell me I was spending too much time looking after my plants, and he actually threw several of them in the garbage!" A vein throbbed in her temple. "Several months later, I gave him a special dinner, and he got very ill and died. So sad." Her eyes glinted. "Fortunately, he had a large life insurance policy. I moved back home to live with my parents and was happy. Unfortunately, my parents both died within three years. My second and third husbands didn't make me happy. But the money they left me when I helped them out of this world certainly did."

Alex's phone had stopped ringing. She hoped whoever had called would realize something was wrong when she didn't answer.

Yvonne continued more brusquely. "By that time, I was really quite rich, but I still thought I needed a husband to feel complete. After all, my parents had had a very happy marriage, and I wanted that too." Yvonne sighed. "Things were going so well with Larry, except for his miserable children, of course, but we'd moved away and hardly ever saw them. Then"—she pointed vaguely toward the television—"he was diagnosed with cancer. Even though the doctor said he had an excellent chance of recovering, there would have been surgery and then chemotherapy. It would have been so hard on him. I knew the right thing to do was help him avoid all that."

Alex strained to hear any noise coming from outside to suggest there was anyone nearby. But the wind was howling and pelting the snow against the windows, making it impossible to hear anything. Yvonne was obviously very disturbed, and it wasn't likely Alex would be able to reason with her. She now understood what Jane had seen in Yvonne's character. Yvonne was selfish and petty and couldn't stand to see someone else have what she wanted.

Yvonne now had a slight edge to her voice. "If it wasn't for his nosy children, I'm sure it would never have caught the attention of the police. Fortunately, I knew they suspected something, so I was able to disappear again and come here. By then, I knew I was destined to be alone. I was never going to recapture the life I'd had with my parents, but I certainly had enough money to live very comfortably. I settled down and was quite content until that nosy woman ruined it all." Yvonne's voice had become bitter, and she gripped the stiletto tightly. "All right. That's enough distraction. It's time to go have your tea. Move!" She indicated Alex was to walk past her through the dining room.

Alex took a step the other way. "I think I've changed my mind." Alex sprang within reach of the umbrella stand and snatched a particularly long, sturdy-looking instrument and brandished it in front of her like a sword. "I think I'll take my chances with the knife after all."

Yvonne's face changed into a grotesque expression of rage. She lunged at Alex, who managed to jump out of the way, and Yvonne, caught off balance, stumbled and knocked an antique vase off a side table. She was fast to recover, though, and lunged at Alex again, who just barely moved out of the way of the blade. They continued to do a dance, as Yvonne lunged and Alex jumped out of the way. The fourth time, Alex wasn't quite quick enough, and the knife nicked her. A warm trickle of blood began running down her arm.

Yvonne moved in quickly to thrust the knife at her again, but this time Alex parried and managed to crash the umbrella down on Yvonne's arm. Yvonne was so shocked she almost dropped her knife, but a second later, she came at Alex like a wild animal. Determined, Alex kept beating her back with the umbrella. In turn, Yvonne thrust and swung the cruel-looking stiletto and almost managed to stab Alex.

Without any warning, Watson sprang from the sofa and, with a low growl, lunged at Yvonne and knocked her over. The knife fell from Yvonne's grasp. Watson stood over her and growled menacingly as Yvonne tried unsuccessfully to reach the stiletto.

A second later, there was a loud crash of glass at the front door, and Gary rushed into the room with a shovel, closely followed by Tom, waving a snow brush.

Yvonne scrambled to get up, but Gary held the shovel over her while Tom indicated that Alex should step behind him. Yvonne made one more desperate attempt to retrieve the knife.

Breathlessly, Gary said, "Don't even think about touching that knife! I've called the sheriff. They'll be here in a few minutes. If you move, I swear I'll bring this down on your head."

Alex called Watson, who promptly ran and hid behind her legs, quivering.

Seeing Gary looming over her, Yvonne sank back to the floor and began to whimper. "I think my arm is broken. We were about to have tea when this madwoman and her dog attacked me."

Gary repositioned his hands on the shovel to get a better grip. "I watched you sneak in the back door. Then I moved to the front porch. I was watching through the curtains. I saw you attack Alex with the knife, so save your old-lady routine for the sheriff. Are you okay, Alex?"

Alex peered out from behind Tom's protective stance. "I'm fine, but how did you know to follow Yvonne?"

"I told you, I'd been keeping an eye out for Jane. I've been watching Yvonne for a long time, ever since I saw her cut the heads off all of Jane's flowers after Jane was elected president of the horticultural society. I was in my kitchen cleaning up the mess from the plant I repotted, and I saw Yvonne sneak through my backyard. I watched her unlock the back door of Jane's house and go inside. I ran to the front porch to see what she was up to."

"I knew I heard a sound on the porch earlier," Alex said.

"When I saw her pull out that knife, I ran back to my house and grabbed the shovel and called the sheriff's office. I came back just as Tom pulled up in front of my house. I told him what was going on, and we both ran to the window and saw her lunging at you. I tried the door, but it was locked, so I had to break the glass, and Tom quickly reached in and unlocked the door. Sorry we took so long, but you seem to have managed."

Sirens sounded in the distance. Tom continued to hold the snow brush as if he wanted to give Yvonne a good thumping with it. Soon Duncan and several other deputies arrived and took Yvonne into custody as she continued to accuse Alex and Watson of attacking her.

Alex had Duncan watch the true-crime show that featured Yvonne, also known as Kathryn Huston and Olivia Doss. Sheriff Summers eventually arrived. Travel was being hampered by what had become a raging blizzard. The sheriff, to Alex's satisfaction, seemed relatively unhappy, considering the resolution of two murders and Drew's poisoning.

Jane's house was once more a crime scene, and Alex, Tom, and Gary went to Gary's house for cups of hot chocolate as Watson sat at Gary's feet and enjoyed a nice piece of steak. Paramedics had fixed up Alex's arm with a few butterfly bandages.

"Gary, I have to ask, why are you so secretive about your past? I thought you were Jane's killer until earlier tonight."

Pressing his lips together, Gary's gaze traveled to the ceiling before resting on Alex and Tom. Reluctantly, he said, "Please keep this to yourselves. I moved here after retiring as a criminal lawyer. I represented a murderer in one of my final cases. During the course of the defense, my client told me about another murder he'd committed but hadn't been caught for. He told me where the body was buried, but to be honest, I didn't believe him. Nonetheless, I went and dug where he'd said the body was, and I found it. I had to leave it there, and I couldn't reveal what he'd told me because of attorney-client privilege. In time, the body was discovered, and the fact I'd known about it. I was arrested and disbarred. I fought the disbarment and won. The court concluded I'd done the right thing, and I was reinstated. It was a key case in upholding attorney-client privilege. Unfortunately, people weren't so forgiving. I debated moving away and opening a new office, but in the end, I decided to retire and do something far less stressful. I won't bother you with any further details, but that's why I don't want any publicity. I hope you'll respect that and this will stay between the four of us." Gary looked at Watson.

Alex apologized for giving Gary a hard time and thanked them all for saving her life. The men both blushed with embarrassment, but Watson had fallen asleep.

Chapter Thirty-Five

Alex and Hanna had disagreed over whether Alex should go to work in the morning. Hanna had wanted Alex to stay home and rest, and Alex hadn't wanted to leave Hanna alone on Christmas Eve, the last shopping day before Christmas. They had agreed to a compromise. Alex would go home an hour early, at one.

Alex had managed to go to sleep the moment her head hit the pillow, despite the excitement of the evening. She woke with her alarm at seven and was in the kitchen forty-five minutes later ready to make something for breakfast. The doorbell interrupted her perusal of the refrigerator.

Tom and Maggie were at the door with their arms full of tin-foil containers. Maggie had made a breakfast of scrambled eggs, bacon, sausage, and pancakes.

Tom gently guided Alex onto a stool at her kitchen island and gazed at her for a moment. He whispered, "I want to talk to you alone later. I have something I want to ask you."

Alex would bet her bacon Tom was planning to ask her on a date, but she didn't have time to linger on that thought, as Maggie was bustling around the kitchen, asking where things were.

Hanna and Watson joined them as Tom and Maggie served up breakfast.

Once they all had their plates full, Tom explained how he had come to be involved in the previous evening's excitement. "Alex called me last night while I was driving home, but I didn't dare answer the phone; the roads were terrible. I listened to the message when I got home and went over to Maggie's. I asked her Alex's question—if she knew exactly when Yvonne moved to Harriston. After some debate, we called Drew, who said it was about ten years ago. Maggie and I both thought it had been longer than that, but Drew said he'd been in charge of researching her family for the *History of Harriston* update. He didn't suggest her as a suspect because she'd been very forthcoming about her background for the book, and there wasn't anything suspicious about her. Plus, he was convinced she was too old to have killed Jane—"

Alex interrupted, "Yvonne, no doubt, gave Drew a completely made-up past. I overheard her telling the clerk in the Black Currant the exact same story she'd told me about her move to Harriston. I knew it sounded odd, memorized, but didn't put it all together until last night. I can't believe after our discussion about women murderers, Drew never told us!"

"Oh, he'll be hearing about that for a long time to come," Maggie warned.

Alex looked at Tom. "How did you know to come to Jane's last night?"

"When I called to give you that information and you didn't answer, I called Hanna and explained about your message. She said her twintuition was telling her you were in trouble and there had to be something wrong if you weren't answering. I hopped back in my truck and got over there as fast as I could. That's when I saw Gary on his porch, and, well, you know the rest."

Alex still couldn't believe Watson had saved her life. She had looked at her arm in the shower this morning and thanked her lucky stars she had only a small cut to remind her of what had happened. "Maggie, will Drew be coming home today? Have you heard anything?"

"I called the hospital this morning. As soon as I can safely make the drive to Swanson, I can pick him up."

The blizzard had stopped, though it would take time to get all the roads plowed. Alex and Hanna decided to open as usual, even though it wasn't likely to be busy.

* * *

After shoveling the snow from the sidewalk in front of the shop, the sisters sat on the bench in the bay window, drinking tea and looking at the picture-perfect view.

Hanna admitted, "I was so worried about you last night. I had a feeling something bad was going to happen."

"It all turned out all right. And I want you to know, if you want to move back to Frankenmuth and work for Mom, I'll understand."

Hanna looked at her in openmouthed amazement. "What are you talking about?"

"I'm not an idiot. I've seen your notes and overheard parts of your conversations. You've been talking to Mom and trying to keep it from me. It's okay. I want you to be happy, even if it means I lose my favorite chocolatier."

"You may have solved two murders, but you have no clue in this case. Mom wanted to send you a special gift and didn't want you to know about it in advance. We've been discussing how best to get it here. I ended up telling her to courier it to Maggie's house."

Alex felt like an idiot, again. "Will you tell me what it is?"

"Nope. You have to open it tonight when we're videoconferencing with Mom."

The front door jingled, and Duncan came into the shop.

"Hi, ladies." Duncan had dark circles under his eyes, but he seemed to be in good humor. "I'm surprised to see you here this morning, Alex. But it saves me making two stops. I just wanted to let you know Yvonne, or rather Olivia, still hasn't said anything, other than asking for a lawyer. She gave up trying to blame you"—Duncan looked at Alex—"for attacking her after we told her we had a search warrant and were heading to her house and greenhouse. We've contacted the FBI, and we'll be coordinating with them regarding the other murders she's suspected of."

"That's wonderful. I'm so glad this is finally over and Jane's and Netta's killer is behind bars. It's great that Zach's name has been cleared in time for Christmas."

"I appreciate what you two did, but you need to leave investigations to the sheriff's department from now on. Okay?"

Alex and Hanna glanced at each other and smiled. The door jingled again as a customer entered.

Oliver stood awkwardly in the doorway. "Say, I was wondering if Hanna could help me find a good book to read over the holidays."

Hanna grinned. "I'll be right with you."

Alex watched Duncan, who got a funny look on his face. He stared at Hanna for a moment before he turned and headed to the door. "Merry Christmas," he said in a subdued voice.

"Merry Christmas!" Alex and Hanna said in unison.

Eyes alight with mischief, Alex said, "This is the first time there's been a murder in Harriston in over a hundred years. What are the chances we'll have another one in our lifetimes?"

Recipes

Hand-Molded Chocolate Recipes
(Absolutely no poison to be used!!!!)

PREPARATION

Tools:

Digital kitchen scale (with metric readings)
Digital thermometer
Glass or plastic bowls
Bench scraper
Silicone spatulas
Disposable plastic piping bag
Polycarbonate plastic molds (mine are from Amazon)
Gloves
Wax paper

* * *

Gather All Your Tools

Your work surface should be clean and dry. Cover the surface with wax paper. I like to weigh out all my ingredients and have them in small bowls beforehand for the ganache.

283

Prepare Your Molds and Temper Your Chocolate

Ensure your molds have been wiped clean with a paper towel or soft cloth and are free of any residue. DO NOT touch the inside of your molds with your ungloved hands; you will leave fingerprints that will mar your finished chocolates. Also ensure your molds are completely dry. Seriously, water is your mortal enemy in the chocolate-making process. Even a drop of water can ruin all your hard work.

Your house should be about 18 degrees Celsius/64 degrees Fahrenheit if possible. If it is much warmer, your chocolate will not set properly. (Found this out the hard way the first time. Had to move the chocolates all around the house and into the fridge briefly on and off. Such a headache.) Ideally, you do not want to put your chocolates in the fridge, as this can cause moisture issues. Remember, water is not your friend. So put on a warm sweater and lower your thermostat or turn up the air conditioning, depending on the season.

We will be using the microwave method of tempering chocolate. Pour about 300g of Bernard Callebaut chocolate Callets (or if using a slab, first chop what you need into small pieces) into a glass or plastic bowl. You can use other good-quality chocolate, but this is not the place to skimp. Quality counts. For Poison Pear Ganache, use dark chocolate with a three-drop fluidity for the mold. For Candy Cane Coniine, use white chocolate with a three-drop fluidity for the mold.

Microwave for 30 seconds; take out and stir. Microwave for 20 seconds and stir. Repeat until most but not all of your chocolates are melted. Don't overheat; better to microwave in shorter bursts. This doesn't take long. When most of the chocolate is melted, stir, stir, and stir some more (about 2 minutes). Movement is essential in the tempering process, as is not melting all the chocolate in the bowl in the microwave. If you accidentally do that, just add a few solid Callets to the mixture and stir until they're melted.

For white chocolate, you need the tempered chocolate to be 29C/84F, and for dark chocolate you need it to be about 31C/87.8F, before coating your molds. Use your thermometer to check the temperature. At the appropriate temperature, a metal spatula coated with chocolate and placed on the counter should be solid in about 1 minute.

Heat your molds briefly with a heat gun—I use an embossing heat gun from my card-making days (a blow dryer will work in a pinch). The molds should be about 2 to 4 degrees cooler than your chocolate.

Pour the tempered chocolate into the mold. Keep your mold tilted at an angle over your bowl. Use your bench scraper and scrape off the excess from the top and sides of the mold back into the bowl. Tap the sides of the mold with the handle of your bench scraper. Then tap the mold on the counter. You want to ensure you get any air bubbles out.

Turn your mold upside down over the bowl so the excess chocolate can drip out. Tap the sides of the mold. Scrape again while the mold is upside down. Place the mold upside down on the wax paper for about 5 minutes. Then pick up one end (but keep it upside down) and scrape again onto the wax paper. You want a nice clean edge on the chocolates. Place the mold upright on the counter or in a cool place, 18 C/64F, for 5 to 10 minutes.

Make Your Ganache

See recipes and instructions after the sealing instructions.

Seal the Chocolates

Once your chocolates have been filled and set, you are ready to seal your chocolates. Have your tempered chocolate ready. Follow the same tempering instructions as above, but you won't need quite as much chocolate. You can just add some new Callets to the leftover chocolate from filling the molds, but ensure you follow all the steps properly.

Briefly heat the filled shells with the heat gun. This will allow the sealing chocolate to stick to the shells. Apply your chocolate over the shells—not too much, but ensure each shell is completely covered. Scrape the mold.

Tap the mold on the counter and check for air bubbles. Add more chocolate and repeat if necessary. Store at 18C/64F for at least 2 hours.

Ensure you have a completely clean work surface and cover it with clean wax paper. You are going to flip your mold over quickly and give it a gentle crack onto the wax paper to unmold it. If some shells stick, move your mold to a free spot on the wax paper and repeat, giving the mold a good crack on the counter, but not so hard you'll break the mold. (And watch that stray fingers don't get caught between the counter and the mold. Yes. Did that.)

Use gloves to turn over the chocolates and put them in containers. I use cookie tins.

Store them at cool room temperature, away from humidity and light, for up to 3 to 4 weeks for the Candy Cane Coniine. The Poison Pear Ganache should be stored for only 1 to 2 weeks.

Check out the tutorials at BernardCallebaut.com to see how the experts make hand-molded chocolates.

Cleaning Your Molds

Don't use soap and water. Ideally, you will wash your molds only once or twice a year with hot water. Wipe the insides of the shells dry so there is no residue from the water. Normally, you can heat them briefly in the microwave and wipe them clean with a paper towel or a soft cloth. Remember, no ungloved fingers inside the mold. Ensure molds are clean and dry before using them again.

Candy Cane Coniine Ganache

Makes 30–40 bonbons (depending on size)
250g white-chocolate Callets (three-drop fluidity) for ganache
125g heavy cream or whipping cream (it should be about
    35% fat)
1 tablespoon white corn syrup
30g unsalted butter, room temperature
3/4 teaspoon peppermint extract
1 six-inch candy cane, finely crushed

Place the pieces of white chocolate in a glass bowl. Ensure you use the right type of chocolate, as discussed in the instructions for tempering chocolate.

Heat the cream and corn syrup in a small saucepan over low/medium heat until very hot but not boiling. Pour the cream mixture over the chocolates and use a spatula to push down the chocolate so it is covered by the cream mixture. Wait a minute or two and then start mixing from the center of the bowl, using small circles at first and slowly moving outward.

Keep the temperature of the ganache around 34–40C/93–104F while mixing so the chocolate will all melt. (I don't check the temperature; as long as everything is melting, it should be good.) You can use a heat gun or put the mixture in the microwave, very briefly, to warm it up if needed. Work quickly. The mixture should have a pudding-like consistency and be glossy and smooth.

When the ganache reaches 35C/95F, add the butter and peppermint extract. Mix gently to incorporate. Ensure the butter is completely melted. Heat with the gun or microwave carefully if needed. Then add the crushed candy cane and stir briefly.

Once the ganache is 28C/82F, pour it into a disposable piping bag. Cut a very small opening at the tip. Don't press hard; you want the ganache to come out slowly. Carefully fill each shell and ensure you leave 1.5mm (1/16 inch) at the top of the mold. Ensure that space is across the entire chocolate. (I overfilled some of mine in the center and couldn't get as much chocolate over them as I would have liked for a really good seal.) Don't spill or smudge the filling onto the chocolate edges of the shells; this can cause problems with sealing them.

Tap the mold on the counter to get out air bubbles. Get down and look across the mold at eye level to see if you have overfilled any shells. Cool at 18C/64F for at least 2 hours.

Poison Pear Ganache
Makes 30–40 bonbons
(depending on size)

75g pear puree
1 tablespoon white corn syrup
75g heavy cream/whipping cream
1/2 teaspoon rum or rum extract
1/2 teaspoon almond extract
1/2 teaspoon vanilla extract
1/2 to 1 teaspoon cinnamon
200g white-chocolate Callets
20g unsalted butter at room temperature

Make your pear puree by peeling and cutting two very ripe pears into small pieces; better more than not enough. Either blend (you may need to add 1 teaspoon water) or finely mash your pear. It should resemble the consistency of applesauce.

Bring your pear puree and corn syrup to a boil in a small saucepan over medium heat. Simmer on low for a few minutes, stirring frequently. Push the pear puree through a fine sieve into a bowl. While you are heating the pear puree, heat the cream to just before boiling, stirring constantly. You can heat the cream in the microwave in short bursts, stirring in between. If a scum forms, remove it.

Mix your pear puree and cream together. Add your spices and extracts. Your mixture should be fairly hot. Pour the mixture over the Callets and ensure they are covered. Let sit 1 to 2 minutes. Stir the mixture until all the chocolate is melted. Add the butter and stir until melted. If the mixture is too thin, add a few Callets and stir. If it's cooling too quickly, microwave in 10-second bursts.

Once the ganache is 28C/82F, pour it into a disposable piping bag. Cut a very small opening at the tip. Don't press hard; you want the ganache to come out slowly. Carefully fill each shell and ensure you leave 1.5mm (1/16 inch) at the top of the mold. Ensure the space is across the entire chocolate. (I overfilled some of mine in the center and couldn't get as much chocolate over them as I would have liked for a really good seal.) Don't spill or smudge the filling onto the chocolate edges of the shells; this can cause problems with sealing them.

Tap the mold on the counter to get out air bubbles. Get down and look across the mold at eye level to see if you have overfilled any shells. Cool at 18C/64F for at least 2 hours.

Enjoy!!!

Acknowledgments

I want to thank my Heavenly Father for all the blessings in my life. Having this book published is definitely one of them. A huge thank-you to every member of my family and extended family for their support and encouragement. Especially my husband, who let me practice killing him over and over so I could get it right in the book. A special hug goes out to Spencer, Chortney, Taylor, and Gloria. You guys rock! To Cheryl, you are not just my friend, you are also part of my family. Thank you so much for being my main beta reader, lifelong friend, and supporter through thick and thin.

To my agent, Dawn Dowdle, you amaze me with how much you do. Thank you for bringing me into the BRLA fold and for helping to make this book what it is today. I appreciate your patience as I find every possible way to misuse a comma. To the great team at Crooked Lane books, thank you for all the hard work and dedication you've put into bringing this book into the world. I have to single out my editor, Tara Gavin. Thank you for believing in me.

Thank you so much to all those authors who took time out of their busy schedules to read and blurb my book! Ellie Alexander,

Acknowledgments

you also gave me a bookish community to gather with on Tuesday nights. You have no idea how much that helped me.

Thank you, Jana, for taking the time to explain how you make your delicious chocolates. I wish every reader could experience them! To Stephan—I've known you all of my life; special thanks for your financial expertise as well as your repartee. My sense of humor wouldn't be what it is without you!

Finally, thanks to the Flathead County Sheriff's Office for answering my questions over the phone back in the summer of 2020. Some things you just can't Google. Thanks to the beta readers who read my first three chapters before I sent them out into the world. And thanks to everyone else who has supported and encouraged me these past few years!